THE PEOPLE OF OSTRICH MOUNTAIN

NDIRANGU GITHAIGA

For Maitũ and Baba

ACKNOWLEDGMENTS

My heartfelt gratitude goes to my dear wife Magda and the three strong, beautiful girls of the Ndirangũ household: Zahra, Imani and Makena. Thank you for your unwavering support through this journey. And to Maitũ, who taught us to love stories, and whose childhood reminiscences provided fodder for my imagination. And Baba, who is no longer with us, for teaching us to dare and never give up—you will never be forgotten. Thank you, Joslyn Pine, for your diligent editing and attention to detail. Lastly, I'm grateful to El Shaddai, the Great Author, whose mysterious and dramatic plotlines remain a source of awe and inspiration.

"If I rise on the wings of the dawn, if I settle on the far side of the sea, even there your hand will guide me, your right hand will hold me fast." Psalm 139:9 – 10

PREFACE

Kenya is an East African country that was under British colonial rule between 1895 and 1963. In 1952, a bloody uprising led by the Mau Mau militia broke out in the region around Mt. Kenya. As a result, a state of emergency was declared by the colonial government, which lasted until 1959. The relationship between ordinary villagers and the Mau Mau oscillated between dread and covert support. Africans perceived as being loyal to the British often suffered gruesome punishment in the hands of the Mau Mau, while those suspected of supporting the Mau Mau faced the prospect of horrific torture, imprisonment and death at the hands of the British. Occasionally, the Mau Mau were referred to by villagers as the 'boys of the forest'. Dedan Kimathi, the leader of the movement, was captured by the British and hanged on February 18th 1957, thereafter being buried in an unmarked grave. Kenya gained independence from the British on December 12th 1963.

PART ONE

Chapter One

"WASH AND LEARN!" Sometimes a word or a phrase will take on a life of its own, achieving far more than was originally intended. Reverend Mulligan had no idea that his misquoted and misunderstood utterance had become a rallying cry, mobilizing the previously skeptical villagers of Kĩandutu to send their children to the mission school.

The reverend was a bald and portly red-faced Scotsman with a look of bemusement permanently etched on his face. Despite his stout frame and a tendency to perspire copiously with the slightest exertion, he seemed to be everywhere, ambling around the mission compound all day long. With seemingly inexhaustible reserves of energy, Mulligan often worked from six in the morning till well after dark. On Sundays, he conducted church services and baptisms, and had over the course of seven years seen the church grow from a small wooden edifice attracting a handful of mostly curious locals, to a congregation of easily three hundred. What brought them to the mission initially was his physical person; most people in the village had never seen someone whose face was the color of the palms of their hands. The fact that he spoke some rudimentary Gĩkũyũ, albeit with a horrendously mistimed intonation, quickly endeared him to the villagers.

1

A Presbyterian by ordination and appellation, Reverend Mulligan was an unabashed Baptist when it came to the rite of baptism. He believed that the ritual was incomplete as long as even a tiny portion of the recipient's body remained above the surface of the water, a notion that put him at odds with the mainstream in his denomination. While baptism by immersion did not run afoul of Presbyterian orthodoxy, it was generally not practiced. His zeal for the method was therefore viewed with some suspicion, and had generated a few murmurs of concern within the cloistered halls of the General Assembly, in Nairobi as well as in Edinburgh. Eventually, though, after much sighing and hand-wringing, it had been determined that he was more of a help than a hindrance, especially considering there wasn't a surfeit of clergymen signing up to leave the familiar comforts of Britain to establish churches in the African bush.

The reverend had more than a little disdain for the aspersion method of baptism, which he felt was completely out of place on the beautiful green foothills of Mount Kenya, where the sparkling icy rivers turned and twisted furiously down the slopes, looking from a distance like strands of shimmering tinsel flowing down the side of a giant Christmas tree. The gasps of the natives as they emerged exhilarated from the frigid streams seemed to validate his strongly held beliefs on the matter.

"Wash and learn!" the Africans would say to each other excitedly, enrolling in the mission school after they had participated in the requisite baptism.

The reverend had been preoccupied with these reflections while he was repairing the legs of a table. His musings were suddenly interrupted by the welcome sight of Deacon Mũhũyũ. "George! How are you this morning?" he called out.

"Oh, hello, Reverend. I didn't see you!" George said, while trying to prop the rickety gate open in preparation for the school day. Despite his thick glasses, he was very shortsighted, sorting through the gray silhouettes of familiar people by voice, gait or mannerism if they were more than four feet away. George was a small man, barely above five feet tall, with a twitchy, restless energy about him, seemingly unable to stand still for more than a few seconds.

As he approached the reverend, George took short, hurried strides; and since his right leg was shorter than the left, he bobbed sideways just a little as he moved. His large gray mustache seemed a little too heavy for his face, adding to the weight of his glasses. "I see you're still working on the table from yesterday," the deacon observed.

"Yes, because I had to stop once it got dark. I'm almost finished, though. How's your family?"

"Thanks for asking. They're fine, Reverend."

"I was thinking that, if we can both find the time, we should work on the wall of the goat shed today—you know, the one that's been leaning over since those two billy goats knocked it awry when they were fighting the other day."

"Sure, Reverend. I'll get Njũgũna to go with me to cut some wood to make poles. I think six or seven medium-sized poles and twice as many smaller ones will be enough—unless you think we need more?"

"That sounds fine, George."

"Very well, Reverend. I'll go and open up the schoolhouse now, and I'll get to work on the goat shed once the students have settled in for the day."

"Before you go, would you mind giving me a hand with this table? I need you to hold it steady so I can hammer in the last nail or two on this leg."

Once the nails were in, Reverend Mulligan set it upright on the ground and gave it a vigorous shake. It remained firm. The two legs that had been added were cut from a twisted tree branch that had been stripped of its bark, so the ultimate success of the enterprise had been in some doubt. "Why, it's as good as new, George!" Mulligan said, beaming with satisfaction. "Watch and learn, my friend!"

Deacon Mũhũyũ managed a faint lopsided smile and nodded in approval. "What time do you want to start work on the goat shed, Reverend?"

He looked thoughtful, reflecting on his day's agenda before answering. "Well, I'm teaching some classes this morning, and then I have a meeting with an official visiting from the Synod. So let's plan on four this afternoon, after tea."

"Okay, Reverend. I'll have everything ready for us by then."

The pair separated, with Mulligan still admiring his work as Deacon Mūhūyū headed towards the schoolhouse.

"Watch and learn!" whispered the deacon to himself. It was his favorite phrase—one that he used liberally among the villagers, where he thought of himself as a projection of the reverend's presence. To the ears of the Agĩkũyũ, where the mission was located, the sounds *tch* and *sh* sounded the same, and could only be differentiated by context. His excessive use of the expression, in and out of the original context in which he'd learned it, had made it impossible for the natives—for whom English was a new language— to differentiate between "watch" and "wash." The life-changing dips into the numbingly cold river probably did much to lend primacy to the phrase that eventually won out and which, curiously enough, was probably the biggest reason for the accelerated growth of the mission after the early lean years of its existence.

〜〜

God save our gracious King

Long live our noble King

God save the King . . .

The children sang shrilly in the schoolyard, their skinny bodies trembling like reeds in their oversize khaki school uniforms, their muddy toes clenched in a futile attempt to recoil from the cold bare earth. A thick fog hung over the slopes on days like this, so that it was impossible to see more than just a few yards ahead; and even the extra sweater worn over the shirt or dress gave scant protection against the penetrating cold. The Union Jack fluttered erratically over their heads in the chilly morning wind, appearing one moment and disappearing the next, like a specter in the mist.

Send him victorious

Happy and glorious

Long to reign over us

God save the King . . .

Wambũi mumbled the words half-heartedly alongside the rest of her schoolmates, keeping her eyes fixed on Mrs. Francis, the headteacher, and Reverend Mulligan, the head of the mission. The pair stood at the front of the assembly, their eyes keenly scanning the crowd for any student whose uniform was unkempt or who was not standing at proper attention.

May he defend our laws

And ever give us cause

To sing with heart and voice

God save the King.

Lately, Wambũi had been thinking a good deal about the

words of that song, and a lot of strange new thoughts had started filling her head. She'd always enjoyed the song before and relished the opportunity to demonstrate that she knew all the words by heart, but now she didn't feel like singing it anymore. It had all started with a discussion about the picture.

The picture was not new. It had always hung on the wall for as long as Wambũi had been a student in that classroom, which was a little over three months. There were other pictures too, but this one had piqued her curiosity from the moment she first saw it. Who was the man on the horse and what was that strange animal he had pinned to the ground with a spear? She had wanted to ask someone, but the only people who knew would be the teachers and she didn't want to annoy them with silly questions. Her usual teacher, Mrs. Bruce, was away for a week in Nyeri and a substitute named Ms. Pennington was taking her place. Ms. Pennington tried to be exciting and make the students laugh, but they were all a little afraid of her— she was not as calm and motherly as Mrs. Bruce.

"You have all done very well this week, so today we are going to do something different!" Ms. Pennington announced triumphantly one Thursday afternoon.

A nervous hush fell over the students as they exchanged puzzled glances.

"I've been asking questions all week, but now I'm going to give you the next twenty minutes to ask me any question you want— and I mean *any* question whatsoever."

An awkward, restless silence followed, punctuated by the sounds of anxious clearing of throats and shifting bodies on creaky seats. About two minutes into it, Wambũi cautiously glanced up, and her gaze inadvertently locked with Ms. Pennington's.

"Well, Lydia, are you going to be the first brave soul to take up the challenge?"

Her mouth went dry. She could feel her heart pounding in her chest. "Um . . . er . . . who is that over there?" she said hoarsely, pointing at the picture.

"Excellent question! That right there, children, is Saint George, the patron saint of England!"

From another corner of the room came the question that all the children had asked themselves at one time or another when they looked at the picture.

"What kind of animal is he hunting?"

Wambui saw that it was Njeri, her normally shy classmate, who had dared to ask this question.

"That is a dragon," Ms. Pennington said.

"Do dragons eat people?" Njeri persisted.

Ms. Pennington nodded, and either knowingly or otherwise, passed up an opportunity to point out the fact that dragons were not real, a piece of information that might have been reassuring to children who lived in a world inhabited by an intimidating array of long-toothed predators that moved stealthily among them like shadows. The image of an animal with teeth and claws like a leopard, with a neck like a snake that also had wings to fly was a terrifying one.

"What is a saint?" Wambũi asked, changing the topic.

Ms. Pennington smiled with self-satisfaction at the children's response to her innovative Q and A session. For all Mrs. Bruce's reputation as a good teacher, it was clear her students had never had a moment of interaction such as this. "Well, if someone lives a pure life and obeys the Bible, they can become a saint after they die."

Wambũi smiled inwardly at the prospect. Was it really that simple? "So, even me, I can be called Saint Wambũi when I die, if I do good things?" she asked excitedly.

Ms. Pennington's expression darkened, and her ears and cheeks suddenly turned crimson. "Even *I*!" she said sharply, "not even *me.*"

The sudden change in her demeanor caught everyone by surprise; they had just started to let down their guard and warm up to her. But now she was no longer smiling, and her voice seemed to have gone up an octave. Her upper lip was quivering. "I don't think there would ever be a Saint Wambũi because it's not a Bible name . . ." She paused in midsentence as the realization dawned that the name George was not biblical in origin either.

Letting out an irritated sigh, she continued, "The names of saints are not usually heathen names, so it would have to be your baptismal name. And look now, we've wasted precious time on idle chatter; let's do some mathematics in the few moments of class we have left!"

Wambũi felt the sharp sting of those words and struggled to hold back her tears. She didn't like being told she had a heathen name, even though she wasn't sure what the word heathen meant. That was the day she decided she didn't like Ms. Pennington. It was also the day she decided that her baptismal name, Lydia, was no longer her real name.

Chapter Two

IF YOU STOOD by the *mũgumo*[1] tree next to Mũthee[2] Karanja's homestead and looked across the valley on a clear day, you would see the mountain, a mysterious cobalt-blue eminence towering silently above the landscape and jutting into the clouds. The white patches on its jagged peaks looked like clouds that had drifted too close and gotten snagged there. That was where Ngai, the creator of Agĩkũyũ, lived and oversaw the lives of the descendants of Gĩkũyũ and Mũmbi, the first man and woman on Earth.

"Maitũ[3], what are those white patchy things on top of Kĩrĩnyaga?" Wambũi remembered asking her mother many years ago.

Her mother's answer—ostriches—had not satisfied her. "If those are ostriches, how come we can't see them moving and why don't they come down to where we are, like other ostriches?"

"*Weh*[4], you have too many questions!" replied her mother with a laugh, her brown upper teeth coming into view. "Maybe we should send you there to find out for us. Then you will see what Ngai thinks when a young village girl walks into his homestead with a

---

[1] Species of fig tree, considered sacred by the Agĩkũyũ people
[2] Respectful way to refer to an older man in society
[3] Mom
[4] "You!" said emphatically either as a warning or to get someone's attention

hundred questions for him."

"Maybe he likes people who ask questions," whispered Wambũi quickly as they approached the *mũgumo* tree. It was where the elders of the village used to come and pray to Ngai, and generally people maintained a reverential silence when they were in the vicinity of the tree. Just beyond it, they headed down a sharp slope and made a right turn after going fifty yards or so until they entered the compound. The homestead measured about half an acre, bordered by assorted shrubs, with two large huts at the bottom of the slope belonging to each wife and her children, and a smaller one at the top of the hill where Mũthee Karanja resided. Even when he was home, and not out tending his goats, Mũthee Karanja made no noise, so one never knew if he was around until he called out to one of his wives or children to bring him something or other. Wambũi and her mother had bundles of firewood strapped onto their backs, which they dropped with a thud once they reached their hut; it was the only sound that broke the silence. Mũthee Karanja's other wife, Nyina wa[5] Kariũki, was probably out working in the garden since there was usually a continuous bustle of activity and conversation emanating from her home when she was around. "Why do you spend so much time arranging the sticks like that?" Wambũi's mother asked for the umpteenth time with a hint of exasperation, as she observed her placing them in neat bundles of five.

"I don't know, Maitũ, I can't help it," she replied

---

[5] Mother of [insert child's name]—respectful way to refer to an adult female, relative to one of their children, usually the oldest

apologetically.

"They're all going to end up in the fire no matter how you sort them."

"Yes, Maitū, I know," she said with a shrug.

A brief silence ensued as her mother piled up some twigs over a small pile of gray embers in a three-stone hearth located in the middle of the hut. Once the sticks were in place she started to blow with slow, long exhalations until an orange glow appeared from among the embers. After a few more breaths, the twigs began to crackle before bursting into a small energetic fire. She rearranged the woodpile over the flaming sticks and, reaching into the dark recess on the far side of the fire, came up with a clean earthen pot.

The task completed, Wambūi saw her chance to bring up the matter that was weighing on her mind. "The other day the teacher was telling us about an animal that looks like a leopard with sharp teeth and wings, and a long neck like a . . . like a . . ." She paused when her mother caught her eye and nodded in comprehension. Snakes were not usually mentioned by name as it was felt that this might be an invitation to them, so they were either referred to by analogy or allusion.

"Where, here?" asked her mother, apparently unsettled by the subject.

"No, where the Athũngũ[6] come from."

"*Ngatho!*[7] Maybe that's why they are coming here to live with us," exclaimed her mother as she lifted a pot half full of water onto the fire, the flames now dancing boisterously and casting interesting shadows on the wall of the hut.

A cheery voice called from outside. "Nyina wa Wambũi, is that you?"

"Yes, Nyina wa Kariũki, it is I," she replied to her co-wife. "I'm here with Wambũi; we're trying to get some *gĩtheri*[8] ready for dinner."

Nyina wa Kariũki appeared in the doorway. She was a tall, heavily built woman with merry brown eyes bordered by laugh lines that were well-formed from years of not taking herself too seriously. Her short hair was all gray, as if she dipped her hands into the hearth every morning and grabbed fistfuls of ash to sprinkle over her head. She'd had her first child around the time of the great flood, when it rained day after day until the waters of the Ragati River left their banks and washed away all the farms and huts on the flatlands, including some on the lower hillsides. She was therefore probably in her fifties, but one wouldn't have thought so from the way she effortlessly hoisted huge bundles of firewood onto her back or brought her hoe crashing down nonstop into the reticent red soil

---

[6] White people (singular—Mũthũngũ)
[7] "Goodness gracious!"
[8] Traditional Gikũyũ dish made of maize and beans

during planting season.

"Your people are well?" she asked Wambũi's mother.

"Yes, everybody is well."

"Wambũi, the white man is still teaching you how to count sticks?" she asked grinning broadly.

Wambũi nodded with a smile. She liked Nyina wa Kariũki, who was also her stepmother—everybody did.

The two ladies engaged in casual banter for a few moments before Nyina wa Kariũki's voice dropped into an inaudible monotone, and an uncharacteristic serious expression invaded her demeanor. Wambũi struggled to make sense of what the two women were talking about; they used ordinary Gĩkũyũ words, but she was unable to make head or tail of what they were saying. She thought she overheard them say, "the boys of the forest," but she wasn't sure. Then as quickly as the tenor of the conversation had changed, the mood lightened again as Nyina wa Kariũki gave a chuckle, and patting Wambũi affectionately on the shoulder, headed off in the direction of her hut to start preparing dinner for her family.

A couple of silent minutes elapsed and then Wambũi, sensing that her three younger brothers would be coming soon, decided to make the most of her limited window of opportunity. "Maitũ, who are the boys of the forest?"

Her mother looked startled and seemed to be fumbling for an

answer when a faint raspy voice called out from the upper corner of the compound. "Go and see what your father is calling about," her mother told her, relieved at the perfectly timed interruption.

≈

Something was happening, but Wambũi didn't know what. It seemed to her that there were suddenly a lot of muted conversations and furtive glances among the adults around her, and the tone often changed to a lighter one the minute they noticed her approaching. Besides this recent exchange between her mother and Nyina wa Kariũki, she'd heard one other cryptic mention of the boys of the forest. She looked up at the dense forest that covered the hillside beyond the mission and wondered who those boys were, and why the grownups were nervously whispering about them.

Who were they and who were their parents? Did they come from another village and why were they living in the forest? The trees there were tall, and it was very easy to lose one's bearings wandering around the dark forest floor; and there were wild animals too, like leopards and elephants, not to mention the ogres that her grandmother had told her about, some with one eye in the middle of their face and others with eyes in the back of their head. Ordinarily, when people needed to go through the forest, they took one of the few paths that everybody used and made sure they stayed on it all the way, usually traveling during the day. Children were not allowed to go there alone, and most of the children in the village had sense enough not to want to go there anyway.

~~~

Wambũi would remember vividly the events of one morning in February, 1952 for the rest of her life. That day, when she got to school assembly, she noticed that the flag was only halfway up the flagpole, which she had never seen before. Had somebody started the task of raising the flag and been called away to do something else? And something else was different. Normally, Mrs. Francis the headteacher conducted most of the assembly, but today it was Reverend Mulligan, and all the Athũngũ teachers' faces were red like the reverend's. His face was always red, whether he was happy or angry. The only other time Wambũi had seen a Mũthũngũ's face turn red was that horrible Ms. Pennington's, when she had called her a heathen. Today, all their faces wore harsh expressions, and some of the teachers, like Ms. Pennington, were sobbing. Wambũi nursed a warm flicker of inward delight and triumph at seeing her unhappy; but the forlorn looks of some of the others, like Mrs. Bruce and Mr. Collins, bothered her.

"Children, good morning—if this day might even be called that," began Reverend Mulligan. "I have a very sad announcement to make . . ."

There was complete silence.

"Last night, our King, George the Sixth, whom we all loved dearly, died unexpectedly."

There were some loud gasps of astonishment, and many of

17

the teachers who'd been struggling to maintain their composure could do so no longer and began to weep openly. The children began to cry as well, even though a number of them didn't fully comprehend what was going on.

Wambũi was puzzled. She felt nothing.

Reverend Mulligan continued. "The successor to the throne is his daughter Elizabeth, who, by the strange workings of Providence, happened to have been in Nyeri when this terrible tragedy occurred, and has now returned home to England to take the throne."

A girl! Wambũi felt an instant surge of excitement, followed by guilt. It was all very confusing.

The reverend led the school in a prayer for the Royal Family and for England, before inviting them all to join in the national anthem. "So, remember, as we sing our anthem, the words today are 'God save our Queen' not 'King.' Please remember that as we proceed in song."

And with that, all who were present burst into a heartfelt rendition of the new anthem at his lead.

God save our gracious Queen

Long live our noble Queen,

God save our Queen . . .

Chapter Three

DEACON MŨHŨYŨ HAD settled in effortlessly when he'd moved to the area about seven years ago when the mission opened. His people were from the other side of Karatina, close to Tũmũtũmũ Mission, the original Presbyterian mission center in the area from which satellite facilities were launched. He had served there as a deacon before being dispatched to assist Reverend Mulligan with the founding of the new post. The two got along remarkably well from the day they met. Despite being strikingly different in outward appearance, they had an almost identical sense of purpose and the ferocity with which they pursued it, so each brought out the other's best efforts by the energy they brought to the task at hand.

The deacon had nine children, ranging in age from a son in his early twenties to a six-month-old who was still strapped in a *ngoi*[9] to his mother's back. Unlike many other men in the village, he had only one wife, which had been a source of perplexity, and sometimes ridicule, when he first arrived in the village.

"Are there not enough girls in your village that you have only one wife?" they often asked in a tone of disbelief often accompanied by a smirk.

---

[9] Baby-carrying harness

"The one I have is just fine. I have no need for another, and I hope that she has no need for another husband either!"

That last remark was usually received with reactions ranging from shock to intense merriment. "Mũhũyũ is a strange man! I wonder if the men from his village talk like him," they would say among themselves.

The word Mũhũyũ means "foam" or "lather," a name that aptly captured the manner in which he went about whatever activity he set his mind to. He had been named after his grandfather, who, from the description of those who knew him, was of a similar disposition. It was not clear if the name had started out as a nickname for the former, or whether the metaphorical congruence of the name with its bearer's personality was merely coincidental.

"Good morning, Deacon *Ma-hoo-hoo!*" called out Mabel, the chirpy administrative assistant for the school as the deacon entered the building.

"Good morning, Mabel," he replied with a smile, "it's good to see you!"

She could not pronounce his name despite multiple efforts to correct her, and not just from the deacon himself. But the unencumbered warmth with which she usually greeted him more than made up for her sloppy pronunciation of his name. Her boss, Mrs. Francis, on the other hand, could say the name perfectly; but she was cold and aloof in her interactions with him, often wondering why Reverend Mulligan insisted on involving him in all the major decisions involving the mission, and by extension, the school.

"Is the reverend here today?" the deacon asked her.

"He was here about half an hour ago, though I heard him say he was going to Tũmũtũmũ this morning—I don't know if he left already. Did you need him urgently?"

"No, it can wait. Just a few issues *pertaining* to the church building." He delivered the word expertly, having practiced it several times since he heard Mrs. Francis use it during a meeting the week before.

"Well, I'll be sure to let him know you were looking for him."

"Thank you, Mabel."

"You're welcome, Deacon *Ma-hoo-hoo*! Have a nice day!"

As the deacon left the school compound, he caught sight of a figure hurrying along the path in the opposite direction. Although he called out to him, he continued walking briskly, possibly picking up some speed. "Mwangi!" he called out even louder.

The individual stopped, turned around and started walking towards him slowly.

"I didn't see you yesterday. I just wanted to see how you are doing," the deacon explained to his son.

Mwangi was a younger, lankier version of Deacon Mũhũyũ,

with bloodshot eyes and unruly hair. His face often wore a sullen expression. "I'm fine," he mumbled.

"Your mother has been worried about you. Please make sure you see her today."

The young man nodded.

"I have some work I'm doing in the church compound today that would move faster if I had an extra pair of hands. Are you available to help me?"

Mwangi shook his head and muttered something about having lots to do.

Deacon Mūhūyū didn't really need the help, but he wanted to give Mwangi something worthwhile to do and also thought his company might be beneficial. He believed the young man kept to himself too much.

"Okay. Well, make sure you go and talk to your mother today," he said as the two parted ways.

As the deacon entered the church compound, his thoughts lingered on Mwangi. He was old enough to have a wife and a home of his own, but instead he lived like a stray animal, sleeping during the day in his *thingira*[10] and disappearing for days for no apparent

---

[10] Traditional Gĩkũyũ hut for men

reason. Sometimes, he smelled of *muratina*[11], such as on this morning. This was not suitable behavior for a member of his household, given his position of responsibility in the church, but Mwangi was a grown man, so there was not much he could do. Young people these days seemed to have odd notions about what it meant to be an adult, he concluded, picking up a stack of prayer books to return to the closet in the vestry.

〰〰

Wambũi and her friends often went together to the river to fetch water. It was a fifteen-minute walk that partly traversed the edge of the forest. Normally they preferred to go in the late afternoon, after school, when the ground had warmed up and was less hostile to one's bare feet. Usually by that time the dense morning mist had been dispelled by the sun's warming rays.

Today as they walked, Njoki and Wangarĩ were having an argument—rare for them—and they were trying to keep their voices down as if to keep the surrounding trees from eavesdropping. It was not a topic they knew much about, but it had been weighing on the minds of all five of the girls in their group for some time now.

"I hope he succeeds and more people join him!" said Njoki fiercely.

"I don't think fighting the Mũthũngũ is the answer, though,"

---

[11] Traditional Gĩkũyũ beer, made from the fruit of a tree bearing the same name

23

Wangarĩ countered hesitantly.

"They're the ones who came here with guns and started forcing our people to move from their homes!" Njoki retorted, starting to sound exasperated. "Do you think they are just going to go away without being forced to go?"

"I don't know. It's just that many people will get hurt or killed if fighting breaks out."

"So, you want to smile and say 'please' and 'thank you' to the Mũthũngũ even as he takes your land and animals from you?" sneered Njoki, shaking her head.

Wangarĩ shrugged.

The brief pause that ensued allowed the heat of flaring emotions to cool down, lulled further by the soft cadence of the girls' feet on the red compacted earth of the footpath. A gust of wind blew through the trees causing the fluttering of leaves and the swaying of branches.

Wambũi had been listening quietly to the conversation and many questions sprang to her mind. Her thoughts went to the man called Kĩmathi from Tetũ. What had made him leave his job as a schoolteacher to go and live in the forest? Was it fair for him to fight for the others while they continued with their lives as if nothing was happening?

"I think the Mũthũngũ should go back to where he came

from and leave us alone!" resumed Njoki, not quite ready to let the embers of the argument go cold.

"Njoki, how is your brother?" asked Mũmbi coyly. She and Wangũ, the fifth girl, had, like Wambũi, been following the conversation between the other two, torn between wanting to hear more and abandoning the topic for a lighter and more pleasant one.

There was excited tittering from the others, all except Njoki who was clearly vexed at the timing of the question. Mũmbi was hopelessly infatuated with Njoki's brother, although it was unclear he was even aware of it.

Wambũi caught sight of a sudden movement in a nearby thicket. Her body went numb and she felt the loud *thump-thump* of her heartbeat.When she turned to look more closely, it had gone still, and all she could see was a dense thicket about twenty yards to the left of the path they were on. Her friends continued to chat and giggle obliviously. As she tightened her grip on the heavy water-filled earthen pot she balanced on her head, she debated what she would do if the movement signified the presence of an attacker or a wild animal. They were about a hundred yards from the edge of the forest, so she could drop her pot and run; but whatever it was could probably outrun them.

She glanced again discreetly in the direction of the movement. Nothing. Heaving an inward sigh of relief, she only began turning her gaze forward when she saw it again. It was a man! She managed to get a glimpse of him scurrying from behind a bush to hide behind a nearby tree. He moved in a half-crouch and had a wild mane of hair falling over his shoulders and back.

Wambũi was terrified. Deciding not to tell her friends, she started to walk very quickly, hoping they would pick up the pace to keep up with her. A short distance ahead she could see where the path opened up into a field right next to the village.

"Wambũi, where are you going so quickly?" Wangarĩ asked.

"I just remembered something I have to do—so let's hurry up!"

The girls quickened their pace, though not without loud protests from Njoki and Mũmbi. When they were within twenty yards of the forest's edge, a large muscular figure suddenly stepped onto the path in front of them. He had an axe over his right shoulder.

"Ndĩritũ!" exclaimed Wambũi, suppressing a shriek just in time. "How are you?" she added, sounding decidedly relieved.

"I'm very well, young ladies. How are you?" Ndĩritũ was the village strongman, usually called upon when an application of brute strength was required in a particular situation, such as cutting down a stubborn tree trunk or separating hot-blooded young warriors who had gotten into a fight. His appearance alone was usually enough to persuade the parties involved to try harder to find a more civil way to resolve their dispute.

As he stepped to the side of the path and let them pass, they all greeted him cheerily.

"Give my greetings to all your people!" he replied.

As the girls crossed the open field to head back into the village, Wambūi wondered about the man she'd seen who'd tried to stay hidden. She was glad that Ndīritū had showed up when he did, not wanting to think about what might have happened otherwise. She had decided not to mention it to her friends, since they would either become anxious and conjecture about it endlessly, or laugh it off as a figment of her unruly imagination.

"See you tomorrow!" she said as they came to where the common path diverged and each girl went in the direction of her home.

≈

That evening, as Wambūi helped her mother with the chores, the mysterious man in the forest kept popping up in her thoughts. She wished she'd managed to see his face, since without it the image she retained seemed more sinister.

As she slept that night, she had a dream. She had gone alone to the river to fetch water, and when she got there her brother Kariūki was sitting on a rock with his legs dangling in the water. The river was a bit shallow and rocky there before it navigated a bend, so that clumps of white foam usually formed on the still surface of the water that was some distance away from the tumbling currents. The

27

clumps gently drifted outwards, diminishing in size until the myriad tiny bubbles popped until the clumps were no more.

"Kariũki!" she called out to him.

He didn't answer. He had a long stick in his hand that he was using to reach out and skim off the clumps of foam as they formed.

"Kariũki!" she shouted again.

He turned around suddenly and she shrieked. He had no face! There was just a dark shadow where his face should have been, surrounded by shaggy braided locks of hair hanging down the sides of his head. She screamed, but no sound came out.

Kariũki lifted up his stick and brought it whizzing down towards her.

Wambũi screamed again, and this time the sound came, waking her up instantly. Her breathing was heavy and her heart was pounding. She looked around the room—it was pitch black. In the darkness, she could hear the sound of the rhythmic breathing of her siblings and her mother. Outside their hut, the night was silent.

She settled herself on her mat and tried to go back to sleep, relieved that it had just been a dream.

Chapter Four

THE WHOLE VILLAGE was awakened by an ear-splitting howl they initially mistook for a wounded animal. But it turned out to be the full-throated scream of a man calling for help. Many of the men shuffled out of their huts, and picking up their *pangas*[12] and bows and arrows, headed to where the commotion was coming from—in the direction of the school. When they got there, they found Reverend Mulligan yelling unintelligibly, his large frame heaving with exertion and his face and neck having turned a deep scarlet, several shades darker than his usual cherry-red skin tone.

He pointed at one of the early arrivals to the scene, a young man known to him who had attended the mission school and therefore spoke English. He managed to find his voice and choked out the words: "James! Run to the police station and tell whoever is there that they need to come here with Inspector Wilcox as quickly as possible!"

The young man immediately sped off, while the curious gathering throng was still trying to decipher the cause of the reverend's initial inconsolable ranting. When they followed his gaze to the ground, they saw an object propped up against the gate, which from a distance looked like a rock. But when the men got closer, they

---

[12] Machetes

noticed the red smudges in the grass around the object—and it was only then they realized what it was. There were anguished gasps of horror as those closest to it jumped back, triggering a frenetic retreat among those behind them, with villagers spitting in disgust at what they had seen.

"What wicked son of the devil would do this!" Reverend Mulligan called out to no one in particular.

By this time, the villagers were conversing in low tones in Gikũyũ, no longer paying attention to him. Someone suggested retrieving the man's family, while another suggested blocking off the area to keep the children away. The group split up, with about five men running in the direction of the deacon's home. Within moments of their entry into the homestead, a loud disturbance ensued, with all the men breaking into frenzied shouting.

Reverend Mulligan started off in that direction, but then hesitated, unsure about whether he should leave the spot where a crowd continued to gather. He looked around for a familiar face. "Josiah," he said to one of the young men, "find something to cover *that*"—pointing at the decapitated head—"and don't let anyone go near it."

"Yes, Reverend."

"And when Inspector Wilcox gets here, let him know I've gone over to the house!"

"I will, Reverend."

At the house, the gory spectacle was far worse than the one he had left at the gate of the school. The headless bodies of Deacon Mũhũyũ's wife and seven children lay in a pile in the main hut, bound hand and foot.

"Oh, my dear God!" the reverend cried out in horror.

The men who had gotten there first were walking around in a daze, wringing their hands and letting out tormented sighs. It was not long before they heard the urgent stomping of boots coming down the path.

"Rob! Are you there?" the inspector called out as he burst through the gate with two of his African constables.

"Over here," Mulligan called out from inside the hut.

The inspector cocked his rifle and stooped to enter the hut, quickly surveying the dim interior. "Oh, dear Lord, have mercy!" he exclaimed as the bodies came into view, an ashen hue spreading over his face. "What sort of beast would do this?"

When Wilcox looked around at the men, he was greeted with total silence.

"This is without doubt the work of those Mau Mau savages!" he declared angrily. "Those animals will stop at nothing, not even women and children!" The inspector turned to the Agĩkũyũ men, pointing furiously at the bodies. "Is this what you people are fighting for? You want the British to leave, so you can go back to murdering

31

each other like this?"

The men looked down, not quite comprehending what he was saying, but sensed that he was directing some of his anger at them. "One of them is not there," said one of the villagers in halting English, trying to be helpful.

"What is that, boy? Speak up!" Wilcox demanded impatiently.

Whether it was the hostile tone or the demeaning way he had addressed him, the man who'd started to speak decided not to proceed. He had noticed that the body of Mwangi, Deacon Mũhũyũ's eldest son, was not present, and he thought that might be relevant; but on reconsideration he decided there was no value in trying to engage with the ill-humored inspector.

The brief interval of silence was disrupted by a sound and some movement from inside the *ngoi* that was still strapped on the back of its decapitated mother.

"A baby!" someone blurted out, as two men reluctantly stepped over to the bodies, not wanting to touch them lest they be visited by the same angry spirit that had wreaked havoc on the deceased. Gingerly, with trembling hands, they fumbled with the knot in the *ngoi*. As soon as they had loosed the knot, the baby tumbled to the ground and began to cry. He was hastily picked up by the person closest, and for a brief moment there were unrestrained shouts and tears of mingled jubilation, sorrow and confusion. Not from Inspector Wilcox, however.

"Has anyone found the heads?" he asked, getting back to the business that concerned him.

There were blank stares.

"Well, let's get to it! What are we standing around here for? Kĩmani, go back to the school gate where they found the deacon's head and see if you can find a body. And I don't want to see a crowd when I get there. You can enlist some of the villagers to help you disperse them, assuming these are not the same Mau Mau miscreants that committed this horrible act in the first place!"

"Yessir!"

Before long, someone found a freshly dug mound of earth in the corner of the garden; and after digging down about a foot, encountered a bundle wrapped in goatskin that contained all the heads. Deacon Mũhũyũ's body was nowhere to be found despite an extensive search of the village and surrounding areas.

"Such hideous beasts!" the inspector muttered aloud to himself. "It's on days like this that I wonder what exactly it is we are doing in this godforsaken corner of the earth."

From the time the police arrived, Reverend Mulligan seemed to go into some kind of trance and silently observed the proceedings. But once the baby was found, he was the one who carried it out of the hut, cradling it as gently as he could in his large arms, fearful he might accidentally crush it and extinguish the last flicker of hope on that dreadful day. Fortunately, his big belly served as a naturally soft ledge on which the infant could rest. But when the baby began to cry uncontrollably, he handed him over to one of the women in the village to look after.

When Inspector Wilcox and his constables returned briefly to Karatina, people congregated in small groups to discuss the distressing events of the morning and commiserate with each other. But later, when a larger contingent of police arrived—equipped with rifles, pistols, barking dogs and a meaner, angrier Inspector Wilcox— the villagers hastily retreated into the sanctuary of their huts. It was clear that nothing would be the same in Kĩandutu village.

Chapter Five

IN THE WEEKS and months that followed, it became difficult for the villagers to decide what they dreaded most about the numerous, relentless night raids by the police—whether it was Inspector Wilcox's vile, expletive-rich outbursts, the gratuitous kicks and blows from his boot-wearing lackeys, or the savage barking and rushing of the police dogs. Simply put, life in Kĩandutu village had turned into hell.

After being robbed of sleep by a raid or lying awake all night dreading one, adults stumbled around all day in an exhausted daze, while the children faced the harsh scolding of an unsympathetic teacher when they dozed off in class. In general, the grown-ups tried to maintain a stoic demeanor for the benefit of the children, but the veneer was thin and it didn't take much to lose one's composure, usually through an inappropriate fit of rage, as anger was socially more acceptable than fear or sorrow.

It was during this time that Wambũi first heard an adult cry. She was walking past Nyina wa Gĩchũhĩ's hut when she heard voices, which turned out to be those of Nyina wa Gĩchũhĩ and Nyina wa Mwangi. She saw them first, and was about to call out a greeting as was customary for the younger party when she realized Nyina wa Gĩchũhĩ was sobbing. Wambũi hastily took a few silent steps

35

backwards until the wall of the hut hid her from view. "These people are going to finish us!" she could hear Nyina wa Gĩchũhĩ saying disconsolately as she quickly tiptoed back up the path to find another way to where she was going.

Seeing an adult cry was a strange and unwelcome experience; and the image of that afternoon kept replaying in Wambũi's mind, so that she went through the day distractedly, leaving tasks half done. That night she lay awake, thinking about what she had heard, tears streaming down her cheeks. From the sound of her mother's breathing, she could tell that she too was awake. Most people had a hard time sleeping, knowing the police could show up at any moment, kicking down doors and making arbitrary arrests.

She thought about Kĩmani and Nguru, Inspector Wilcox's constables. They were both from Karatina, yet they went around with their loathsome boss terrorizing people who were sometimes related to them, or were old enough to be their parents. It was shameful enough to speak back to your elders, but they had the audacity to verbally and physically abuse men who were their fathers' age. Nguru's family was from a village about a ten-minute walk from Kĩandutu, Kĩmani's a little further out, but their people were well known to the villagers.

Kĩmani was much nicer than Nguru, and he tried as much as he could to maintain decorum and show some respect for the village folk, though this was sometimes difficult when he was in the company of their spiteful boss who never hesitated to land his cane or boot on anyone he considered less cooperative than was suitable. Nguru was a snarling hyena, effortlessly matching or outdoing Inspector Wilcox's callous and brutish behavior. Before signing up with the incipient colonial police force, he had been a good-for-nothing layabout in his village, shirking hard work and hell-bent on being an embarrassment to his parents. It was as if in this job he had seen an opportunity to get even with all those people who had regarded him with scorn before the British arrived. It was a little less clear why Kĩmani joined the force, although it may have been for the same reason that the village children attended the mission school; it was possible he hadn't foreseen a day when he would be required to impose the will of an invading power on his people. Neither of their families had much to do with them after the police raids began, seeing them as traitors to their own people.

Wambũi's home was searched only once, but it was a terrifying experience. Late in the night, long after everyone had gone to bed, the sound of a barking dog and stomping boots were heard approaching. They pushed open the gate and headed directly to Nyina wa Kariũki's hut, which was the closest.

"Open up here!" shouted Nguru.

"Who is it?" Nyina wa Kariũki answered timidly from within.

"Open up, it's the police! Stop wasting our time!" he bellowed.

There was the sound of a commotion in the hut as Nyina wa

Kariũki and her children scrambled to get dressed and out of the house. A loud kick brought the door down and there was screaming from within. "Come outside and line up out here, on your knees with your hands behind your head!" yelled Nguru. Inspector Wilcox and the police dog were directly behind him.

Wambũi and her family were listening quietly from the next hut, knowing their turn would come next. They heard the police dog barking and snarling, struggling to free itself from the grasp of the inspector, who had seized it firmly by the collar. Waitherero, Nyina wa Kariũki's youngest daughter, aged about three years old, began to wail uncontrollably as they shuffled out of the hut.

"*Kira*! (Shush!)" her mother hissed at her, and almost instantly the crying stopped.

"Where are the men of this house?" asked Inspector Wilcox when they were all outside.

There was silence, interrupted only by the impatient growling of the dog. Kariũki, the oldest child in the household, about eighteen years of age, was kneeling on the ground as ordered, next to his mother.

"*Mwĩna thayũ* (Do you come in peace)?" came a gravelly voice from the shadows at that very moment, about ten yards to the right of the hut.

Inspector Wilcox cocked his gun and pointed it in that direction.

Mūthee Karanja's stooped silhouette was visible in the moon-bleached darkness. He was leaning against a cane, covered in a blanket.

"Get down here!" the inspector demanded.

The old man did not move.

"Bessie, sic!" Wilcox ordered the large Alsatian still straining feverishly at its collar, pulling the inspector along with him in the direction of Mūthee Karanja. As soon as he let go, the dog shot from his grasp like a rocket towards the old man, barking and growling. Then something strange happened—as soon as it got to within two feet of where its would-be victim was standing, it let out a whimper and lay down on the ground. The policemen stared in disbelief, as did Mūthee Karanja's family, since everyone had expected the frail old man would be ripped to shreds by the vicious animal. For what seemed like a sizeable chunk of eternity no one spoke, then Inspector Wilcox called out to the dog. "Come here, Bessie!"

The dog did not move.

"*Coka na harīa!* (Go back there!)" the old man whispered calmly to the animal.

Bessie got up instantly and trotted back to the inspector.

Nguru couldn't stand to see his boss humiliated in this way. "Get down here right now, old man!" he shouted angrily, signaling for Mūthee Karanja to join the rest of his family who were still kneeling outside the hut.

Mũthee Karanja didn't move, then slowly raised a gnarly index finger that he pointed at Nguru. *"Nĩdakũgeithia!* (I greet you!)"

In everyday parlance this expression was a simple greeting; but when it came from a displeased elder in an ominous tone, it signified something totally different. Everyone felt a chill travel down their spine, and even Inspector Wilcox realized there was not much to be gained by hanging around there any longer.

"All of you, get back in your huts!" he yelled, turning around and walking away, with his two constables forced to follow.

No one in Mũthee Karanja's house discussed the incident in the days that followed, everyone carrying on with tortured curiosity, trying to decipher in their minds the meaning of what they'd seen. A lot of perplexed looks were directed at Mũthee Karanja's hut, but no one had the temerity to ask the old man for an explanation of the events of that night. Inspector Wilcox and his constables did not discuss the incident either; and if Bessie had any clue to offer her human handlers about what had happened, she chose not to share it, carrying on with regal nonchalance and poise in her subsequent duties.

If Nguru woke up the next morning thinking that the brilliant sunshine would dissipate the haunting dread of the old man's parting words to him, he was mistaken. Something happened when he and Kĩmani were heading to the police station from the small house they shared, about a ten-minute walk through the woods. When Nguru picked up his pace and got ahead of Kĩmani, he heard his colleague call out to warn him about a dead tree limb that seemed ready to fall into his path. But it was not a branch that landed on the ground with a soft thump, and then raised its head towards him before turning around and slithering into the bushes.

Nguru screamed and babbled hysterically, turning around and hurtling in the direction from which they'd come, the dark semicircle of moisture on the front of his shorts not escaping Kĩmani's notice as he hastily stepped out of the way to let his colleague pass before joining him in a frenzied sprint back to their house.

After that day, Nguru and Kĩmani always found a way to avoid doing night raids on Mũthee Karanja's property, and Inspector Wilcox seemed not to notice.

Chapter Six

REVEREND MULLIGAN DIED the day the Mũhũyũ family was murdered—but not literally. He continued wandering around the mission compound in a trance, listlessly going through the motions of his daily duties, apparently drained of all vitality. No longer was he seen tinkering away at one odd construction project or another; and when he conducted the church service on Sundays his voice was monotonous and bereft of conviction, so that it would have been difficult for a casual listener to distinguish whether he was reading from a Bible or a dictionary. At night, the rhythmic lullaby of his loud snoring was no longer the sedative the nearby villagers fell asleep to. It was replaced with a restless, nervous silence, punctuated by the not-so-distant cackling of hyenas, which sounded much closer than they ever had in the past.

The lack of sleep took a toll on him. On one occasion, he was invited back to the pulpit to give the benediction at the end of the service and instead gave the whole sermon again, almost word for word, not having realized he had given it twenty minutes earlier. Initially the congregants were amused, then a little irritated, before wearily resigning themselves to the unexpected encore performance, some of the cheekier members mouthing the words of his emphases and punchlines before he got to them. Nobody felt it necessary to make him aware of that act of double commission—they all knew he had a lot on his mind. There was also the time when Deacon Tate was leading the congregation in the Prayer for Peace, and the loud grating crescendo-decrescendo emanating from where the reverend sat began to drown him out, much to the merriment of most and the embarrassment of one, namely the deacon. For the villagers who lived close to the reverend, there was some comfort in knowing he was at least able to get some sleep, the inopportune circumstances of this consummation notwithstanding.

He traveled at least once a week to the village that Deacon Mūhūyū had come from—to the home of the late deacon's sister and her family, for that was where the baby had been taken. From the reports of those present in that household, it was the only time the sun's rays seemed to penetrate his cocoon of despondency, eliciting an occasional crooked smile or a chuckle as he held out his chubby index finger for the baby to grasp.

At the school, the unsmiling Mrs. Francis ran the entire morning assembly in addition to taking on some of the other roles that had hitherto been exclusively Reverend Mulligan's to fulfil. He would stand there silently with the other teachers as she led the assembly, always relieved to be a silent participant at any gathering. Most of the teachers were very distressed by the recent acts of violence, and some had started to question the purpose and suitability of the mission. A silver lining for Wambūi in all of this was that Ms. Pennington, the teacher who had called her a heathen, had returned to England, overwhelmed by the specter of marauding Mau Mau attackers making a meal of her on one moonless night in the not-so-distant future.

Wambũi arrived on the assembly grounds one morning and was surprised to notice the flag wasn't there; and that the slender wooden flagpole on which it usually fluttered had been cut down, leaving a stump about a foot high. But Mrs. Francis proceeded with the assembly as if nothing was amiss.

"Good morning, children. Let us sing our national anthem and express our gratitude to the Good Lord for bringing us to the start of this day."

God save our gracious Queen

Long live our noble Queen . . .

Wambũi wondered what had happened to the flag, but no mention of it was made by Mrs. Francis, and most people hadn't even seemed to have noticed. The next day the flag was up on a new flagpole, a supple slender tree limb from which the bark had just been stripped, with the fresh stumps of the branches that had been cut off still visible. Two days later, that flagpole had been cut down; and once again Mrs. Francis successfully navigated the morning assembly, managing to keep everyone's attention on anything but the missing flag.

Since the night-time police raids began, a number of young men had disappeared. Some had been arrested by the police, while others had presumably run off into the forest, not wanting to wait their turn to be arrested. People spoke in whispers and there was fear

44

in their eyes.

Now Wambũi and her friends had to take the long way to fetch water from the river, to steer clear of the forest. This route took about twice as much time as their usual one, but considering the new dangers afoot, this was the only safe option.

"What do you think happened to the flagpole?" Wambũi asked her friends in a whisper as they sat in the grass, taking a break on the way back from the river.

"What flagpole?" Wangarĩ replied, a quizzical look on her face. The other girls also looked unsure of what she was talking about. Njoki's reaction was somewhat different—she didn't even look up, but continued staring abstractedly at the ground, her nimble fingers weaving three blades of grass into a braid.

"The one in school," Wambũi explained. "On Monday there was no flag at assembly and there was only a stump of a pole. Tuesday there was a new pole with a flag. Thursday, there was only a stump again . . ."

"*Haiya*[13]!" exclaimed Mũmbi, "I never noticed anything. What happened to the flag?"

Wambũi groaned inwardly. Mũmbi was a little dull, and it was reactions like this one that discouraged her from bringing up certain topics.

---

[13] Exclamation of surprise

"I think the Mau Mau did it!" whispered Wangũ nervously.

Their conversation was interrupted by the appearance of Nyina wa Mwangi and Nyina wa Njoroge, two of the village mothers, coming up the path with large creaking bundles of firewood strapped to their backs.

"Are you well, young people?" Nyina wa Mwangi called out in greeting.

"Yes, we are well," they chorused.

"Greet your people when you get home," said Nyina wa Mwangi with a smile as the two ladies walked on.

As the girls got up to resume their walk, first giving the older women a chance to put some distance between them, Wambũi wondered about Njoki's silence. Of late, she seemed disinterested in their conversations, even when it came to subjects she would normally be very passionate about. On most days, she would have had something to say about the flagpole incident, but today she had only sat by silently. Yet Wambũi was certain she was listening keenly.

Njoki's behavior caused Wambũi to wonder if her friend had taken the secret oath—those who had joined the Mau Mau, but continued to live in the village, serving as the ears and eyes of the boys of the forest. For the young men in particular, the setting of the sun brought the dread of surprise night raids with the possibility of being arrested and brutalized by the malevolent Inspector Wilcox and his sociopathic sidekick Nguru. In view of that, many decided to leave. Njoki's older brother was one of the young men in the village who had vanished into the forest just as the police raids began, presumably to join the Mau Mau. Even Ndĩrĩtũ, affectionately known among the villagers as the gentle giant, had walked out of his hut one evening and not returned.

Wambũi's half-brother Kariũki, the eldest son in the household, also disappeared one day, bringing rare tears of anguish to his stricken mother's face. It was hard to see how this mild addlebrained fellow would be of any use to the forest fighters. He had a hard time focusing on even simple tasks as he'd amply demonstrated several times when he'd gone out to pasture in the morning with his father's goats, and returned at the end of the day without them and no idea where they went—or even that he'd taken them in the morning. Such tasks that should have been routine for a young man his age were now assigned to his younger siblings and half-siblings.

He had a very charming personality and no one in the household could stay angry with him for more than a few moments. So on the day he failed to come home in the evening, the whole family was concerned that something terrible had happened to him. Nyina wa Kariũki checked in with all his friends, but none remembered seeing him apart from much earlier in the day. Mũthee Karanja rarely displayed any emotion, so it was difficult to tell what he was thinking, but he seemed to spend a lot more time in the dark recesses of his hut than he did before Kariũki's disappearance.

"Maitū," Wambūi said hesitantly to her mother one day when they were alone, "the day before Deacon Mūhūyū . . . um . . . the day before it happened, we were coming from the river and I saw a man hiding in the forest."

Her mother looked at her expectantly, apparently waiting to hear more.

"Maybe if I had told someone, it might not have happened."

Her mother squinted for a moment, then shook her head and let out a short mirthless laugh. "Told who? That mad hyena Wilcox or his mongrel son Nguru? The one who sent his dog to attack your father in his own home?"

Wambūi's mother was a mild-mannered woman, but she uttered the words with extreme disdain and spat in disgust. This was a side of her that Wambūi had never seen.

"The Mūthūngū is not here to help us. He is here to take things for himself—and dogs like Nguru are helping him instead of helping their own people!"

Wambūi paused for a moment, unsure whether she should pursue the conversation given her mother's unexpected emotional eruption; and then decided to take advantage of the fact they were alone, which didn't happen much nowadays.

"But if Nguru is working against his own people, what about the people that killed Deacon Mūhūyū and his family? Aren't they working against their own people?"

"Whatever happened to Deacon Mūhūyū was a terrible thing, and if the Mau Mau did it, they did a bad thing. I think that worthless son of Mūhūyū was behind it. How come he was not there that night and has never been seen since?"

"Do you think our Kariūki joined the Mau Mau?"

Her mother's voice quivered and she brushed back a tear. "Kariūki is not a fighter. I hope he comes back soon."

As her mother took a sharp stick and poked it into one of the arrowroots that were boiling in a pot to see if it was ready, Wambūi heard the loud running footfalls of her three younger brothers, Kariūki, Mūgo and Wahome. Mūgo stuck his head in the doorway, putting an end to their conversation.

"You're back?" Wambūi's mother asked.

"Yes, Maitū, we're back."

Wambūi considered that customary greeting rather silly as there was only one possible answer if the person being asked the question was present.

Throughout that evening, Wambūi could tell from the way her mother spoke to her that their relationship had suddenly shifted to a deeper level. After dinner, as the younger siblings were settling down on their mats to sleep, her mother grabbed her hand, and in the dim light of the glowing embers pointed towards the door.

Wambũi quietly headed in that direction, and her mother followed.

"Take this basket and put it down right there against the fence!" her mother whispered, handing her a heavy basket filled with beans, sweet potatoes and arrowroots, before returning to the hut.

There was only a sliver of moonlight in the sky, and Wambũi could vaguely discern the shapes of the trees and bushes, but her feet knew the path well, having trod on it frequently over the years. She got to the fence and looked around nervously.

"Just put it down there," a male voice half-whispered to her.

She set the basket down.

"Thank you. You can go back," the same voice said.

She peered into the darkness as she turned around, but could not make out any human form in the darkness. Restraining the impulse to break into a terrified sprint, she walked back to the hut at a brisk pace.

Chapter Seven

THE SKY WAS a nondescript gray that morning, with no hint of the impending daybreak. Wambũi crouched against the wall of her hut, gritting her teeth as the sharp chill of the mountain air burrowed deep into her bones, making her shake uncontrollably. She wore a threadbare sweater, the only one she had, which provided little protection from the biting cold.

"Let's go!" whispered her mother, stepping quietly out of the hut.

The two set out on their walk, keeping their footfalls light so as not to wake up anyone else in the household. A rooster crowed unexpectedly as they reached the outskirts of the village, causing Wambũi to jump with fright. Her mother strode on, unfazed, not even turning back to make sure her daughter was keeping up with her.

It would be about an hour before they made it to the train station. Wambũi gripped her almost empty wooden suitcase nervously in her right hand; in her other hand were five shillings that she clutched as though her life depended on it.

~~~

"Maitũ, I've been accepted to Alliance Girls!" she had announced breathlessly to her mother two months earlier, after dashing all the way home from school. When the results of the national examination were released, letters had been mailed out to the primary schools indicating which high schools the final year students had been selected to attend. She was the only one who received an acceptance letter from Alliance Girls, a prestigious boarding school located in Thogoto, a half-day's journey by train.

"*Haiya*! Is that so?" her mother exclaimed, clapping her hands gleefully, letting her usually shy brown-stained upper teeth come fully into view.

"I was the only one from our school who was selected," Wambũi declared triumphantly.

"Well done, my daughter! I'm so proud of you."

They sat together at the hearth in blissful silence, sipping hot fermented porridge that her mother had just finished preparing. Her mother made the best fermented porridge in Kĩandutu, and that was not just Wambũi's opinion. Some people made it too sour, so that it almost tasted like *mũratina*, the alcoholic brew that brought mirth and merriment to gatherings of old men. Most people made their porridge lumpy, with the solid clods showing up unceremoniously in the drinker's throat when they expected it least, causing some to gag or swallow hard even while maintaining an outward polite demeanor so as not to offend their host. When Wambũi drank porridge at other people's homes she did so cautiously, with gritted teeth, in anticipation of the lumps she knew were coming. In her mother's hut she didn't have to do that—the steaming brown, velvety liquid never hid any unwelcome surprises.

"Thogoto is far away," her mother said in a flat inscrutable tone, staring towards the far wall of the hut.

"Yes, Maitū, it is far."

No other words were exchanged on the subject that day or in the days that followed. At some point Wambūi wondered if her conversation with her mother had even happened. Multiple times she found herself opening up the now well-worn acceptance letter and reading it again for reassurance, so that eventually she found she could recite the contents by heart.

One day, about two weeks later, Mūthee Karanja called for her. She ran up the slope behind the other huts to reach him, and found him seated on his stool outside his hut, his cane propped up next to him against the wall of the edifice.

"Your mother says you have been accepted to the school in Thogoto," he said, and from his tone it was unclear if it was a question or a statement of fact.

"Yes, Baba[14]."

Without saying much else, he held out a downturned fist in her direction and she opened her hand palm-up underneath it. When five coins tumbled into it, she let out a faint gasp. She had seen

[14] Dad

money from a distance, but had never before held it in her hand.

"Go and represent us well!" he declared with an unsmiling nod and dismissed her. For a brief moment, their eyes met before she hastily redirected her gaze to the ground.

It was only the next day that Wambũi realized that Kairũ, one of her father's billy goats, was no longer in the compound. All his goats had names, and Kairũ, a jet-black frisky two-and-a-half-year-old with a white patch on its right foreleg, was his favorite. From the day he could walk, he seemed drawn to the old man and would often leave his mother's side and come to graze around his feet. Mũthee Karanja could often be heard speaking to him in a low crackly voice, and he would stop grazing and look up sometimes, as if in response to what had been said. In fact, there were times Kairũ seemed to be nodding in agreement with what he was saying. Mũthee Kahũthũ, one of the old men in the village, had asked Mũthee Karanja numerous times if he was interested in selling Kairũ, but the answer had always been that he would sell any other animal in his herd except Kairũ. When Mũthee Karanja sent word out of the blue that he was now willing to sell him, Mũthee Kahũthũ felt ecstatic, suspicious and remorseful all at once.

"But why have you decided to sell him now?" he probed politely, as he scrutinized the animal for any signs of disease.

"I'm sending my girl to school in Thogoto; I need the Mũthũngũ's money," Mũthee Karanja rejoined.

A puzzled look came across Mūthee Kahūthū's face. "You're sending your girl away for more school? But she already went to school here!"

Mūthee Karanja was becoming a little impatient, though it was difficult to discern from the steady, impenetrable gaze that remained fixed on his friend, so that Mūthee Kahūthū finally looked away and simply asked how much.

They haggled briefly and settled on a price. By this time, Mūthee Kahūthū was convinced that his windfall was genuine, although he was still befuddled by Mūthee Karanja's explanation for why he wanted to sell the animal.

"The ones who continue going to school, at what point do they get married?" Mūthee Kahūthū said with a smirk, unable to hide his delight as he gripped the halter around the animal's neck and started heading off. The silent stare from Mūthee Karanja had made it clear that the transaction and any related conversation were over and it was time to leave.

{{mmm}}

As Wambūi and her mother approached the outskirts of Karatina, the sun was coming up and the light fog was clearing. They walked through brush and maize fields, avoiding the main road, treading lightly and communicating when needed in signs and whispers. Wambūi could make out the cluster of buildings that defined the town about a quarter of a mile ahead of them. The railway station was at the edge of it, so they would not need to go into the town and risk being harassed by the police for not carrying a pass, the identification document that every African adult needed to have, and which her mother did not. An occasional car roared down the dirt road a short distance away, intermittently coming into view when the wall of vegetation that hid them thinned out in places.

"Halt!" a loud voice bellowed a short distance away.

They froze, spinning in terror towards the direction the voice came from, which was the roadside beyond the bushes. Wambũi turned nervously towards her mother and saw a look of dread and helplessness on her face.

"Come here!" the voice commanded.

They slowly started walking towards it, then stopped abruptly when they realized they were not the ones being addressed. Peering through the bushes, they saw Inspector Wilcox and his two constables Nguru and Kĩmani, at the side of the road. A man was shambling towards them—and Wambũi recognized him. It was Ithe wa [15] Mũnene, the father of one of her younger brother's playmates.

"Show me your pass!" Inspector Wilcox growled.

The man held up his open palms and shook his head slightly, as if to indicate he had no pass but no bad intentions either.

---

[15] Father of [insert child's name]—respectful way to refer to a man, relative to their child, usually the oldest

"Where is your pass?" barked Nguru.

He gave no answer.

"Get down on your knees!" Nguru again.

No response.

"I said get down on your knees, old man!" Nguru screamed, lifting up his baton and swinging it angrily down on the man, who cringed and raised his arm to block the blow. In the process, he stepped forward so that his forearm connected with Nguru's wrist, blunting the impact of the baton, which landed weakly on his back.

"Leave me alone, you dog! You traitor!" Ithe wa Mūnene yelled as Nguru raised his baton and took a second swing. He pushed forward against the man who was thirty years his junior, and the constable stumbled backwards. Then there was a loud bang, and the man fell to the ground limp.

Wambūi gasped in horror as she saw Inspector Wilcox's smoking pistol at the end of his still outstretched arm. She turned to her mother, tears filling her eyes. "They killed him!" she mouthed the words silently.

Her mother's face was taut with suppressed anger. Signaling with a slight tilt of her head, she indicated to Wambūi that it was time to get moving, and the two noiselessly made their way through the vegetation, avoiding treading on any dead leaves or twigs. Wambūi was numb with shock as she followed her mother, who weaved like a ghost between the maize stalks until they came within sight of the station. This was as far as her mother could go. She pointed to the gate of the railway station at the end of the barbed wire fence. A few people were already trickling into the station.

"Go well!" her mother whispered.

Wambũi choked back tears and started walking forward. As she stepped out from the edge of the maize field into the open and crossed the road, she looked back one more time to say good-bye to her mother, but she was already gone.

Chapter Eight

THE MAN SELLING tickets was in his sixties, with graying hair and a merry twinkle in his eye.

"Where are you going today, young lady?" he asked, noticing her anxious, timid demeanor.

"Thogoto."

A puzzled expression came to his face. "Hmm, Thogoto, are you sure? I'm not aware of a station called Thogoto."

Wambũi looked around helplessly, before fumbling in her pocket for her acceptance letter from the school.

The man scrutinized it, then his eyes brightened and he nodded slightly. "Oh, I see! The station you're going to is Kikuyu[16]. Once you get there, you can ask them to tell you how to get to Alliance Girls. The fare is one shilling and sixty cents, but you have to purchase a return ticket too, so it will be three shillings and twenty cents."

She gave him four shillings, and he returned the change and the ticket, adding, "You will use this portion for going, and then

---

[16] In this narrative, Kikuyu is refers to a particular town in Central Kenya, while Gĩkũyũ refers to the Wambũi's tribe—in reality the words are interchangeable.

remember to keep this other portion safe as you will need it when you are coming back."

"Thank you," she said, "where do I go now?"

"Over there," he replied pointing over his left shoulder. "When you get to where the path divides, you will go left until you get to where you see people like us on the platform waiting to board the train."

"Thank you," she said once again.

"Good luck in school," he called out to her as she walked away.

She stayed on the path of beaten dirt until she came to where it split. To the right there was a sign that said WHITES ONLY. She turned left and continued walking. She could see a group of Africans clustered together on a platform with a sign above it that said GOODS TRAIN. After she joined them, she hesitantly approached a woman in her mid-twenties who was sitting at the edge of the platform, staring into space. "Is this . . . is this where I catch the train?" she stammered.

"Yes," the woman answered, looking up at Wambūi and noticing the quizzical expression on the girl's face. "The goods train is for us; the other train is for the Athūngū," she said nonchalantly.

"Is it going to Kikuyu?" Wambūi asked.

"There is only one train and it goes to Nairobi. Once you get to the station in Nairobi, you will find the train to take you to Kikuyu."

She thanked the woman and walked over to sit down on one of the upturned crates that functioned as benches. Moments later the platform attendant arrived and announced in a loud voice: "Train for Nairobi is arriving shortly, please make sure you have your tickets for boarding!"

The passengers all roused themselves from their quiet ruminations and fumbled in their bags or pockets for their tickets. Wambũi clutched her ticket as the rumble of the approaching train grew louder and louder until it stopped with a deafening screech at the platform. Boarding was a rapid affair, with the passengers filing past the stationmaster as they handed him their tickets for inspection before proceeding to the three open cars adjacent to the platform. Wambũi peered into the dimly lit car as she stumbled inside. There were loaded sacks arranged in low piles towards the rear of the car; and after watching what everyone else was doing, she sat down on one of them that was up against the wall. Nobody spoke. She glanced around to see who her companions were. Apart from one other girl who might have been about fourteen, Wambũi's age, or perhaps a little older, the rest were adults, all apparently deep in thought.

The side door of the carriage reached only partway to the top; and when the stationmaster slid it shut with a loud bang, there was still enough light coming in so Wambũi could see the trees and the sky. Moments later, there was some jerking and lurching as the train began to move, gradually transitioning into a steady, rhythmic thump, as Wambũi watched the *muratina* trees and their oblong, sausage-like fruit start slipping away faster and faster from right to left.

〰

The journey seemed to take forever. Wambũi cycled between staring outside, dozing off, daydreaming, shifting position and glancing at the other passengers, who were all doing a similar routine with some variations. She poked her finger against the sack she sat on, which was pretty firm, trying to guess what was in it—maybe maize or beans, or even rice. She made a fist and punched down on it, finding it hard and unyielding, like a rock. The dull pain in her hand that she felt afterwards discouraged her from making a second attempt.

Her mind started wandering and settled on her family. By now the household was up, and her brothers were probably starting to miss her already. She hoped her mother had gotten home okay. When thoughts about the violent incident they'd witnessed by the side of the road came into her head, she pushed them away; but the heaviness she felt inside that came along with them didn't. It was a very bad feeling, a kind of emptiness that hurt but was unrelieved by tears. She felt she couldn't cry even if she wanted to.

Changing trains in Nairobi was much easier than Wambũi anticipated; and after a three-hour wait, the train to Kikuyu departed, arriving at her destination a little over an hour later. As the train pulled in, she felt a knot of anxiety in her stomach, as she wondered where she would go after she disembarked.

Only a handful of people got off with her. The station was a short, dusty wooden platform with a small ticketing office close by, and a dirt path leading from the platform past the office into the adjacent settlement comprising rickety tin-roofed buildings.

"Alliance Girls?" a well-dressed woman in her twenties or thirties called out to Wambũi as she hesitantly followed the five or six fellow passengers who were heading out into the town.

Wambũi nodded and began to walk in her direction. The lady had in her company another girl about her age, also carrying a small suitcase.

"Hello, my name is Alice Njũgũna, and you are . . . ?" the lady said with a big smile, stretching out her hand to shake Wambũi's.

"Lydia Karanja," Wambũi replied nervously, for some unknown reason feeling compelled to use her official name, which sounded totally alien and unfamiliar to her.

"Nice to meet you, Lydia—say hello to Rispa Oduor. From this moment on, think of her as your sister."

Rispa was short, dark and chubby, and had beautiful white teeth with a small gap between her two upper front teeth. She had a warm smile. The girls shook hands.

"The school is about a three-mile walk from here, and there's no other train coming into the station for at least two hours," said Alice, "so we can start walking."

Along the way, Alice did most of the talking, explaining that she worked in the school's administration office, and in the last few days, she and another lady named Joyce had shuttled back and forth to the train station to meet the new girls who were coming in from different parts of the country to attend the school. They walked on the path along the dirt road, and as Wambũi looked around, the landscape reminded her of Karatina, with lots of trees and bushes everywhere. She learned that Rispa was from a place called Nyanza, on the shores of a big lake called Lake Victoria, which Wambũi remembered having seen on a map in geography class, and recollected there were a lot of mosquitoes there. Rispa seemed like a very happy person—she smiled and chuckled a great deal. After about forty-five minutes of walking, they arrived at a wooden gate bordered by a tall *kaiyaba*[17] hedge. The large sign on the gate said, ALLIANCE GIRLS HIGH SCHOOL, and underneath it was an insignia bearing an image of a flaming torch superimposed on St. Andrew's cross, an X-shaped white cross on a navy blue background. Below it was a motto which read WALK IN THE LIGHT.

A man appeared from behind the gate, holding a wooden club, and he smiled at Alice. "You brought more girls, eh?" he said to her in Gĩkũyũ.

"Yes, Mũhoro, I did," Alice replied.

Wambũi felt a thrill of surprise to hear her native tongue, albeit with odd pronunciations, such as the way the watchman

---

[17] Kei-apple shrub

pronounced the "t" in *airītu*[18]. The language seemed out of place in this context. She noticed that once they got past the watchman, Alice immediately went back to conversing in English.

"Well, girls," she said triumphantly, making an arc-like sweeping motion with her right arm to indicate the clustered buildings, hedgerows and well-kept lawns facing them, "welcome to the place that will be your home for the next four years!"

---

[18] Girls

Chapter Nine

WAMBŨI SLEPT POORLY that first night. It was partly due to her excitement about the next day, but there was also the bed. The metal-frame bunk beds had a wire lattice that held a two-inch sponge mattress. When she climbed hesitantly onto hers, it felt wobbly and uncomfortable, and she was terrified she would fall through and land on Doris, the girl underneath. Whenever she changed position, it started rocking and squeaking, so she found herself trying to lie still as much as possible. Through the thin mattress, the wire frame pressed unyieldingly against her skin. By the time morning came, she was tired and sore, thinking about how much more comfortable she had always been sleeping on the dirt floor of her mother's hut.

There were twelve girls in her dormitory, three from each grade level, and the older girls seemed to take seriously their responsibility for helping the new girls settle in. At registration, she had received three complete sets of school uniforms, right down to her underwear, as well as bedding, soap, bathtowels, a toothbrush, and the like. She was excited about her new clothes, and looked forward to wearing them.

"Students are not allowed to wear shoes," Alice had explained to her and Rispa as they completed their registration, "because there is not enough money to buy everyone shoes, and not every family can afford them. The school does not want some people thinking they are better than others just because their parents were able to buy them shoes."

It had not occurred to Wambũi that some students might prefer to wear shoes on a daily basis, as that had never been an issue in Karatina; but she felt inwardly relieved when she heard the rule, knowing full well which category of families she belonged to. But if the weather in Kikuyu was anything like Karatina, there would be many mornings when all she could think about would be minimizing the amount of time her feet made contact with the ground.

The dark green *kaiyaba* hedge, which consisted of dense opaque foliage that grew from branches studded with thorns, completely surrounded the school. It provided an effective deterrent to any person or animal who considered burrowing through. Beyond the hedge, in most directions, all one could see was the sky, although to the north there was a small hill with a copse of *mũkindũri*[19] and blue gum trees, a second layer of green stretching out to the horizon, in continuity with the first. Wambũi wondered if there were Mau Mau fighters in that forest; if so, nobody here seemed to be thinking about them.

Edith Njeri and Mary Wekesa were the other two Form One girls in Wambũi's dormitory. She and her year-mates had each been assigned a housemother, a girl in Form Four who would take the new girl under her wing and help her settle in. In fact, everyone in the

---

[19] Croton tree species

higher classes made a concerted effort to help the newcomers feel welcome. That is, of course, everyone except Constance Muthengi.

Constance was the daughter of a wealthy senior chief in the colonial government. This fact was usually revealed within twenty minutes of one-sided conversation with her. She made no effort to conceal her disdain for those from less prosperous backgrounds, which was pretty much everyone else save for one or two other girls. In no way was it more apparent than the manner in which she addressed people using the pronoun "you," rather than their name.

Wambũi had heard enough about Constance before they met so she had no doubt who it was when a tall girl rushed into the dormitory, looking somewhat frazzled, carrying an untidy clump of bedsheets that she had just pulled off the clothesline.

"You," she said with a small jerk of her head, looking at directly at Wambũi, "would you mind grabbing these and putting them on the bed in that cubicle at the end of the hallway? I need to go outside and get some more."

Wambũi politely agreed, and approached her to receive the crumpled bundle of linen. She glanced up and got a good look at her face up close. Constance had smooth, light-brown skin and short-cropped coal black hair that was less than an inch long, in keeping with school regulations. Just below the righthand corner of her mouth there was a tiny black dot—a birthmark—that stood out pleasingly against the surrounding skin. Her nose was small and pointed, with an ever-so-slight upward tilt that gave an impression of aloofness. She was very pretty; but her favorable attributes were eclipsed by the downturned corners of her mouth that signaled perennial disapproval, and her general mean-spiritedness.

Not once did she make eye contact with Wambũi, or thank her for doing what really had been a favor.

Later in the evening, the girls in forms One and Two gathered before bedtime, and the topic of Constance came up. When Wambũi asked them a question, the older girls delightedly embraced the opportunity to pass on a juicy tidbit of dormitory lore, just as it had been passed along to them the year before.

"Does she always talk like that to people?" she asked.

Susan, one of the girls in Form Two, rose up with a mischievous snort and began to do an imitation of Constance, standing with her fists clenched against her hips and screwing up her face into a scowl. Then in an exaggerated deep voice, her right arm outstretched, she pointed at each of the girls in turn: "You . . . take these clothes and put them over there! You . . . stop staring at me! You . . . it's your turn to clean the bathroom floor, why are you still standing around here? You . . . why are you laughing?"

The older girls shrieked until they cried with tears of laughter. Wambũi was the only one of the new girls who had experienced the insulting behavior, and she thought the caricature was uncannily accurate. She laughed softly. The other two new girls smiled in solidarity, if nothing else.

When the Form Two girls were finally able to catch their breath, Susan turned to Edith Njeri and said sympathetically, "I'm sorry you ended up with Constance as your housemother. Don't worry, we'll all be here for you."

Edith nodded gratefully.

"It's hard to imagine," began Doris, one of the other Form Two girls, "that her sister Charity is so nice and down-to-earth. Such opposites!"

"True," echoed Susan. "Charity is a wonderful person."

Wambũi came to look forward to the evenings after study time, when the older girls were still in class and the younger ones had the dormitory to themselves. She was starting to make friends and welcomed each new day with pleasurable anticipation.

〜

Mathematics came naturally to Wambũi; it always had. Even before she learned to count in Standard One, she had already developed an unconscious habit of counting things that didn't need to be counted, or sorting them in numeric clusters. If any of her siblings came across an arrangement of sticks or pebbles arrayed in multiples of three or five, or any other number, they could reliably deduce she had been there before them. Thanks to her, her friends in Kĩandutu all knew the number of *mĩthandũkũ*[20] trees on the old route to the river

---

[20] Black wattle tree

through the forest, just as she now knew there were seven jacaranda trees between her dormitory and the administration building, three on the right and four on the left. She made no special effort to count—it just happened naturally, in much the same way someone might casually observe a flower to be red or a sky blue. Initially her mother had berated her for it; but it soon became obvious that coaxing and cajoling had only transformed the obsessive computation into a silent, brow-furrowed whisper.

Ms. Atwood, the math teacher, was a petite lady with short brown hair and an intense gaze. Her eyes were a strange color, like that of very light brown clay, which made one want to keep staring into them while at the same time being discreet enough not to get caught doing so. She had a serious demeanor, and her smiles came infrequently, usually when someone solved a difficult problem on the blackboard. You could always tell when she was getting annoyed because her ears started turning red very quickly.

Wambũi was not sure she liked her. For one thing, she reminded her of Ms. Pennington, the sharp-tongued primary school teacher who once called her a heathen. There were some similarities in their build, hair color, demeanor—maybe even their voice. For Wambũi that was enough, so she tried for the most part to remain just another face in the crowd, speaking only when spoken to. But that changed one day in February, the day of their first continuous assessment test.

Ms. Atwood had gone over the instructions in painstaking

detail: one hour of allotted time, no speaking or looking at someone else's work, raise your hand if you need something, etc. The students nodded nervously—this was their first test in high school, and in most people's least favorite subject no less.

A deep hush fell over the room as the teacher gave the signal to begin, interrupted only by the hurried *scritch-scritch* of pencils as the young minds anxiously tried to decipher the coded mysteries on the test sheet, racing against the clock. Ms. Atwood had taken her seat and began to go over the lesson plan for her class with the Form Three students later in the day, when from the corner of her eye she saw a hand go up. She made a surprised face and showed two upturned palms as if to say, "What?" But the girl said nothing and kept her hand up. She beckoned her to approach her desk.

"Yes, what is it?" the teacher whispered.

"I finished."

"You what!" she exclaimed. "But it's only been twenty-five minutes."

The girl was silent.

"Well then, go back and check your work. It's no use finishing in a hurry and making mistakes, is it?"

The girl nodded and went back to her seat. Ms. Atwood watched her from the corner of her eye. After exactly two minutes of scanning through her answer sheet, the girl turned it face down and leaned forward, burying her head in her arms.

When the hour was over, the girls were instructed to hand in their tests on the way out. Ms. Atwood had intended to single out the one from the student who'd finished early, but there was a flurry of activity as several girls handed them in at the same time, so she wasn't able to see the girl's name.

Later that evening, Ms. Atwood sat down after supper, burning with curiosity, and began reviewing the tests, trying to identify that one in particular. She expected it to have unanswered questions or wrong answers, likely both, so she was somewhat surprised when she finished marking all of them and none fit that description.

"Hmm, that's odd!" she thought, slowly leafing through them one at a time. There were a handful of tests with all the questions correctly answered, and many with a wrong answer here and there; in general, the overall performance of the girls had been good.

During the next math class, she called out the name of each girl to come up and retrieve the graded test, scrutinizing each one carefully even though she could match about half of the girls to their names by now. "Anne Wambugu . . . Susan Cherotich . . . Sophia Mwamburi . . ." she called as one girl filed forward after another. "Lydia Karanja . . ." Ms. Atwood's heart fluttered with excitement, as the mystery was finally solved. She casually glanced down at the test as the girl approached. It was a perfect score, with all the steps in every calculation neatly written down without a single step or number crossed out.

"Well done!" she said, smiling at the girl, who returned an awkward half-smile as she took the piece of paper and returned to her seat.

Chapter Ten

EILEEN ATWOOD WAS from Surrey, England. She was an only child, doted on by her parents. From the time she was five years old she had told them she wanted to be a teacher. They had no objection to her chosen career, but didn't want her to feel bound to a decision she'd made at an early age if she changed her mind. So they neither encouraged her nor discouraged her.

When Eileen was eleven, a missionary from Africa visited the church her family attended. It was a small brick church with a congregation of between fifty and a hundred people who showed up every Sunday mainly out of a sense of duty to one another. The vicar was an unexpressive man who delivered drab and esoteric sermons that would put even the most vibrant and energetic soul to sleep. One day, a Scottish missionary visited and delivered in fifteen minutes what the vicar had been unable to do all year. The whole congregation listened, enthralled, as he told them of the beautiful green hills of Kenya, and of the cheerful but benighted natives who needed to hear about Jesus and who badly needed education and medicine. Eileen, who usually spent her time during the Sunday service coloring or writing poems on the church program, listened transfixed. She imagined herself walking around in the splendid lands the missionary had described, teaching the native children English, holding their little babies . . .

"When I grow up, I am going to be a missionary teacher in Kenya!" she announced enthusiastically to her parents later that afternoon.

Judith, her mother, grimaced and held her breath. She shot a desperate look at her husband Harrold. He struggled to maintain his composure, inwardly cursing the missionary they had all regaled earlier.

"Now Eileen, you're still very young and a lot of things may change between now and when you grow up. Even if you don't end up being a Kenyan missionary yourself, there are still many ways you can support their good efforts, like sending money. In fact, I think your mother and I will look into doing just that."

"It's wonderful you want to do that, Daddy," Eileen said. But before her parents could relax and congratulate themselves on a crisis averted, she added, "While you and mummy send them money, I will be out there in Kenya!"

Over time, her parents' attitude morphed from desperation into despondency, followed by a resigned acceptance of her decision. "I suppose there are more dishonorable choices she could have made," Harrold would say to his wife occasionally, trying to sound a positive note.

Most people live their lives one day or one year at a time. Not Eileen Atwood. In the years that followed, everything she did seemed to be in preparation for the destiny she had chosen for herself.

During high school, when other girls were thinking about boys and getting jobs in London after they graduated, she listened with detachment, inwardly dismissing their ambitions as vain and vacuous. Conversely, her friends considered her plans inordinately reckless, but felt it prudent not to say what they thought—at least not when she was around.

While still at university, Eileen feverishly sought information on different missionary organizations and eventually felt drawn to the Alliance of Protestant Missions, which ran a boarding school for boys in Kikuyu, Kenya, and was in the process of opening one for girls. But first, she worked for four years at a private school in Surrey, which was considered a highly desirable position among her peers. These, however, were the longest years of her life as she merely went through the motions of her job, eagerly awaiting the day she would leave England and finally begin the work she had dreamed of for so long.

♒

Wambũi did not like the way the math teacher kept picking on her, asking her to answer questions. Her classmates had noticed and had started making fun of her.

"Why does she keep calling on you to answer questions?" Susan Chege asked, when a group of them were sitting in the grass during a twenty-minute recess, trying to catch the faint warmth of the sun as it appeared from behind the clouds, breaking the mid-morning Kikuyu chill.

"I don't know," shrugged Wambũi, nonchalantly.

"*Weh!*" said Lydia Oyoo in her booming voice, smiling broadly and waving her arms energetically as she usually did when she was trying to make a point. "In the beginning, every time I would hear the name Lydia, my heart would stop because I usually don't know the answer and I thought she was calling on me. But now I'm starting to get upset that she's acting as though there is only one Lydia in the class. I feel like putting up my hand and saying, 'Ms. Atwood, would you mind clarifying which Lydia you mean?' "

The girls laughed. Wambũi was smarting with embarrassment. She didn't like the attention, and she didn't like the way the teacher kept calling her by the name Lydia. It was a name she tolerated and responded to, but something about the way this teacher said it kept taking her back to Ms. Pennington and the day of St. George and the dragon.

As the bell rang, signifying the end of recess, the girls got up and proceeded to class. They had another math quiz today. Time was flying—the last test seemed like it was only yesterday.

Ms. Atwood went through the instructions as she had the first time, except she seemed a lot less intimidating now. "Alright girls, you have one hour to complete this test. Check your work once you're done to make sure there are no silly mistakes. It is ten thirty by my watch. You may begin now."

The teacher sat down at her desk to review some course

material. After about twenty minutes she looked up—everyone was still working on the test. But when she checked again five minutes later, she noticed Wambũi had her head buried in her arms on the desk and appeared to have finished. Ms. Atwood looked up every minute or so until Wambũi sat upright and their eyes met. Ms. Atwood nodded and signaled her to approach.

"Are you finished?" she asked.

Wambũi nodded.

"You can bring your paper up here if you like."

As she walked back to retrieve it, Ms. Atwood felt her heart race as she anticipated what she next had in mind for her student.

"If you don't mind, Wambũi, I'd like you to try doing this test," she said as she handed it over. "Just do the best you can. It won't count against you."

Wambũi looked confused and slightly exasperated, but she nodded and obediently took the paper and returned to her desk.

Chapter Eleven

AT THE END of the first term, Wambũi brought out the return ticket stub she had been holding onto for the past three months; and after saying good-bye to her friends at the train station, she boarded the train to Nairobi on her way back to Karatina. Return journeys always seem shorter, and the trip that had previously felt long and unrelenting now seemed to pass by quickly. She arrived in Karatina about three o'clock in the afternoon. As she exited the train station, a familiar gloom and apprehension returned to her. She crossed the road and walked briskly along the roadside, until she neared the spot where the incident with Ithe wa Mũnene had happened months earlier. From there, she cut through the adjacent farm onto a side path, not wanting to risk an encounter with the colonial police.

"*Ngatho*! Is that you, Wambũi?" her mother screamed in delight when she saw her daughter entering the homestead, and she rushed over to embrace her.

Nyina wa Kariũki, her stepmother, emerged from her hut and also gave her a big hug. Some of her siblings were home, and they also came out to greet her. In the excited chatter, Mũthee Karanja emerged from his hut and carefully tottered down the slope to join them. The voices subsided to a hush as he approached, walking slowly and deliberately, leaning on his cane.

"You have come back?" he asked, in the peculiar conversational formality of the Agikũyũ—asking certain questions that had obvious answers.

"Yes, Baba, I have come back," she smiled and said politely, before shaking the wizened hand he held out to her.

He seemed a lot older and frailer, unlike her mother and stepmother who hadn't changed at all. The grass on the compound didn't seem as green as she remembered it, or at least not as lush as the meticulously groomed lawns in the quadrangle at Alliance Girls. And there was now a shiny new barbed-wire fence surrounding the village.

"I saw a *thĩgĩngĩ*[21] fence when I was entering the village," she interjected amid the joyous conversation.

There was a long awkward pause, and the general mood seemed to darken, especially among the adults.

"They are treating us like goats now," Mũthee Karanja muttered with dismay as he dismissed himself and began to shuffle back in the direction of his hut.

"Wambũi, tell us about Kikuyu!" cried Wahome, her youngest brother, excitedly.

"Yes, tell us about Kikuyu!" her mother echoed.

---

[21] Barbed wire

Wambũi began to describe her experiences to an enthralled audience: the train ride, the girls in her school, her fleeting impressions of Nairobi . . .

At some point, Nyina wa Kariũki brought out a stool for her to sit on, and a calabash of steaming porridge. Being the center of attention was an unfamiliar experience, particularly when her mother and stepmother were among the audience. She cautiously sipped the hot beverage, grimacing slightly as a thick curd managed to slip through her partially clenched teeth.

"So, you have to speak Gĩthũngũ all the time?"

"Yes, Maitũ, many of the girls are not even Agĩkũyũ; they're from other tribes."

"Is that you, Wambũi? I greet you!" a loud deep voice bellowed from the gate, and they all turned in that direction to see Kariũki, Wambũi's younger brother.

"Kariũki, I receive your greeting!" she exclaimed, getting up hastily to hurry over and shake his hand. He had changed a lot in the short time she'd been away, and he towered over her now. His voice had also matured from one scratchy with erratic fluctuations in pitch to a smooth pleasing baritone.

He beamed at her, clearly surprised and thrilled to see her. "You have come?"

She nodded emphatically, while grinning broadly.

The rest of the evening was spent in pleasant conversation, with Wambũi having to retell some of her experiences two or three times as other family members and fellow villagers showed up. She could sense an undercurrent of gloom and resignation, but nobody seemed willing to relinquish the topic of where she had been and what she had done in the preceding three months. But slowly, clues emerged the next day.

Wambũi had always been accustomed to hearing the goats bleating after the sun came up. When this didn't happen on her first morning back, she waited until her mother was alone and asked her in hushed tones, "Maitũ, where are Baba's goats?"

Her mother glanced around quickly and then dropped her voice to a whisper. "We woke up one day and found they were gone. The gate of their enclosure had been left open. We looked for them all day, but never found them. It was around the time the Athũngũ had come with their men to put that fence around the village, and there were a lot of strange people working for them—brown people like us, but many of them were not from here, and some did not speak our language. It was not only us—many other people lost their animals."

"And the police . . ." Wambũi began, before a sharp look from her mother withered the words on her lips.

"Which police? You mean Nguru and Wilcox, those scavenging hyenas? They were the ones in charge of the people putting up the *thĩgĩngĩ* and were probably behind the thefts of the animals. As for that idiot Kĩmani, he follows them everywhere and thinks he can remain innocent while walking around with murderers . . ." She made a loud clicking noise with her tongue, indicating extreme annoyance, then bent down and picked up a pot of dirty water that she intended to pour out into the grass. "Let's go outside," she said abruptly.

It was about nine o'clock in the morning and the sun was up. The other members of the household had left the homestead to do their errands, except Mũthee Karanja who had not yet emerged from his hut. The sky was clear, with the serene mountain below it commanding the distant landscape.

"How is Baba?" Wambũi asked hesitantly.

Her mother shook her head and sighed. "He has not been the same since the goats went missing. Those animals were like his brothers. Sometimes he will come out and sit outside his hut like in the old days; but sometimes he will stay in there the whole day, and we have to keep checking on him to make sure he is still alive."

"He's looking much older than he did when I left," observed Wambũi.

"That is true."

"Did you ever hear anything more about Kariũki of Nyina wa Kariũki?"

"Nothing," her mother said looking downcast. "And nobody

likes to talk about it anymore. There is too much sadness already."
After a short pause, her mother said in a slightly more upbeat tone,
"Something interesting happened while you were gone. Remember
the Mūthūngū who used to be in the mission? The one with a big
belly, whose snoring used to wake up the people in the corner of the
village?"

"Who—Reverend Mulligan?"

"Yes, that one . . . Mūrīnga, is that how you say it? I can
never say his name properly. He went back to his country and they
brought another man to replace him, but the new one is not as
friendly as he was. And do you know, he took Deacon Mūhũyũ's
little boy home with him."

"The baby?" Wambũi looked surprised.

Her mother nodded.

"But what about Deacon Mūhũyũ's people? Why did they let
him do it?"

Moving closer, her mother whispered conspiratorially, "I
think they were very happy that he went with the boy. Some of them
felt that keeping him would bring them the same kind of *mũtino*[22] that
had befallen his family, so they were relieved when he offered.
Besides, he had become like a father to the boy—he used to go and
visit him almost every day towards the end. That was the only time

---

[22] Bad luck

he behaved like his old self; otherwise, he would walk around looking lost. Many times, when he preached, people could not follow what he was saying."

"That *is* interesting," Wambũi said, nodding. She was feeling very proud to have a grown-up conversation with her mother.

At this point, her mother started looking around for a *jembe*[23] to take with her to the fields. "*Haiya*! I have to go and prepare the ground for the planting season. Nyina wa Kariũki is already there, so I don't want to be too late. You can come with me or you can go and visit your old school friends. Your friend Mũmbi is getting married soon, did you know?"

"What!" exclaimed Wambũi, her eyes opening wide with surprise. "To whom?"

"A man from a nearby village. He already has one wife and five daughters. I think he is trying to have a son so that his father can be named."

Wambũi was flummoxed. She started to speak, but she couldn't decide what she wanted to say.

In the pause, her mother continued. "I was about her age when I got married, and Nyina wa Kariũki was about the age of that man's first wife, so it is not as strange as you might think. Still, when I was young, nobody was going to school, so as soon as you were old

---

[23] Hoe

enough to have children and take care of a home you left your parents' house. From what I have heard, Mũmbi was not interested in going to school year after year like the rest of you."

Wambũi was still in a daze when her mother set off for the *shamba*[24], looking somewhat amused at her befuddled look. "Don't stand there all day—you might grow roots and turn into a tree," her mother called out playfully as she exited the compound.

Wambũi thought she might try to visit her friends. But Wangũ and Wangarĩ were still attending Tũmũtũmũ High School, and it would not be closing until the end of the week. Her other friend, Njoki, had apparently disappeared into the forest, following her brother to join the Mau Mau. She hesitated for a moment, then started walking in the direction of Mũmbi's house, but after a few steps she abruptly changed her mind and sauntered back towards home.

---

[24] Farm

Chapter Twelve

WAMBŪI ENJOYED THE April school holidays, and they went by fast. She fell back into the rhythm of village life, eventually reconnecting with all her friends, and helping out her mother and stepmother with household chores. She spent time with her five younger siblings, particularly her younger sisters Nyokabi and Nyairero. Nyina wa Kariūki's older children had moved out of the homestead. Mūgo was working as a cook for a Mūthūngū in Nyeri, and Wambūi, her half-sister with whom she shared a name, was married and living in another village. Only Kiarie and Waitherero were still living with their mother.

She had not even considered where her train fare would come from, now that her father no longer had any animals to sell. Occasionally, her mother and stepmother would make fifty cents here and there from selling arrowroots and potatoes at the open-air market on the outskirts of Karatina, and Wambūi made several trips there with her mother that April. One often did better by exchanging items directly, rather than selling them for the Mūthūngū's money, as most of the people in the area didn't have any money. The trading post was located a safe distance from the town, where people could avoid the prowling colonial home guards who were always looking for villagers who did not have a pass.

On the day before she was to return to Kikuyu, Mũgo of Nyina wa Kariũki visited her home. As he was leaving, he took Wambũi aside.

"Here is money for the train," he whispered, pressing four one-shilling coins into her palm. "Have a safe journey back!"

She thanked him graciously.

"We help each other where we can," he said with a charming crooked smile, before he turned and started down the gentle slope towards the gate.

The next day as she sat on the train, Wambũi couldn't stop thinking about what Mũgo had done. Where would she have gotten the train fare if he hadn't come by on the day that he did? Had Mũthee Karanja sent for him—or had it been Nyina wa Kariũki? She was glad for the money, but it made her aware of a problem that would likely keep cropping up, one that she hadn't previously given any thought to.

There was no Alice Njũgũna to meet her at the train station in Kikuyu, as it was assumed that, by now, the girls would be able to find their own way to the school. She joined the stream of girls walking along the footpath in the direction of the school, each of them carrying a wooden or sheet-metal suitcase, most of them silent, although a few were engaged in conversation. When she got to the dormitory, only Susan and Edith had arrived, each of them emptying out their suitcases while they chatted quietly.

"Hello, Lydia, welcome back!" Susan called out cheerily as she and Edith stopped what they were doing to greet her.

Wambũi placed her small suitcase on the bare mattress on her bed and began to catch up with her dorm-mates. A short while later, Doris appeared, and then Elizabeth. One by one, over the course of the afternoon, more girls entered the dormitory, until the sound of their excited conversations filled the building.

The kop-kop-kop sound of shoes at the entrance of the dormitory made the younger girls turn towards the door and a couple of the older girls roll their eyes.

"You two, please take these suitcases over to my cubicle," directed Constance Muthengi when she appeared in the doorway. She was pointing at Edith and Wambũi, the only Form One girls in the room.

They all stared at her feet. She was wearing a pair of shiny black shoes with a slightly raised, pointed heel.

Wambũi was rather annoyed by her condescending manner, but that feeling was eclipsed by being perplexed about her shoes. She and Edith obediently went over to Constance's impassive, slightly built servant, and each took a heavy suitcase from him.

"Why was she wearing shoes?" Wambũi asked Susan later when Constance was out of earshot.

"It's not illegal to wear shoes before the first assembly of the school term, just as, technically, you are still allowed to wear the clothes from home you traveled in. Nobody else does it, though, except her. I think because she wants to show everyone that she is better than us."

Wambūi shook her head disapprovingly.

"Just remember that part of our education in this school is learning to live with strange people," Susan remarked sagely.

∿

Once the second term was underway, the girls adapted smoothly to the new routine. Wambūi was enjoying all her classes, as well as the company of her growing number of friends. She joined the volleyball team and began to look forward to the practice sessions and games at the end of the school day.

But there were challenges nonetheless, like the prevailing weather during the months of May through July. Cold stretches and gloomy, overcast days were a frequent occurrence, enough to dampen the mood of even the most high-spirited individual; when bare feet making contact with the frigid, hostile ground became hard to ignore. It was also during this same period that homesickness, that erstwhile banished companion, began to make an unwelcome comeback. On one such day in June, things did not go so well for Wambūi in math class.

The subject was geometry—sines, cosines and tangents—and as Ms. Atwood's voice droned on and on, the girls struggled to stay awake, casting occasional glances out the window at the unappealing gray environs, where the steady drizzle that had begun before dawn continued unabated.

Wambūi still resented Ms. Atwood for singling her out for special attention—she felt she was just picking on her, and her classmates continued to tease her about it. But she'd stoically managed to keep her composure until now, when she finally reached a tipping point. As she sat hunched over to keep warm, she felt the cold air through her sweater, adding another irritant into the mix. So when Ms. Atwood called on her for the fourth time, she was as surprised as everybody else at her reaction.

"My name is not Lydia!" Wambūi snapped.

There was an astonished reaction from her classmates, who all turned to look at her in disbelief. This was not the gentle, easygoing Wambūi they knew.

"I beg your pardon!" Ms. Atwood exclaimed angrily.

Wambūi wished she had the power to make herself disappear at that instant, but all she could do was bury her head in her hands instead.

"Lydia Karanja, is there something you would like to say? If so, I'm giving you the chance to say it right now!" Ms. Atwood said, with a steely edge to her voice. By now, her whole face was flushed red.

"I'm sorry," Wambũi mumbled in a shaky voice as the tears ran down her face, which was still hidden in her hands.

"You will see me after class!" said Ms. Atwood curtly, before resuming the lesson.

Nobody really paid any attention to the remaining fifteen minutes of the class. And even though they kept their eyes fixed on the teacher, their thoughts were elsewhere—wondering about what had just happened, and anticipating an opportunity later in the day to tell the story to their friends.

The class ended, and as her classmates silently exited the room, Wambũi sat quietly at her desk waiting in dread of what was to come. After everyone had left, Ms. Atwood approached her.

"Look up!" she said sternly.

Wambũi raised her face from her hands. Her eyes were red and tears were still streaming down her cheeks.

"What *is* the matter?" asked Ms. Atwood.

"I'm sorry . . ." blurted Wambũi, as she gulped deep breaths of air to control her sobs.

"Telling me you are sorry does not explain what you did. I would like an explanation for your outburst. Is Lydia not your name? Have I been mistaken all this time?"

Wambũi shook her head.

"Then what is the problem?"

There was a long silence, punctuated only by Wambũi's sniffling.

"What do they call you at home?" Ms. Atwood asked softly, sounding a more conciliatory note.

"Wambũi."

"Is that what you prefer I call you?"

Wambũi nodded.

"Very well, Wambũi. I'm not sure I understand the meaning of all this, but I will address you by the name you prefer. But please be warned that any other episodes of rude and disruptive behavior will not be tolerated. You are a very gifted mathematics student, but that means little if you are poorly behaved—do you understand?"

"Yes, Ms. Atwood."

"You are dismissed. Now, hurry along to your next class!"

☲

A few days after the incident, Eileen Atwood arranged to meet with Mrs. Barbour, the school principal. She was a tough, iron-willed woman in her mid-fifties, with short, meticulously groomed curly brown hair that was graying at the temples. She was a stickler for the rules that kept the school running like clockwork, and attitudes towards her generally ranged from dread to respect, the latter often tinged with admiration. She was undeniably the engine behind the success and reputation of the school, having been present from the day it opened its doors.

"Good morning, Eileen. You wanted to see me?" she asked.

"Yes, Mrs. Barbour. I need your advice regarding one of my students."

"I hope it isn't a disciplinary issue, is it?"

Eileen laughed nervously and began to explain the situation. When she finished talking, there was a puzzled look on Mrs. Barbour's face.

"I'm not sure I understand the problem."

Eileen cringed inwardly and tried to clarify the meaning of what she'd already shared. But Mrs. Barbour stopped her before she got very far.

"I understand that part; you already explained it. She completed a quiz in thirty minutes instead of an hour and got everything right. And you gave her a second quiz in the time left, and she completed it in the remaining time and got everything right . . . indicating that she works twice as fast as her colleagues and is a clever mathematician. Is there more?"

"Er . . . yes. That would be impressive enough, Mrs. Barbour. But here's what's different. The second quiz was for the Form Three students, and I had them do it on that very same day. Despite completing it in half the time that it took the Form Three students, she was the only one who got all the sums right. The next highest score was eighty-six percent."

Mrs. Barbour's eyebrows rose and she leaned back in her chair. "Is that so?"

"Yes. Most of the questions on the test covered material that she has not been taught."

"Hmm, that is very impressive!" rejoined Mrs. Barbour with a nod, followed by a long pause.

"What should I do?" asked Eileen, breaking the silence.

"Keep challenging her, that's for sure. I do foresee a problem, though. At the rate she is going, there will be nothing else to teach her by the end of her first year, and that is assuming she cannot already work out what the Form Four girls are learning. That is certainly an unusual situation."

"Are there special schools for students like her?" Eileen ventured. "And should we think about steering her along a certain career path?"

Mrs. Barbour appeared to bristle at the first question, when she heard the words "special schools." "This is the premier school for girls in the region, so she is exactly where she needs to be. The question regarding careers is a much more complicated one, I think."

"How so?" asked Eileen.

"Let's pretend for a moment that this girl was called Emily Watson, a young lass with blue eyes and golden curls, born in Kensington. What career opportunities might she have?"

Eileen grimaced and her eyes narrowed as she pondered the question. "Well, I suppose she could study mathematics at Oxford or Cambridge and become a distinguished scholar . . ."

"Yes, absolutely. But besides being a scholar or a teacher, can you think of any other opportunities where this girl's talent might be considered welcome. Note my use of the word 'welcome' rather than 'useful.' "

Eileen felt a flush of anger and embarrassment as she finally understood the direction of Mrs. Barbour's discourse.

Mrs. Barbour continued unrelentingly. "Now, if she had been born Peter Wilson with a similar or even lesser talent, there would have been a wide array of interested parties, such as the Royal Air Force, the Navy, companies that specialize in research and development—areas where a quick mathematical mind would be a winning asset. Unfortunately, that mind has to be in the body of a man. I don't agree with that premise, but that's the way the world is right now."

"Well, it makes me very angry!" Eileen exclaimed.

"Me, too. When I was growing up, I wanted to be an engineer. But it was made very clear to me from a young age that the obstacles along that path might be difficult to overcome, so I chose to be a teacher instead. I was encouraged to go in that direction by one of my own teachers whom I respect and revere to this day. I don't regret my decision—I like to think I'm making a difference in this world."

Eileen rose to leave, thanking Mrs. Barbour as she did. But the principal still had more to say.

"Do you think the Africans have intellectual capabilities equal to ours?"

"I most certainly do!" Eileen said, her eyes flashing angrily.

"Please calm down," Mrs. Barbour said, noting the abrupt change in her demeanor. "The only reason I ask is because it is possible to do this job, and very effectively, with a different expectation from our students here than we might have from our students in England. In many ways, it's comparable to our teachers there, many of whom were gracious and taught us very well, but deep down didn't think we were as clever as the boys in many subjects."

"This is a long way to travel if you don't believe in what you do," Eileen suggested, somewhat aggressively.

"Oh, our teachers believe in what they're doing—they may just hold different beliefs and expectations from yours! As far as I'm concerned, as long as they do what's expected of them, which is to teach with the same rigor as they would back home, then maybe what they believe on the inside doesn't really matter in the end."

"How about you, Mrs. Barbour," Eileen asked somewhat hesitantly as she headed towards the door. "What are your beliefs?"

"I'm willing to give the natives a chance to prove themselves to me, one way or the other," Mrs. Barbour said with a shrug.

Chapter Thirteen

As THE END of the second term approached, and hints of the warm sunny days of August began to appear, Wambũi had something on her mind and she was not quite sure who to talk to about it. It was the kind of thing that a friend or classmate would not be able to help with, but it was not suitable to discuss with a teacher either. She had been mulling it over for a number of weeks, and the day she ran into Alice Njũgũna her question was ripe for asking—and Alice seemed to be just the right person to ask.

After exchanging a few pleasantries, Alice was about to break away when Wambũi spoke up.

"Er . . . who normally does the work around the school when we leave for the holidays?"

"What kind of work? You mean, like my work?"

"No. I mean like weeding the flowerbeds, cleaning the administration building . . . things like that."

Alice looked puzzled. "Normally, we have the school workers do it, and if we need extra help for the duties you girls usually perform, we hire casual laborers from the nearby village. That's a strange question. Why do you ask?"

Wambūi squirmed and hesitated briefly, before she answered. "Um, I can't afford to take the train each holiday, so I was thinking that maybe I could stay around in August and earn some money, then go home in December."

A serious look came over Alice's face. "Is everything okay at home?"

"It's just . . . it's just that . . . when I was last there . . ." Wambūi's voice trailed off as she felt a mixture of sadness and embarrassment beginning to well up inside her.

"It's okay, Lydia. I'll check with Mrs. Barbour and see what she thinks. We've never done this before, so I don't know what she will say. Where would you stay, though? The dormitories are usually locked up over the holidays, you know."

Wambūi was silent. She hadn't gone that far in her planning.

"Here's what we'll do," said Alice decisively. "If Mrs. Barbour says that it's okay, you can come and stay at my place. We have a small one-bedroom house. You would have to sleep on the floor in the living room as the chairs are neither big nor comfortable; so maybe we could put a blanket on the floor you could sleep on. Also," she added with a twinkle in her eye, "you should know that my one-year-old wakes up sometimes at night and all of us with him."

Wambūi's eyes lit up with excitement. "Thank you. Thank you, that would be very nice!"

"Don't thank me yet. I don't know if Mrs. Barbour will even agree to this plan."

Mrs. Barbour's response turned out to be favorable. And so, on the last day of school, as the other girls filed towards the gate, making their way to the train station, Wambũi discreetly veered off in the direction of Alice Njũgũna's house. She would receive one shilling a week for her work, which meant she wouldn't have to worry about her train fare back to school after she went home in December.

The school was lonely after the other girls left. Wambũi felt strange walking along the same paths she walked every day, but with a different purpose and identity. There was a lot to be done, and she moved energetically from one task to another until at some point the sweat was dripping down her face and her back began to ache. By the end of the first day, Wambũi was exhausted; and after having dinner with Alice and her family, she curled up in the corner of the living room and fell fast asleep.

On the second day, Mrs. Barbour surprised her by stopping to talk as she swept the walkway to the administration building. It was an odd experience because normally the only time you spoke to Mrs. Barbour as a student was when you were in trouble. She was smiling, and she called her by name.

"Is everything going okay, Lydia?" she asked cheerfully.

"Yes, Mrs. Barbour," Wambũi replied nervously.

"Keep up the good work! I admire your resourcefulness," she said as she entered the building.

Wambũi's heart swelled with pride and she threw herself back into her work with renewed energy. At about eleven o'clock, a familiar voice called out to her.

"Wambũi?"

She turned around to see Ms. Atwood.

"I thought that was you. What are you still doing in school?"

Wambũi unabashedly explained her situation. By now, after the validation she'd received from Alice and Mrs. Barbour, she no longer felt any shame or hesitation.

"Where are you staying?" the teacher asked quizzically. "The dormitories are closed, aren't they?"

"Yes, I'm staying with Alice Njũgũna."

"God love Alice! She's a beautiful soul. How's her little boy?"

"He is doing very well."

"Well, I'm sure I'll see you around," Ms. Atwood said, starting to resume her walk. After taking a few steps, she turned back to Wambũi. "I don't know if Alice would be offended, but I have an extra bedroom in my house and you're welcome to stay there if you like."

Wambũi shook her head. "I'm fine, but thank you very much."

"Let me know if you change your mind."

"I definitely will. Thank you."

Two days later, after dinner, Alice and Wambũi were talking.

"Ms. Atwood mentioned to me today that she would like you to consider her offer to stay at her place. She wanted to make sure it was okay with me first because she didn't want to offend me or have me think she went behind my back."

Wambũi looked up at Alice, not sure what to say.

Alice continued. "Eileen is a good person. She means what she says, unlike some of the others. I would not feel slighted if you wanted to stay with her. Besides, she mentioned that she could use your help around her house and is willing to give you an additional fifty cents a week, alongside the one shilling a week the school will pay you. Between you and me, I don't think there's that much work around her house—I think she's just making up an excuse to give you some extra money."

But Alice could tell that her young companion had some lingering doubts. "Lydia, if I'd heard that request from half the teachers in the school, I would have said no. Many of them will smile at you, but have something completely different going on in their heads from what you see on the outside. I know Eileen and I trust her. Besides, think of it this way—if you plan on doing this again on any other school holiday over the next four years, it would be better for you if you had a room with a bed, rather than sleeping on my hard floor."

"Okay," Wambũi said, sounding reassured, "if you think that I should do it, then I will do it."

Chapter Fourteen

MŨTHEE KARANJA OCCASIONALLY had strange thoughts and dreams about things that ended up happening days, weeks or even years later. This didn't happen very often, but when it did there were usually indications that what he had seen in his mind's eye was more than just the product of an overactive imagination.

Once, as a boy, he had awakened from a scary dream about a big, shiny snake with smoke coming out of its head. His heart was pounding when he awoke, and he had been relieved when he realized it was only a dream. Later in the day, he had mentioned it to his mother.

"Maitũ, last night I dreamed about a big, shiny snake . . ." he began, only to be cut short by his mother.

"Don't talk about things like that!" she said brusquely. "If you do, they might think you are inviting them to come and visit you."

Karanja felt duly chastised and didn't bring it up again. Nor did he mention the strange-looking man in that same dream, whose skin was the same color as the palm of his hand. It wasn't until about ten years later that people began talking about the arrival of a tribe of people with light skin who spoke as if through their nose. When he first saw the train steaming across the countryside, he felt a frisson of disquiet and foreboding as his thoughts flashed back to the giant snake of his childhood dream. He remembered how frightened it had made him feel.

Most of the time, he kept his unusual thoughts to himself, though sometimes his friends would observe an occurrence they recalled him having mentioned in passing weeks before. They also noticed that he often talked to animals, including their own goats and sheep, in a way that was a bit strange. Of course, many people talk to animals, and would like to believe the animals are listening. And some even train their animals to respond in a specific way to certain words or gestures, which is gratifying to the human, as it fulfils one of the basic cravings of human beings, which is to be heard. But with Mūthee Karanja, it was a distinctive kind of communication.

One day, while he and his friends were out in the forest grazing their animals, a deep guttural roar from atop one of the trees caused them to freeze in their tracks. Even before the spotted eminence peeled itself away from the bough it had been imperceptibly intertwined with moments earlier, the boys knew they were in major trouble. It was no use trying to outrun a leopard. Their goats had heard the warning roar and were running helter-skelter into the trees—some possibly headed into the jaws of another predator.

"Owner of many spots, receive my greeting!" the young Karanja had called out calmly, to the surprise of his terrified companions.

There was a long, low-pitched growl as the fearsome feline effortlessly made its way down the tree branch.

Karanja had started to say something else, when the beast abruptly leaped five feet to the ground. By the time it landed, his companions had erupted into a mad dash, headed toward the village. The leopard sauntered over to Karanja and rubbed its head against his thigh, then flopped down lazily at his feet. His friends didn't witness that final interaction because they were sprinting for their lives. When Karanja returned to the village half an hour later with all the herds intact, they were amazed and confused, but too ashamed to ask him how he'd avoided getting mauled by the wild beast.

Mūthee Karanja's wives both knew there was something amiss the night they heard a large branch snap off the *mūgumo* tree. When he emerged from his hut the next morning, he looked haggard and despondent. It was clear he hadn't slept all night.

"They have killed Kĩmathi!" he announced to them as if it were a matter of fact.

Wambūi's mother let out an involuntary gasp of shock and glanced at her co-wife who flinched but said nothing. A heavy dread descended upon them as Karanja left the compound and began to walk slowly towards the village, leaning against his walking stick.

"What shall we do?" Wambūi's mother asked her co-wife.

"Is there anything to do except to be sad? That is all we are able to do these days."

It wasn't until two days later that the news came to the rest of the village, as someone returning from Nyeri arrived and started telling everyone what he had heard. A few people broke into tears, but for the most part the faces of the villagers bore the same grim expressions they had gotten used to wearing every day.

≈

After four years at Alliance Girls, Wambui and her classmates continued with the next phase of their studies at Technical College in Nairobi, which offered the advanced level classes of Form Five and Six. Wambũi had just started Form Five when she heard the news about the death of Dedan Kĩmathi. She managed to put on a brave face throughout the day, but when she lay in bed that night she cried uncontrollably. Most of the other girls had carried on through the day like she had, pretending that nothing had happened, only waiting for an opportune moment to discuss in whispers what this meant and how it might affect their lives.

Wambũi's time at Alliance had gone well; and she had excelled in her studies and made many friends. She had spent her April and August holidays at Ms. Atwood's house, working in the school compound; and by Form Two, she was making two shillings and fifty cents a week, which meant that when she did go home there was money left over to give her parents and not just to pay for the train. The looks on the faces of her younger siblings had been priceless the first time she came home with a handful of *sukari wa nguru* (molasses cubes) that she had purchased for them for twenty cents at the train station on the way home.

As the state of emergency dragged on, with random arrests, searches and killings, life seemed to get darker and more hopeless by the day. It was more difficult now to go to the farms to plant or harvest; and sometimes when one planted, especially if it was something like maize, someone else would harvest it and reap the benefits. Fortunately, unlike the sheep and goats that had been easy targets, neither the colonial home guards nor the Mau Mau had any interest in spending time digging up tubers, such as arrowroots or potatoes. Every time Wambũi came home there seemed to be something new to worry about. She felt guilty, because at school she did not have to think about those things.

At Technical College, she wore her first pair of shoes. The experience was anticlimactic. She wasn't sure what she'd been expecting, but joy and comfort were not among the adjectives she would have used to describe her experience. Still, everyone was wearing shoes there, so it would have been a bit odd if she didn't. She observed that many people preferred to take a break from them over the weekend, in much the same way an executive might choose not to wear a necktie on their days off.

As her two years at Technical College progressed, there was much discussion about the next step that would follow. Many people were considering enrolling in degree programs at the prestigious Makerere University in Uganda. It was assumed that this was the path Wambũi would take as well. After all, she had never seen any grade less than an A in mathematics, and she had been the head girl at Alliance in her final year there, which was an exceptional honor. Wambũi herself had lived every day under this assumption, receiving strong encouragement from Ms. Atwood as well as Mrs. Ogolla, her mathematics teacher at Technical College, who also happened to be the career advisor.

Sometime during the course of her final year, an unusual thought began to gnaw at her. She wasn't sure where it came from, and initially she dismissed it out of hand; but the more she thought about it, the less illogical it seemed. Maybe it was the trips home, where she stepped back into her family's abject poverty, noticing more and more the helpless, despondent looks of her mother, stepmother and Mũthee Karanja, seeing their shame as they struggled to put a meal before her, sometimes needing to borrow potatoes or flour from a neighbor. Before she went to Alliance, there was usually something to eat in the morning and in the evening. Now, having one meal for the day was an achievement. She saw that her mother would serve the children and Mũthee Karanja first, and eat only if there was food left over.

The fighting had destroyed most people's property and livelihood, and there was no indication that things were about to get better. Wambũi's feelings of guilt deepened because she would visit for a few weeks, and then return to her comfortable life where there were three meals a day and where she didn't have to worry about home guards or Mau Mau coming in the middle of the night. And the shoes made her feel even worse. So she decided she didn't want her family to see them, as they would have been an obvious marker of how different her current life was from theirs. She therefore got into the habit of taking them off when she debarked from the train in Karatina, and donning them once more either on the return journey or when she arrived back in Nairobi.

She was feeling quite nervous when she knocked on the door of Mrs. Ogolla's office.

"Hello, Lydia—please come in!" she called out from behind her desk when she saw Wambũi's face as she cracked open the door.

Wambũi entered the room and sat across the desk from her.

"How are your studies coming along?" she inquired casually.

"Very well, thank you."

"How may I be of assistance today?"

"I . . . er . . . I would like to find out about getting a certificate in teacher training."

"You have a relative who wants to pursue a teacher training course?"

"Um, actually it's me."

Mrs. Ogolla's eyebrows arched in surprise but she quickly regained her composure. "You?"

"Yes, Madam."

"Why? I thought you were planning on going to the university."

Wambūi swallowed hard. "I was, but my family is struggling . . ." Her voice trailed off. She took in a deep breath.

Mrs. Ogolla spoke softly in sympathetic tones. "I'm sorry, my child; I'm sorry to hear that. We're living in troubled times, and it is sad when a young person like you has to carry the weight of an entire family on her shoulders. I do understand your predicament." So she proceeded to explain the process of obtaining the certificate, which would require only one additional year of school, and would qualify Wambūi to teach in primary school, and possibly even some high schools.

Wambūi listened intently, and the more she heard, the more certain she became that this was the best option for her.

"Well, then," Mrs. Ogolla said as she wrapped up the conversation, "I wish you every success in this endeavor. Please remember, if things settle down in future, it is never too late to go back to the university. A brilliant mathematician like you would be an asset worth boasting about for any university."

Chapter Fifteen

THE EXTRA YEAR Wambũi needed to complete the teacher training program went by much faster than she'd anticipated. And she had no trouble getting a job as a math teacher at Tũmũtũmũ High School. While it was a comfort to be back in familiar surroundings, it also seemed like everything there was much smaller and a lot less impressive than she remembered. She felt a twinge of regret when she thought of her friends who had gone on to Uganda to get their degrees. But those feelings were short-lived when she thought of all the needs of her family that simply couldn't wait any longer.

Her first month's salary was quickly swallowed up by the sundry expenses the impoverished household required. It was like the first rainfall arriving unexpectedly on the parched soil after a prolonged drought, bringing sighs of relief and proud tears along with exclamations like, "I never gave up—I knew it would come!"

But she withheld her surprise for her father until she felt the security situation was favorable enough, as the state of emergency sputtered to its eagerly anticipated end. The look on his face was priceless when she walked into the compound one day with a brown and white nanny goat sauntering nonchalantly behind her at the end of a rope. His squinting rheumy eyes lit up with excitement and his wrinkled leathery face cracked a smile as she tied the rope around a tree and the goat promptly began munching on the grass in its vicinity.

"This one is for you, Baba!" Wambũi announced triumphantly.

"Very good!" he said nodding emphatically, "very, very good!"

The neighbors in the village had congratulated Mũthee Karanja's family on their daughter's return as a schoolteacher, which instantly elevated their status, as teachers were a rare and highly respected lot. The fact she had so immediately began to invest precious shillings in her family's well-being was quickly noticed, eliciting numerous murmurs and nods of approval among the adults in the village. Some of the old men who now openly admired her achievement were the same ones who had shaken their heads in disbelief when the maverick Mũthee Karanja inexplicably sold his prize goat to send his daughter of marriageable age to school, choosing to forfeit a dowry of many goats that would have been his to claim. These men's daughters were married now, but whatever they had received from their dowries was no longer evident. Back then, Mũthee Karanja's stoic but irrational defiance regarding Wambũi's education had amazed them, and they were certain that his stubborn, unconventional perspective would be his undoing. They now regaled him as a farsighted genius who had made his move based on an improbable but ultimately accurate prediction.

Most of the teachers at Tũmũtũmũ were Athũngũ, but there

were quite a number of African teachers there, some of whom had come from as far afield as Embu and Kitui. Wambũi recognized many of the students who had come from Karatina by their family names. They all knew about her and were in perpetual awe of her, having already heard from their parents and relatives about the Karanja girl who had gone to school in Kikuyu. Tũmũtũmũ was one of the biggest schools in the area, so there were also children from Nyeri and even Mũranga. Even when all the students from outside the Karatina area were considered, the entire student body was from the Agĩkũyũ community.

At Alliance she had met girls from all the different tribes of Kenya, which had been an exciting experience for her, as they all spoke with distinct accents and described homelands that were starkly different from hers. Some were from warm, muggy lands close to the ocean or a lake—full of mosquitoes—but places where it was so warm that there was no need to bundle up even when they were outside at night. Some of the others had described desert-like places where it was unbearably hot even in the shade during the day, and so extremely cold at night they might have been even colder than Karatina. All the girls had undoubtedly returned home and told their fascinated families about their friends and where they came from; and the ones who went on to Makerere would have a completely new experience to relate after their encounters with students from the other countries in East Africa.

Wambũi had always enjoyed math, but she soon found out that she hated teaching it. Everything that seemed obvious and intuitive to her was met with blank looks and occasional groans of despair. She made every effort to be patient, but she often found herself wondering with a strong sense of trepidation if this was how she was going to spend the rest of her life.

After Wambũi had given her students their first quiz, she realized that her doubts and misgivings were not unfounded. The highest score was sixty percent, and there were a few in the forty percent range. But more than half the class had scored zero, which meant they might just as well have not shown up for the test. It may not be obvious to a non-teacher, but failure is as much the teacher's problem as it is their student's. Had she rushed them too quickly through the lessons or had she prepared a test that did not accurately cover the material she had taught? She reviewed their answers, scanning for a logical pattern, but there was none.

The students bravely accepted their scores and promised to do better the next time, a few of them trying hard to suppress the tears brimming in their eyes. In the weeks that followed, Wambũi slowed down her presentation of the material, and frequently asked questions to make sure everyone was moving at the same pace. Her students, who were in Form Three, made every effort to engage with her through the lessons and nodded whenever she made an important point, indicating they were still in sync with her. When the next test came there was one score of seventy-five percent and a number of students in the fifty and sixty percent range, much better than the first quiz results. But she could tell there was still a problem, as she had deliberately made the test easy in her estimation, asking very straightforward questions.

Tūmūtūmū was about an hour's walk from where her family lived. She lived in a small one-bedroom house on the school campus and usually spent her weekdays there, traveling home to be with her family on the weekend. Usually she could hitch a ride with one of the few teachers who owned an automobile, or with Ng'ang'a, the van driver for the nearby hospital, who was from her village. On some occasions, when the weather was nice and she had the time, she would go on foot, cutting through farms and villages, following paths she knew well from her childhood.

One Saturday, about a year after she returned to Karatina, she went into town to look around a hardware store, one owned by a Gikũyũ shopkeeper, on a backstreet. What she had in mind was the possibility of building small houses of wood and aluminum sheets to replace the mud and thatch houses that Mũthee Karanja, her mother and Nyina wa Kariũki lived in. She had absolutely no idea what it took to build a house, but she figured there was no harm in taking a look around and seeing what ideas she could come up with.

KĨNG'ORI AND SONS HARDWARE SHOP—a small handwritten sign on the door of the store boldly proclaimed. Most of the stores in Karatina were owned by Athũngũ and Ahĩndĩ (people of Indian origin); but a few adventurous Agĩkũyũ were starting to try out this new mode of commerce which was not very different from that of the traders who bartered merchandise in the sprawling shade of mũratina trees in the days of old. She stood hesitantly at the door, feeling somewhat intimidated, when she heard a voice call out to her in Gĩkũyũ from the inside.

"Please come in. There is no charge for looking around!"

Aware that someone had been watching her, she sheepishly stepped into the dimly lit room that was about a thousand square feet in area, densely stacked with an untidy assortment of wooden planks, iron pipes and plastic tubs filled with nuts, bolts and screws. It had a musty, woodsy smell. The person who'd addressed her was a slender dark man in his late fifties with a graying mustache and sideburns; he had a calm demeanor.

"Are you looking for something in particular?" Mr. Kĩng'ori asked the bewildered-looking customer.

"What do I need to build a house?" she blurted, wishing she could retrieve the awkward words the minute they left her mouth.

The shopkeeper looked confused for a moment, but then saw an opportunity. "You mean a house of wood and *mabati* (corrugated aluminum sheets), not like the usual traditional houses? We have all the supplies here, and whatever we don't have we can get for you. Also, we can help you find a *fundi* (builder) if you don't already have one."

Her eyes brightened. "How much would a small house cost? One that is about the size of a *thingira* (man's hut)?"

Mr. Kĩng'ori leaned forward and peered closely at the visitor, realizing that a serious transaction was in the making, and he pulled out a large sheet of squared paper and a pencil. "Are you from Karatina?" he asked casually as he started drawing up a list of building materials.

"Yes," she said, smiling now.

"Who are your people?" he asked with undisguised curiosity.

"My father is Mũthee Karanja, the one who lives on the hill near the big *mũgumo* tree."

"Oh, yes, I know of Mũthee Karanja, he is a respected elder. Isn't he the one who sent a daughter to the school in Kikuyu?"

Wambũi smiled self-consciously, never quite having come to terms with her own notoriety. "Yes, I am that one," she said meekly.

This last revelation lit up the room, and the conversation transformed from a cautious, respectful interaction between strangers to a relaxed and jovial conversation between people who had never met but were supposed to know each other. Mr. Kĩng'ori drew up a list of materials and estimates as they chatted, sharing news about different families and prominent people in the town. A loud noise from the back interrupted them as a man in his twenties appeared, carefully gripping a stack of *mabati* that he was transporting to a corner of the store. He didn't acknowledge their presence at all, so focused was he on finding a spot for the sheets in the tight space that was their destination.

"Mwangi, come and say hello to Mwalimu (teacher); she is the daughter of Mūthee Karanja who went to school in Kikuyu."

Mwangi was a carbon copy of Kĩng'ori, just a couple of decades younger. He didn't speak much, but he was very polite when he did; and he stayed and listened intently to the conversation between his father and Wambũi.

When Wambũi left the hardware store an hour and a half later, she was elated. She felt as if the house that had seemed like such an abstract and half-baked notion earlier in the day was starting to seem like a very real prospect.

≋

It did not take long before the collective angst of Wambũi's math students became a source of concern among other members of the staff. Not that the students themselves had complained—far from it; they were all humble and respectful, highly motivated with regard to their education, hoping to eventually land jobs in Nyeri or Nairobi so they could support their families. The fact that the arcane discipline of mathematics was apparently terrorizing all of them seemed to impart solidarity and bolster their determination. But at the end of the term, the numerous C's, D's and E's alongside only a few B's and a rare A in math raised a red flag.

Maureen Livingstone, the headmistress at Tūmūtūmū, sent for Wambũi one day. It was her sixth month of teaching. She'd spoken to Mrs. Livingstone once before on her first day at the school but not since. The headmistress was unpredictable, so most who knew her thought it wise to keep a respectful distance. She'd been known to yell at fellow teachers in public, but had also drawn shocked gasps and guffaws from students and teachers alike for sudden spontaneous actions that were considered totally unbecoming to a person of her stature, such as when she decided to join in the 100-yard dash on Sports Day at the school.

During one of the heats, there were two open lanes, and nobody thought much of it when the headmistress approached the athletic director, Mr. Phillips, and started chatting with him. They watched as his demeanor stiffened and a puzzled expression came over his face, followed by a resigned shrug. At that point no one had any idea what was going on, and it was only when Mrs. Livingstone kicked off her shoes and took her place alongside the other runners that a hush fell over the crowd, while people exchanged incredulous glances. The whistle blew and off she went, all 250 pounds of her, clad in a flowery print dress that fluttered comically in her wake. She moved a lot faster than anyone could have imagined.

Unbeknownst to her audience, she had been the 100-yard champion at her high school several decades earlier. Between that and the fact that her fellow competitors were so flummoxed at the sight of her unexpectedly in their midst, she came in second. The next five minutes were filled with hoarse cheers of "Livi! Livi!"— which was her nickname—with girls and teachers alike doubled over with laughter and excitement.

Wambũi knocked nervously on the door of Mrs. Livingstone's office. Her palms were moist, and she could feel her heart pounding. When a voice answered from the inside, she pushed the door open and walked in.

The headmistress was sitting at her desk, and she peered over her glasses as she continued writing. "Hello, Lydia, come in and have a seat."

Wambũi sat down quietly. A few stretched-out seconds followed in which the headmistress continued writing; finally, she put her pen down and took off her glasses, and stared directly at Wambũi.

"How is your work coming along?" Mrs. Livingstone asked in a neutral tone.

"It's fine, I think."

"Any particular challenges so far?"

"Not really."

Mrs. Livingstone leaned back in her chair. "Your students seem to have done worse than would be expected in their end-of-term exams. Any thoughts as to what the problem might be?"

Wambũi gulped nervously and shook her head, shifting her gaze to the floor.

"Do you remember Ms. Atwood, your former teacher at

Alliance?"

Wambũi looked up and nodded, surprised at the mention of her former teacher's name.

"Well," Mrs. Livingstone continued, seeming to have derived some satisfaction from the baffled look she had brought to Wambũi's face. "Ms. Atwood and I met at a teacher's conference a few months ago and she was very excited to have news of you. She thinks very highly of you, although she did express some concern that you might have trouble teaching others what comes naturally to you."

Wambũi started to relax a little, the favorable mention of her former math teacher bringing with it some reassurance that her job wasn't in jeopardy.

Mrs. Livingstone went on to share some tips and cautionary tales—drawn from her own experience—of how to make the best of this early phase of her career. "You're going to need to watch and listen to your students, Lydia," she summed up, after a half-hour of discussion where she did most of the talking. "Your students will teach you to become a better teacher, but only if you listen to them."

Wambũi left the office relieved and invigorated, unlike many others she'd seen who'd emerged with stony countenances and occasionally bloodshot eyes. She felt very grateful to Ms. Atwood for having put in a timely good word on her behalf.

〰
〰

The estimate from Mr. Kĩng'ori gave Wambũi a timeline of about two years of saving before she could afford to put up a basic structure—although there was also the option of building it bit by bit, paying for each piece of work as she obtained the funds. But ultimately she decided on an option that was in-between. She would save up for a year and get the bulk of initial materials ready, then continue paying monthly and adding to the structure until it became habitable.

She hadn't yet breathed a word of her plan to her family—she didn't want them to get their hopes up and then be disappointed if things didn't work out. Her trips to the hardware store left her feeling excited and motivated, and made up for the problems she was having in her struggle to make the transition from being a good student to a good teacher. But she felt she was making some progress in that area, too. By asking her students to solve problems on the blackboard, she was able to observe how they processed information; she tried to refrain from jumping in to help them unless they went totally off-track, which happened often enough. All in all, the students seemed to enjoy their new sense of empowerment, but there were still a fair number of dull, distant looks.

One day when Wambũi was home visiting for the weekend, Mũthee Karanja sent for her. Since her return, she'd felt the change in their relationship—from a vertical one in which she spoke only when spoken to, to one that was more horizontal and engaging. She was clearly his favorite child, but since he was a wise man, he tried not to let it show.

"A certain man by the name Kĩng'ori was asking about you yesterday . . ." he began.

She looked startled, but said nothing. Was he talking about the hardware man? If so, she hoped Kĩng'ori hadn't ruined her surprise by telling her father about her plan to build him a house.

"Kĩng'ori is a good man, I know his family. He has a son called Mwangi who knows about you. They would like to come and visit."

A marriage proposal! Traditional marriage etiquette dictated that if a young man was interested in a girl, then his father would gather a group of elders and they would visit the girl's house, usually stating the purpose of their visit in vague and meandering euphemisms. "Our young man here was passing by this household and he saw something that made him think it may be a good idea to pay a visit . . ." someone might say by way of introduction to their presence.

If the initial visit was favorable, there would be subsequent visits with dowry negotiations, eventually culminating in the wedding. The process was delicate, and words were chosen carefully—any misunderstanding risked derailing the process or adding a punitive surcharge to the bride-price. Normally the people appointed to speak on behalf of the families were good orators and negotiators, having earned their reputations from previous weddings or other social events.

Wambũi was stunned. In all her visits to the hardware store, she had been single-mindedly focused on her project and had spoken for the most part with Mr. Kĩng'ori. His son Mwangi often joined them but he usually didn't say much. Never in her wildest imaginings had she considered the possibility of being married to him, or that the jovial shop owner whom she enjoyed exchanging ideas with would one day be her father-in-law.

"I will only let them come if you want them to come," said Mũthee Karanja reassuringly.

Her eyes were misty, her thoughts all jumbled up. She didn't know how she felt; this was completely unexpected.

"Yes, Baba," she said finally in a shaky voice, "tell them to come."

〰〰

There had been nervous waiting on the part of other family members regarding the fact that Wambũi had returned from Nairobi seemingly oblivious to the expectation that it was time for her to "settle down." Indeed, failure to undergo this significant rite of passage would have emboldened the now-silent naysayers who had predicted that having sent her to Kikuyu to learn the ways of the Athũngũ would result in her total unmooring from who she was and what the community expected of her. It was true that she hadn't really given much thought to courtship and marriage. What with her family's difficulties and the acute awareness that she was the one best positioned to help, how could she be expected to plan for a life away from the people who depended on her? But events unfolded in spite of her, and after her conversation with her father, she decided it all felt right.

Wambũi and Mwangi's wedding was remembered by the villagers as one of the first weddings in her village where tea and bread were served to the guests at the reception. At the time, these were considered exotic delicacies enjoyed exclusively by shoe-wearing city types. Traditional wedding fare at that time usually consisted of dishes like *ndũma* (arrowroots), *ngwacĩ* (sweet potatoes), *njahĩ* (mashed black beans) and goat meat, all respectable staples but without the allure of the fancy new foods that had arrived with the Athũngũ. Also unique about their wedding was the number of shoe-wearing, non-Agĩkũyũ guests in attendance. There were a number of people who had come from Nairobi and Kikuyu, including Mrs. Ogolla and Ms. Atwood, as well as former classmates of Wambũi and her current colleagues at Tũmũtũmũ.

Once they were married, the subtle pressure to "name" their offspring would begin. The first son would be named after the paternal grandfather and the second after the maternal grandfather, with a similar pattern applied for daughters with respect to their grandmothers. Once the grandparents' names were taken, the names of the parents' siblings would be used, from eldest to youngest, paternal alternating with maternal. The first son would therefore be Kĩng'ori, after Mwangi's father, while the first daughter was Mũthoni, after Mwangi's mother; the second son and daughter would be Karanja (after Mũthee Karanja) and Wanja (after Wambũi's mother), respectively. Four children, two boys and two girls, would therefore be ideal to carry on the name of both the bride and groom's parents. Most regarded this custom as sacred, and some went as far as considering the grandchild an incarnation of the person for whom they were named. As a result, an illogical partiality might sometimes be observed with a spouse showing a predilection for children named after their own parents over siblings named after their spouse's parents.

Wambũi settled down into married life and continued working on demystifying the cryptic philosophy of mathematics to her students. When she wasn't teaching, she was usually at the hardware store, working with her husband and father-in-law. Kĩng'ori soon realized she had an unusual knack for predicting what items they needed to stock up on before his customers came asking for them; and concepts about managing the business that had taken him years to learn seemed to come to her naturally. For her part, Wambũi found herself thinking about the store all the time, longing for Saturday to come, and feeling a strange, almost electric buzz when she arrived there and took her place behind the counter.

PART TWO

Chapter Sixteen

RAY AND MŪTHONI had always been close—although she was six years his senior. There had been a sister midway in age between them, but she died tragically at the age of two. She had climbed into a bathtub that was half full of water where some towels had been left soaking and drowned. Wanja had been her name. They still had baby pictures of her. Mūthoni remembered her but only vaguely—she was five when it happened. She recalled playing with a baby and singing to her, and then Mom crying a lot and Dad silent and brooding. Friends and family came to visit, and she remembered getting lots of hugs and attention from numerous relatives, some of whom she didn't know well. She had no recollection of the funeral; she had seen herself in pictures at the event, but she remembered nothing.

It was only after the funeral when the commotion settled down that Wanja's absence became noticeable. Mūthoni often looked at the big smiling baby pictures on the wall and wondered where she went. Whenever she asked her parents, they would tell her she had gone to heaven and they would point to the sky. She didn't understand it, but after a while she learned not to ask that question, because her mother always seemed to send her off on a previously forgotten errand whenever she did. It was not until Mūthoni was twenty-three that she had a meaningful conversation about Wanja with her mother.

Ray was born about fifteen months after the tragic incident, and his arrival brought warm, pleasant rays of renewal into the Mwangi household. "What shall we call him?" Wambũi had asked her husband at the hospital after the baby was born. Throughout the pregnancy, they had been reluctant to discuss possible names for the unborn infant, afraid that such presumption might bring bad luck; but now, as they held the normal, healthy baby, they had to come up with a name. They hadn't expected a boy, so there hadn't been much thought given to boy-names.

"I think we should call him Raymond," Joel Mwangi announced triumphantly, after they had reviewed and dismissed a handful of other possibilities.

Wambũi cringed. "Raymond? Er . . . I'm not so sure about that one."

Mr. Mwangi was undeterred. "I think Raymond is a very good name. It sounds dignified."

"But what does it even mean? And why do we need to give him an English name?" Wambũi pushed back gently, trying to hide her exasperation.

"He needs a Christian name, and I really like the sound of 'Raymond.'"

After several hours of labor, Wambũi was worn out and didn't have the energy to engage in a battle over this. But they needed a name for the birth certificate and it was an issue she had strong feelings about.

Three years earlier, she had officially discarded the name "Lydia" after walking into a law office in Karatina to sign the paperwork. "Why do you want to change your name?" the clerk had asked, sounding surprised, having never before received such a request.

"I don't like it. It's not my name," Wambūi explained. Her husband had tried in vain to dissuade her—after several heated conversations, it was clear their differing viewpoints on the matter were irreconcilable.

"So, are you going to take on another Christian name?" he asked.

"My name is Wambūi," she said with conviction, letting that be her answer.

The clerk looked puzzled for a moment and was about to ask another question. But he changed his mind and shrugged when it occurred to him that Wambūi was paying for the service.

When Mūthoni, their first-born daughter was born, Wambūi had acquiesced to the name "Janet," resolving inwardly never to call her daughter that. She had been successful in that endeavor, and the name only existed in a document that was in her safekeeping, surfacing just when official paperwork was required. So all in all, Wambūi felt the dispute over names was still worth having.

She loved her husband and recognized that he had a different perspective. He was simply not one to go against the grain of established thinking. After hitting an impasse on the first day, Mr. Mwangi assured the nurses as he left the hospital they would choose a name before the baby left on the following day. But as far as Wambũi was concerned, he already had a name—based on his birth order, he would automatically be named Kĩng'ori after her father-in-law, and she was more than happy with it. That she genuinely liked her father-in-law made it easy.

The next day, when they were preparing to leave the hospital, the lady from registration approached them to finalize the details for the birth certificate. "Congratulations on your baby boy!" she said enthusiastically. "I just need the names we'll put on the birth certificate. You'll be able to pick up the document at the County Hall in about two weeks."

The couple exchanged glances. Wambũi held the sleeping infant in her arms. She sighed, shrugged and then gave her husband a slight nod.

"His names are Raymond Kĩng'ori Mwangi," Mr. Mwangi said proudly, with a wide grin on his face.

~~

Mũthoni was a hot-tempered child; so when Ray attended primary school, his identity as her younger brother conferred him with automatic protection from bullies. She had cemented her reputation as one to avoid confrontation with when she took on a boy two years older than herself and won.

When she was in Standard Four, a notorious bully named Patrick Gĩthĩnji had picked on a younger boy, who had been playing quietly on his own. Patrick was in Standard Six and he was a big lad, at least a head taller than Mũthoni. He had picked up the other boy by his collar while tightening his grip, choking the terrified lad as he lifted him slowly off the ground, so he was standing on the tips of his toes.

Mũthoni had been jumping rope with her friends a short distance away, and they watched her suddenly take off like a rabid dog, making a beeline for Patrick. He didn't see it coming. A sharp kick to his right shin caused him to release his victim and turn around in surprise, where his face met the palm of Mũthoni's hand, making a loud smack. Next she landed a solid punch to his belly, and he doubled over, gasping for breath before letting out an anguished yell.

By this time, Mũthoni had begun to have second thoughts about what she had done, but it was too late to back down. If she ran away now, she would spend the rest of her time in that school running away from him. A crowd of excited children had flocked to the scene, eager to see more action. Mũthoni screwed up her face, rolled up her sleeves and then took a step towards the bully. He scrambled to his feet and beat a hasty retreat, putting about ten yards between them. She pointed her index finger at him menacingly, and in a trembling voice uttered, "*Weh!* If you ever touch him again, I will come and find you!"

Mūthoni became a legend that day. All the children held her in awe, and word got around to the other bullies that they should stay away from the wild girl in Standard Four. The school suspended her for two days, but that only served to bolster her reputation. Her parents scolded her for getting into a fight, but inwardly they were proud she stood up for a helpless child. She never got into a physical altercation again—there was no need to.

Even after Mūthoni left the school, Ray continued to enjoy immunity from bullies. He needed it. He was a fat, nervous, awkward boy with a stammer who struggled to make friends and was often teased by his playmates.

"Raymond, go outside and play soccer with the other boys," his father told him repeatedly on weekends or evenings, if the sun was still up.

Ray gave it a try, but he hated the sport at first. He was not very good at it. Often, he would swing his leg and miss the ball, to the exasperation of his teammates.

"How can you miss the ball? It's so big!" he would hear one of them muttering from time to time.

He wished his father would stop making him go outside and play all the time. He was usually much happier reading a book or lying on his bed and letting his mind wander when he had the chance.

"I don't know what we are going to do about this boy. He's too fat—he needs to lose weight," Mr. Mwangi whined to his wife.

"He eats the same food as we do, and never takes a second helping," Wambũi rejoined calmly, "and he is always outside playing with his friends. Maybe we just need to accept that his body is different."

But Joel Mwangi remained relentless in his efforts; and while there was no visible impact on the boy's physique, Ray, over time, became quite adept at playing soccer and even began to enjoy it.

Both the Mwangi children went to high school at Alliance, with Mũthoni attending her mother's alma mater, while Ray went to the boys' school that was five minutes away. Shortly after he started there, he learned there would be tryouts for the soccer team, and all interested parties were welcome. At four o'clock, on the day they were scheduled, he showed up in his brand-new sports uniform alongside almost thirty other boys. The prospective candidates were mostly from forms One and Two.

"This is a large crowd indeed!" exclaimed Mr. Juma, the head coach, to his assistant, Mr. Mbogo.

The players already on the team—older boys in the senior classes—were on the pitch warming up and kicking the ball to each other. All of them were quick and muscular, confidently tapping the ball to each other and showing off their ball-handling skills.

"Gather around here," Mr. Juma called to the group of

anxious prospects huddled along the sideline. "We're going to assess your physical fitness and how you handle the ball. While I am pleased to see such a big turnout, I would like to make it clear that most of you won't make it onto the team. Even if you don't, you will still have the opportunity to play for your house, or to participate in the numerous noncompetitive matches played every evening after class."

He seemed to be staring at Ray, who self-consciously raised his shoulders and inhaled, slowly sucking in the rounded prominence of his belly.

"Alright boys!" the coach continued. "When I blow my whistle, I want you to run all the way to the white line marked at that end of the field and back. A trip there and back is one lap. I would like you to do ten laps—so run there and back ten times. If anyone stops to rest, walks along the way or does not complete the exercise by the time I blow my whistle after six minutes, they will automatically be dismissed. Ready, set, go!"

The shrill whistle set off a chaotic clamor, as the boys set off to prove their mettle. By the third lap, the first casualty dropped out and others soon followed. At the end of the drill, twelve dejected boys walked off in the direction of their dormitories. Ray was not one of them.

"Okay, boys! The next step will assess your ball control. I'm going to have you play a test match against those fellows over there," he said, pointing to the individuals on the school team. "Since there are seventeen of you, I'll use a rotation system so all of you will have a chance to play."

There were silent groans and feverish prayers as the terrified boys assessed the daunting challenge, most wishing they would not be among the first eleven boys chosen. Some were still inhaling and exhaling heavily, trying to catch their breath after the earlier run. Ray was among the first selected. Within minutes, they were running around frantically, trying to counter the smooth, well-coordinated attacks of the opposing team. Ray managed to make contact with the ball multiple times, including one time when he cleverly dispossessed the lead striker of the opposition as he tried to position himself to take a shot at the goal. A number of boys were called off as others came in, but he played to the end. The final score was 0–3. Ray and his teammates were vastly relieved that the loss had not been as steep and humiliating as they'd anticipated. Following the game, an additional five prospective players were discharged from any further obligation to attend practice with the team.

"We started with twenty-nine, and there are twelve left!" Mr. Juma announced in a booming voice. "This is not the end of the selection process, but you should be pleased you have made it to the second round of this process, tomorrow at four-fifteen sharp. You are free to return to your dormitories, or you may sit on the sidelines and watch the rest of the practice session. It will not count against you if you choose to leave at this point."

As the twelve boys—who'd had enough for one day—slowly headed towards the dormitories, someone tapped Ray on the shoulder and he turned around. It was one of the midfielders on the team, his arm outstretched to shake his hand.

"Good job on the field. You're very quick for a fat guy!" he said.

"Thank you," Ray replied, shaking his hand with a bashful smile.

∿

Ray made it onto the soccer team, where he usually played as a substitute defender. Practice lasted two hours a day, Monday through Friday, and as the regional tournament approached, Saturday morning practice was added to the schedule. He earned the nickname "Kifaru," the Swahili word for rhinoceros, due to his surprising speed and agility in spite of his size. As the team progressed through the season, Ray was content, along with the other newbie teammates, to watch the matches from the bench of substitutes, as their more seasoned colleagues worked to pick apart one opposing team's defenses after another while endeavoring not to yield any goals.

The team made it through the divisional, regional and district stages, until they reached the final match in the provincial tournament. It was a high stakes game, and the opposing team had come out on top in the provincial stages for the last three years, qualifying for the national championships where they had on one occasion won the national trophy. The Alliance team were clearly the underdogs; but they were a very skilled and well-coordinated bunch, and the lead striker—Phillip Wekesa—was in excellent form. He had scored a goal in every single game to this point, creating opportunities where no one anticipated they might exist. He could artfully dribble the ball so that it appeared, from a distance, as if it was taped to his foot—that is, until the moment he decided to dispatch it into the net. While he was an exceptional player in terms of technique, he had a foul temper and was prone to explosive emotional outbursts.

It was the seventy-fifth minute of the game, and the teams were still in a goalless tie. Both teams were starting to become rather frantic in their efforts. If the game ended without a goal, they would go into overtime; and if that didn't yield a winner, it would be followed by a dreaded penalty shootout where luck was often as important as skill, if not more so. A ball was looped from the opposing side and picked up by one of the midfielders, who quickly tapped it to the left winger and then raced past the Alliance wingback to receive it back from the winger who had flicked it forward in anticipation. Suddenly, loud feverish cheers erupted as the midfielder, who was now unmarked, received the ball and broke into a relentless sprint towards the goal. Victor Oloo, the fullback—who was somewhat off position—had been caught flat-footed, so he scrambled to intercept the approaching attacker. Amid the deafening screams and cheers from the fans of the opposing team who were playing at their home stadium, Ray and his teammates watched in horror as the attacking player raced towards the goal and prepared to fire off a shot. Victor stuck out his foot in a desperate attempt to make contact with the ball just as the player slammed his foot into it. The interference changed the ball's direction ever so slightly, so that it whizzed harmlessly over the crossbar. The goalkeeper hadn't even been close to where it passed by; and had it not been for the deflection, the ball would have found the back of the net.

As Ray and his colleagues heaved a sigh of relief in the midst of the collective groan of disappointment from the home-team supporters in the stands, everyone's attention turned to Victor and the attacking player who were lying on the ground. There had been a collision. Play was stopped for a few minutes while the referee, first-aid team and the players close by rushed toward them to assess the situation. After a short while, the attacking midfielder hobbled to his feet, but Victor lay on the ground, rolling from side to side and grimacing in pain. Coach Juma ran onto the field, and after conversations with the referee and the medical personnel, Victor was placed on a stretcher. Next, the coach headed briskly towards the substitute bench, a somber look on his face. He scanned the players on the bench quickly, and then his eyes locked on Ray.

"Kifaru, start warming up, you're going on," Coach Juma said.

Ray froze momentarily.

"Good luck, man!" murmured someone behind him. "Don't let them score, otherwise that might be your first and last game."

That last remark was greeted with mirthless laughter from

142

those who heard it. Ray wasn't one of them, since seconds before he'd scrambled off the bench and arrived on the sideline. He warmed up hastily and then ran onto the field. The feeling was surreal—he was the only junior on the team. The whistle blew and play resumed. There were only about twelve minutes left. He made contact a few times with the ball—a pass here, a block there—and after a while the dry mouth and numb legs were forgotten.

The midfielder who had collided with Victor had recovered from his injury and was causing trouble again, repeatedly outrunning and outmaneuvering the person who was supposed to be marking him. It wasn't long before he managed to make another break for it, and Ray rushed forward to intercept him. As he reached him, the player made a sharp right turn with the ball, throwing Ray off balance; but he managed to stretch out his left foot and block the ball before it could go past him, sending it rolling between the attacker's legs. Ray regained his balance, and before his opponent could turn back to recover the ball, he swept it with the outside of his foot towards the sideline. As the ball rolled towards it, Ray rushed forward and landed a solid kick, sending the ball upfield. It soared towards Phillip Wekesa, who started running towards it, with two of the opposing team's defenders sticking close and running in lockstep with him, determined to deny him any opportunity to mount an attack.

"Useless shot! Aim better next time!" he yelled angrily at Ray, as he realized the ball was too high and out of his reach.

There were only two minutes left in the game, and as the ball sailed past the trio of Phillip and his defenders, the goalkeeper stepped forward and positioned himself to catch it on its downward trajectory. His steely, determined expression turned to one of horror as he leaped into the air and realized the ball was an inch or two out of reach. It continued past him, spinning downwards, before landing on the ground behind him and bouncing firmly into the net.

"Gooaaalll!" the Alliance team and their fans screamed in surprise and jubilation.

Ray smiled awkwardly as he was mobbed by his ecstatic teammates, as all their fans on the sidelines burst into chants of "Kifaru! Kifaru!" With only about a minute and a half left, victory was all but certain. It was the first time in the school's history that their team made it to the national championships.

Chapter Seventeen

RAY AND HIS classmates were seated around the room, their attention riveted on Mina Qureishi as she read out one question after another from the study guide. It was almost midnight and they had been at this for almost two hours. A coffeemaker on a table in the corner was in the process of producing its third pot of the evening. But judging from the intermittent blank stares and involuntary head bobbing, the potent dark liquid it offered had lost its power to energize and animate this group.

It was the final year of medical school, and the weekly study group provided an opportunity to connect with others and take refuge in camaraderie as the decisive end-of-year examination approached. The stakes were high; anyone unfortunate enough to be among the handful of individuals who failed the exam would have to repeat the whole year. While testing medical knowledge was one of its goals, it seemed to have another, deeper purpose—to determine one's ability to hold firm under pressure and think on one's feet, key qualities for a physician to possess.

༄

During Ray's six years of medical school, a number of students had either dropped out or been kicked out, mostly in the first two years when the most consequential adjustments were necessary. There had been a few who had seemed on track to complete their studies, until something happened in their lives that abruptly derailed them.

Fred Mutuku was a quiet, brilliant student who suddenly stopped coming to class and ward rounds, and was seen wandering the hallways of the hostels all night and crouching furtively amidst the shrubbery in the daytime. When his friends called out to him, he didn't recognize them, and what he said didn't make any sense—he was apparently conversing with invisible people around him. He was subsequently diagnosed with paranoid schizophrenia. Attempts were made to medicate him, but only got him well enough to where he refused further medication and failed to follow up with his psychiatrist.

Fred came from a peasant family from Kitui, and they were totally overwhelmed with grief by his illness, convinced he had been bewitched. After trying unsuccessfully to talk sense into him, his mother and father boarded a bus and headed back home, heartbroken. Since he wasn't dangerous to others, there was no pressure to institutionalize him involuntarily. So he remained a skulking presence in the student residence for a few months, before wandering off into the streets of Nairobi—a disheveled specter with matted untidy hair, wild restless eyes and filthy tattered clothes.

Amina Juma was another student who didn't make it. She was found lifeless in her bed after her friends, worried because they hadn't seen her for two days, broke into her room. An open empty bottle of paracetamol sat on her bedside table, with a note that said simply, "I can't do this anymore. Sorry." No one had seen it coming. It was true she'd complained about the long study hours and the impossible expectations, but that was everyone's constant refrain. Even after an offhand remark to her closest friend Mary that she'd had about all she could take, her friend thought she was referring to quitting medical school, which seemed especially foolish considering she'd made it through five out of the six years. Mary had resolved to have a heart-to-heart chat with Amina at the first opportune moment, but they both had busy schedules and that moment never arrived.

Ray next recalled William Mũnene, who—in just the previous year—announced out of the blue to perplexed friends, family and colleagues, that God had called him to be a missionary in Lodwar in northern Kenya, and that he needed to leave right away.

Besides Ray and Mina, the other members of the study group were Joshua Odongo, Peter Kilonzo, Vikram Patel and Kwamboka Onsongo. Joshua was a quick-witted, bombastic fellow with a distinguished goatee who, when the occasion demanded, could recite verbatim entire paragraphs from Harrison's *Principles of Internal Medicine*. This had earned him the moniker "Kasuku," which is the Swahili word for parrot. Kilonzo was laid-back and seldom flustered, always managing to accomplish just enough to get from one year to the next, and not an iota more. When everyone else was losing their mind from sleep deprivation and anxiety about exams or malevolent professors, Kilonzo was the calm person you wanted to be around, as he casually shrugged off worries with a nonchalant, "That's life! What can you do?"

Ray, Joshua and Kilonzo had become friends during their first year of medical school when pure happenstance threw them together. It was a chilly gray Friday afternoon in July, and they were attending a lecture given by Professor Mwasi. It concerned skeletal muscle physiology, and the professor was energetically moving his laser pointer over a diagram of a muscle cell, when suddenly the sound of shouting and running could be heard from outside. When someone sitting close to the front door got up and opened it to see what was causing the commotion, an object that looked like a can crashed onto the ground a few feet away and began spewing thick fumes that escaped into the lecture hall. Instantly, there were screams and shouts as students scrambled to grab their books and exit the room, while those closest to the door experienced fits of coughing and choking.

"Teargas! Everybody leave!" someone shouted.

A stampede ensued, with 100 students trying to push through any of the three remaining doors, one at the opposite end from where the teargas canister had landed, and two in the back. Once outside, the students were met by a menacing horde of GSU— General Service Unit— officers clutching their clubs and shields. They were a paramilitary force, somewhere between police and military, who were deployed to deal with anything from street protests to terrorist attacks. Usually when there was a riot at the university, the regular riot police were adequate to getting the job done; the appearance of GSU usually signaled an ominous escalation.

A group of about six officers was advancing from the direction the teargas canister had come from. Fifty yards ahead of them, where the concrete sidewalk met the tarmac, there were two large trucks fronted by about two dozen helmeted officers standing behind their wall of shields. In between these two teams, a group of about eight young men, probably students, was walking hesitantly towards the officers in front of the truck, arms raised as they dropped the rocks they had been carrying. They were sweating and their chests heaved with exertion; they gasped and choked as they tried to put some distance between themselves and the pungent fumes emanating from the canister on the ground behind them. From the way they hung their heads, it was clear they had been cornered. An officer with a bullhorn made a loud announcement.

"Welcome, troublemakers!" he bellowed malevolently. "We have been waiting for you! You thought you could run away! I want you to walk in single file directly into the back of that lorry! We will take you downtown, where we can discuss why it's a bad idea to throw rocks at law enforcement officers. As for those of you coming from the lecture theater, I want you to move in that direction"— pointing to the dormitories—"and proceed as fast as you can to your residence halls. You are required to vacate this part of the campus immediately. You have thirty minutes. Anyone who is still on the grounds at the end of that time will be arrested!"

An atmosphere of panic and urgency ensued, as the students walked briskly towards their dorm rooms, where they collected their valuables and identification papers—and in some cases a change of clothing. Everything else was left behind, in the hope it would still be there when they were allowed to return, whenever that would be.

As Ray was out in the hallway locking up his room, Kilonzo and Joshua, who at that point were only nodding acquaintances, emerged from their rooms at about the same time.

"Going down the main road is probably a bad idea as everyone will be headed in that direction," said Kilonzo. "It might be better to take the back route to Westlands, and try to catch a *matatu* (public minivan) into town via Hospital Hill."

Ray and Joshua took that as Kilonzo's invitation for the three to travel together, and they nodded to signify they were in. When they got to the gate of the campus, a huge swarm of people turned left, walking towards Uhuru Highway, which was half a mile away. Normally, there would have been *matatus* waiting at the gate of the campus; but whenever there was a riot, they steered clear as it was not uncommon for students to stone cars or set them on fire.

The GSU officers waited a short distance away, keenly watching the minutes count down on the clock. Ray, Joshua and Kilonzo turned right and went in the opposite direction from everyone else with Kilonzo in the lead. About two hundred yards down the road, he made a sharp right turn onto a footpath that Ray had never noticed before. Following him down the winding path then up a hill, they suddenly emerged in Westlands, an upmarket suburb where life went on as usual, oblivious to what was happening just a short distance away.

As they hopped into a *matatu* that began making its way downtown, Ray realized he had a problem. He had nowhere to stay in Nairobi; and given the uncertainty and the hour of the day, he was not sure about traveling to Karatina. Without knowing exactly what was going on and why they'd been sent off campus, he didn't want to travel all the way to Karatina, only to turn around and come right back in a day or two. Also, he didn't know when they'd be allowed to go back and collect the rest of their personal belongings. The same thought was going through Joshua's mind—but his situation was much worse than Ray's. While Ray lived about an hour and a half away, Joshua's home was in Sondu, which was about a seven-hour road trip.

Kilonzo read their minds. "Where are you guys going?" he asked.

Ray and Joshua laughed nervously.

"Me, I have no idea," replied Joshua.

"You're both welcome to come with me," Kilonzo offered. "My mother's house is in Imara."

There were grateful nods and sighs of relief.

Kilonzo's mother and his two siblings gave a warm welcome to the unexpected guests. Before long, Ray and Joshua found themselves telling embellished tales about campus life to Kilonzo's enthralled younger brothers. It wasn't until a few hours later that they learned what caused the incident at their school earlier in the day.

As they'd suspected, some students from the main campus had decided to join a political demonstration in Uhuru Park that had escalated to the point where a number of rioters started throwing rocks at passing cars. There were several thousand people at the gathering, and when the riot police tried to contain them the situation deteriorated, with demonstrators lobbing rocks, Molotov cocktails and teargas canisters back at the riot police. As the GSU arrived, the students, and probably non-students as well, retreated onto the grounds of the university and into the residence halls, causing total mayhem. The medical school campus might have been spared any involvement, had it not been for a number of rioters choosing to flee in that direction, shouting loud taunts at the GSU officers in the process.

Later that night there was a televised announcement from the dean of students indicating that the university would be closed indefinitely. The student residences would be temporarily open on Monday for students to collect their belongings and then clear out. Ray and Joshua spent the weekend with Kilonzo's family, and returned to the school on Monday morning to pack up their remaining possessions before heading home.

It would be a long nine months before the university reopened, and it wouldn't be the last unexpected closure they would have to deal with. Some interruptions lasted two days, others could go on for months. The students whose lives were periodically upended simply learned to accept the disruptions, and to always have money and identification documents readily available in case they had to leave immediately without first gaining access to their rooms at the school.

〰

Mina was trying to keep the study group's attention on the task at hand, despite the lateness of the hour. "Answer true or false: the following are typical features of post-streptococcal glomerulonephritis except . . ."

"Odd one out is D!" Joshua cut in, enthusiastically.

"Mr. Odongo, kindly refrain from interrupting the examiner," said Mina without any hint of exasperation. "Please explain what the other choices are and why D is true."

"I'm sorry, Mina, but I've seen that question a hundred times! Proteinuria of greater than three grams per twenty-four hours is the wrong answer. All the other answers, namely decrease in C3 activity, presence of crescents on microscopy, no symptoms and antecedent pharyngitis are correct. However, you can have nephrotic range proteinuria in some rare cases, so D is technically incorrect, but who am I to correct the person writing the exam?"

"Those 'except' questions are annoying," grumbled Kwamboka irritably; "why can't they just ask the questions directly?"

"You're absolutely *not incorrect*, my sister," agreed Mina, smiling wryly.

Vikram was dozing off, intermittently letting out a soft snore.

It was already ten minutes past midnight. He generally had no ability to fend off sleep when it overwhelmed him, falling asleep mid-sentence and then vehemently denying he had been sleeping—explaining he had merely closed his eyes to formulate what he was going to say next. Kwamboka brought her hand to her mouth to hide a yawn.

"Alright everyone," Mina declared, closing the book. "It's bedtime and we have a long day ahead of us. Twelve weeks left to the end of the world; it's too late to quit at this point."

∿

Ward rounds with Professor Kisilu were guaranteed to be nerve-wracking or vastly entertaining, depending on whether you were in his line of fire or not. He was a small energetic man with a quick mind who spoke with exuberant urgency. He also had an impeccable memory for names and details, much to the chagrin of the medical students who would have much preferred the comfort of anonymity or generic identity. Often, when someone presented a case to him, he would seem to listen with his attention elsewhere, stopping the presenter to seek clarification on a seemingly minor detail that had escaped everyone's notice, which was often the one instrumental in making the diagnosis. Most students considered themselves fortunate to have the opportunity to rotate through his ward.

This was Ray's last clinical rotation in medical school, and Professor Kisilu made frequent mention of this. The clinical team comprised three final-year medical students, two fourth-year students

154

in their junior clerkship, an intern, two registrars (specialty physicians in training), a nutritionist, occupational therapist and two or three nurses.

Ray was presenting the case of a fifty-six-year-old man who had been brought in by his wife because he was acting strangely. He had been fairly normal until a week or two earlier when he had complained of a dull headache and started behaving erratically, intermittently becoming confused and not recognizing his wife, while being lucid the rest of the time. Sometimes he would make grunting noises and rock his head and upper torso back and forth, talking to people who were not present.

". . . his wife says he drinks one to t-two beers a week and used to work as a t-t-tailor in K-k-kitui until about eight months ago. He doesn't smoke. He and his wife have three grown children . . ." Ray explained apprehensively to Professor Kisilu.

"Why did he stop working?" asked the professor.

Ray started to speak, then realized he didn't have an answer. "I'm sorry, I didn't ask."

Professor Kisilu turned to the man and asked him the question in Kamba, the man's native language—since, fortunately, he and the patient were from the same ethnic group. The man gave a long-winded response that only Professor Kisilu and one of the nurses understood, the rest of the team waiting patiently as the conversation became more animated. At one point the nurse tittered uncontrollably, and the others looked at her quizzically. Professor Kisilu continued the conversation a little longer and then nodded to the man, shaking his hand appreciatively. The man seemed exhilarated by the attention he had received.

"He says he stopped working after his neighbor bewitched him," the professor said, sounding surprisingly matter-of-fact. "They have been at odds for a while. A little under a year ago, he started finding it harder and harder to control the pedal of the sewing machine as he felt as if he was stepping on air, to use his description. He is convinced that his neighbor cast a spell on him so as to destroy his business. He did not feel that piece of information was relevant to the recent events that brought him to the hospital, so he did not see the need to tell you about it. It is, however, very relevant. Continue your presentation, Kĩng'ori; what else did you find and what do you think this man has?"

Ray's mind raced. He delivered the remainder of his presentation, struggling to incorporate this crucial piece of information, but he was having a hard time seeing where this new clue fit into the whole picture.

"Kĩng'ori here has proposed vasculitis and atypical meningitis among his differential diagnoses. Let's all agree that the patient's problems did not start two weeks ago as he and his wife originally stated. And we have learned that the patient is not diabetic and his HIV test was negative, so we can put the lazy thinking aside. Alright, let's explore the diagnostic possibilities, starting with your other final-year colleagues, and then moving up to the intern and registrars."

Normal pressure hydrocephalus, Wernicke-Korsakoff syndrome, tuberculous meningitis, conversion disorder . . . the other members of the group called out different possibilities.

"Did you observe his gait?" the professor asked Ray.

Ray shook his head apologetically.

Professor Kisilu turned to the man and asked him to walk across the room. The patient got up unsteadily on his feet and proceeded to walk slowly across the room, fixing his eyes on the floor, moving with each step as if he was stepping over an invisible wire that was three inches off the ground. He walked about twenty feet and slowly turned around and returned to his bed.

"Well?" asked the professor, "the man has handed you his diagnosis, which is . . . ?"

One of the fourth-year students said something timidly within his hearing, and he turned to her. "Say it loud, so they can all hear," he said excitedly.

"Tabes dorsalis."

"That's correct! This is most likely tabes dorsalis!" Professor Kisilu announced triumphantly, taking care to use the Latin name for syphilis of the spinal cord so as to exclude any stray ears that may have been following the conversation. "Let's make sure there is a CSF VDRL ordered on the spinal fluid."

That particular test had already been ordered but not on account of any revelation that had been present prior to this discussion. It was a test that was often ordered on the spinal fluid in patients with unusual neurologic symptoms, and Ray had never seen it come back positive.

Rounds continued in this way, with more and more reminders of just how much additional information they were supposed to pack into their already overloaded brains before the fast-approaching final exams. But the written exam was not nearly as intimidating as the viva voce (oral exam), where a patient would be presented just like Ray had done, only he would be on his own this time, with maybe two or three senior physicians quizzing him. A student couldn't pass the final exam if they failed the viva, and because of its wild unpredictability, all the hard work of several months could go up in flames in a matter of minutes.

$$\approx$$

The week of exams finally arrived in early October. Everything seemed like a blur at this point, starting off with written exams, most importantly those in internal medicine and surgery. After the written exams, the viva exams followed; the best preparation for students this late in the game was to ensure they were well rested and immaculately dressed, with their hospital lab coat a spotless white.

Ray's first case was a seventy-year-old diabetic man with kidney disease and neuropathy. It was a fairly unremarkable case in terms of the degree of mystery, though his gastroparesis (impaired movement of food through his stomach) might occasion an interesting footnote in the conversation. The man gave a straightforward history and did not wander off into apocryphal speculation as some people were wont to. He had some abnormal sensory findings in his legs that Ray was easily able to identify and describe. As he scribbled down his thoughts, waiting for the examiners to come in, he surmised that the discussion would focus on the complications of diabetes and he quickly ran through them in his mind, organ by organ.

The curtain opened and three consultants walked in. He recognized Dr. Abdallah and Professor Kisilu. The third person was unfamiliar. She was introduced as Professor Shilu, the external examiner, who was visiting from the University of Dar es Salaam in Tanzania.

"Alright, soon-to-be-doctor King'ori, what do you have for us?" began Dr. Abdallah amicably. He was well-liked by students and had a calm, reassuring demeanor.

Ray started off hesitantly, then relaxed and went through his presentation. Next he was asked to point to abnormalities that were physically apparent on the patient's body, which he did. Then the questions came, and just as he had expected, most of the conversation revolved around the complications from diabetes. Everything went well, and he thought he saw Professor Kisilu give a slight nod of affirmation at the end of the session.

In the following encounter were three shorter cases where

Ray would spend a few minutes with a patient, ask some questions, do a brief assessment and then discuss his findings with the examiners. He had a different set of examiners this time, one of whom was Professor Owino, the ill-humored, malevolent supremo of the department, accompanied by two unsmiling associates. The questions this time seemed vaguer and more concealed, and his audience gave him nothing more than stony stares, so he couldn't tell if he was on track or not. He tried on two occasions to get clarification on a question he'd been asked, only to have it thrown back at him in the same form as before.

After completing his third short case, Ray left the building with an unsatisfied feeling. He felt pretty good about the first case, but the second part of the viva made him feel uneasy. His last examination, the surgery viva, was scheduled for the following day, and after that it might all be over depending on how he performed.

He caught up with Mina on the walkway leading to the residence halls.

"One more day, Kĩng'ori, one more day, then it's all over!" she said excitedly.

"Me, I don't know," he shook his head. "I just got grilled by Owino and I don't feel so good about how it went."

"That man is nasty! I think his mother ate too much *pili pili* (red hot peppers) when she was pregnant with him. He did my short cases too. It's impossible to tell what he's thinking. I had one blind guy wearing regular clothes . . ."

"Oh, you mean the guy in the purple shirt?" Ray asked in surprise. "I had him too!"

"Post-herpetic neuralgia. That was sneaky to make him wear a regular shirt so we couldn't see his rash!" whispered Mina conspiratorially.

Ray let out a loud groan. He hadn't asked the man to take off his shirt. The patient had been admitted with complaints of chest pain on his left side that had been present for six months. Ray had asked him all manner of questions to which he'd responded in the negative. His lungs sounded clear when Ray listened with a stethoscope. He concluded that his symptoms might be indicative of something like a bone or pleural tumor, and decided a CT scan was in order to help identify the source of pain. Because the man was blind, he hadn't seen the shingles rash when it had first showed up six months prior, but the dark characteristic scar had remained in the exact location of the pain. Had the man been wearing a hospital gown, Ray would have noticed it immediately when he listened to his lungs from the back. Having him wear street clothes ensured that only those who took that extra step were rewarded with the correct diagnosis.

For the rest of the day, Ray tried not to dwell on his disappointment over that particular case. All he had needed to do was ask the man to take off his shirt—and the answer was right there! He decided he wouldn't discuss anything else about the exam with his colleagues lest he make another unsettling discovery. There was still one final hurdle tomorrow, and he needed to focus on getting through that one.

Chapter Eighteen

THE MORNING AFTER Ray completed the surgery viva, he hailed an early morning *matatu* headed for Karatina. It would be about a week before the exam results were known, and he had no intention of hanging around the medical school and replaying "what ifs" in his mind. When he arrived at his destination, he showed up unannounced at the hardware store at about nine thirty in the morning, much to his mother's surprise and elation. She bolted from behind the counter and gave him an affectionate hug.

"Kĩng'ori, what a surprise! Are the exams over already?"

He smiled and nodded.

All the employees knew him, and once his presence there was known, they gathered around and greeted him warmly. Grandpa Kĩng'ori heard the commotion and emerged from the back to welcome his namesake, his excitement apparent.

Wambũi now worked at the store full-time. In fact, she ran the place. After about ten years of feeling trapped and unfulfilled despite her best efforts to thrive as a schoolteacher, she finally quit her job and went into the family business. It hadn't come as a surprise to either her husband or her father-in-law, since right from the start working at the store clearly lifted her spirits. She spent a lot of time in the evenings thinking about ways to improve the business, and the two men recognized early on that her energy and innovations were a valuable asset.

Initially, when the store was in its original location, she had suggested that in addition to hardware, they needed to carry farm supplies, like pesticides and simple farming equipment. She reasoned accurately that most of the local farmers would rather patronize their store than travel to Nyeri and struggle to explain their needs to a Mūthūngū or Mūhĩndĩ in one of the fancier shops there. The foot traffic increased from about fifteen to twenty people a day to about forty or so, the number climbing higher at times—like the start of the planting season. Before long, she suggested that the store was too small and they needed to expand. Next door, there was a lackluster bar and restaurant that had managed to limp along over the years, apparently the wrong sort of business for that particular location. When the owner died, his wife and sons were only too happy to offload the property into Wambũi's hands at a throwaway price, and the hardware and farm goods store doubled in size.

Next came the name change. Wambũi's husband, Mwangi, remarked one day that the name "Kĩng'ori and Sons Hardware Shop" was hardly appropriate. Mwangi did have a brother who was a university lecturer in Nairobi, but he had no interest or role in the business. They all agreed that "Karatina Hardware and General Goods Store" was more fitting, and installed a large sign displaying the new name that lit up at night, unlike most of the other stores on the street whose signs were visible only during the day.

After a while, Wambũi became restless again with the status quo, and proposed they look for a location closer to the main Nairobi-Nyeri thoroughfare that cut through Karatina. When an impressive modern building was erected near the bus terminus, she made inquiries to the owner regarding a prospective lease. There was some back-and-forth initially as he tried to extract more money from her than she was willing to part with, but she wouldn't budge. Eventually, with no other offers in sight, the owner capitulated and sent her a message accepting her offer. She waited three days before sending a reply.

The store moved up to the main part of town, and rather than sell the old building that they owned, Wambũi convinced Mwangi and Grandpa Kĩng'ori that it made more sense to convert it into apartments for the growing number of people who worked in town, many of whom were not from Karatina. She had an uncanny ability to spot a business opportunity and actualize it before anyone around her saw it for what it might be worth.

One day, Jaswant Singh, a prominent contractor from Nyeri happened to notice the store in its new location, and decided to stop by and check it out. The prices seemed competitive—cost was an important priority for him—so he decided to get an estimate for some building materials he wanted to purchase. Wambũi and her father-in-law sat down with him at a table in the back room, and as he read out a list of what he needed, she wrote down each item on a sheet of paper with a price next to it. Mr. Singh then pulled out his calculator and started keying in the numbers as Wambũi read them aloud from her list, whispering to herself as she did the computations.

"11,420 shillings!" she announced to him as his index finger skipped back and forth between the keys of his calculator.

He looked up at her, skeptically. "*Mama* (Madam), how could you have counted all those numbers in your head? Let me finish my calculation here." A few seconds elapsed as he completed his computations, then looked at her mystified, having come to the selfsame total as hers. He shook his head in amazement, and his gaze shifted from Wambũi to her father-in-law.

"She counts in her head and I have never seen her make a mistake—not once!" her father-in-law said matter-of-factly.

Mr. Singh didn't ask for any discount. And in the months that followed, there seemed to be more and more builders from Nyeri stopping by the store to make purchases. With Nyeri being the larger town, things generally flowed from Nyeri to Karatina, but in this case the reverse was happening. Once, one of the visitors from Nyeri asked if they made deliveries outside Karatina. Although they'd never had a delivery service even within Karatina—most people transported their purchases themselves—Wambũi didn't miss a beat. "If you buy items worth more than ten thousand shillings, we can arrange to deliver them for you, but there will be an additional charge."

Many people still called Wambũi *Mwalimu* (teacher) even

though she no longer thought of herself as one. When she made her decision to quit teaching, she was greeted with some surprised and disappointed looks from her colleagues. But their unspoken feelings were mostly pity and ridicule, since they regarded her as someone who was walking away from a sure thing to follow a path that seemed to lead nowhere.

At the time of her decision, she had been keeping in touch fairly regularly with Eileen Atwood, her former teacher. Over the years, they had morphed from a mentor-mentee relationship into something more akin to that of an older-younger sister. When Wambũi wrote to Eileen to tell her she was leaving her teaching job at Tũmũtũmũ, Eileen telephoned her at the school and told her she wanted to pay her a visit in Karatina the following weekend. Eileen arrived that Saturday in her bright yellow Volkswagen, bracing herself for a long and difficult conversation.

The two of them sat in a restaurant, sipping tea and making small talk about how things were going at Alliance. It was about seven years since Kenya's independence from the British, and some of the white teachers were starting to talk about moving back to England, while a few had already left.

"So, Wambũi, I don't mean to intrude, but I was surprised to learn about your decision. I was hoping to hear more about it, if it's alright with you."

"I've tried teaching for ten years and I still don't like it. I don't think it's the right career for me," said Wambũi resignedly. "I think I was meant to be a businesswoman."

Eileen managed a joyless smile; she wasn't convinced. "Don't you ever think of going back to school, to the university?"

Wambũi shook her head, starting to look a little exasperated. "What for? My parents and my husband's parents need me here. I can't just leave them and move to Nairobi or Kampala. And what would I do about the baby? Leave her here for other people to take care of her?"

Eileen sighed wearily. She was struggling to overlook the thought of such prodigious talent going to waste, but she was careful not to push too hard. One of the things she had learnt about Kenyans is that they might smile graciously and nod politely over a difference of opinion, while vehemently disagreeing with you on the inside.

Wambũi cleared her throat and continued. "You know, you Wazungus[25] don't have to worry about taking care of your relatives; everyone just thinks about themselves."

Eileen looked at her friend, somewhat startled, but she kept silent. Wambũi had never referred to her as a Mzungu before.

"You see, Eileen, I have to take care of my people. My father and mother and stepmother, as well as some of my siblings and their children need my help, as do some relatives on my husband's side. If

---

[25] White people (Swahili); singular—mzungu

there's a child who needs school fees or books, or if money is needed to buy seeds for planting, I have to make a contribution. All of us who are able to bring in some money have to help. And when the time comes that I need help, they will be there for me. That is how it is done."

"I know you have always wanted me to go to the university and maybe someday become a professor of mathematics, but how is that going to help me or my people right now? They need me now, not ten or twenty years from now. I didn't stop my education because it was difficult or because . . ." Her voice suddenly trailed off. She hastily brought a handkerchief to her eyes and took a deep breath to regain her composure. An awkward silence ensued with the two women staring into the hot light-brown liquid in their teacups, each wondering what was going on in the other's mind.

"How is the shop going?" Eileen ventured, sensing it was high time to change the subject.

Wambũi's eyes lit up, and with considerable excitement she began to describe the plans she had for the place, talking about a "four by four" piece of lumber with the same enthusiasm that a child might in describing cake and ice cream at a recent birthday party. Eileen had seen the store and thought it wasn't much to look at, at least not without Wambũi's magical lenses.

Chapter Nineteen

ON THAT LONG-AWAITED Friday afternoon in October, the atmosphere was heavy with suspense in the hallways of the administration building. Small groups of people tried to carry on conversations, but they were distracted and cast frequent furtive glances in the direction of the boardroom, two doors down from the dean's office. Wrists flicked in nervous repetition, displaying watches that seemed to bring time to a grinding halt, aggravating the existing sense of dread. Conversations grew increasingly disjointed and segued rapidly from one topic to another, a vivid demonstration of the collective state of inattention from the growing number of people waiting there. There was an occasional burst of loud laughter, but it sounded forced and fake.

It was four thirty in the afternoon. What was taking so long? The door had been shut since about two o'clock, with no one going in or out. But they were still in there.

At 4:43, the door swung open and the group emerged, making a sharp left and heading down the hallway into other offices in the building. A tense hush fell over the onlookers, and knees became weak and lips dry. But their attention wasn't focused on the powerful group that had exited; all eyes were riveted on the open doorway, waiting for the room's final inhabitant to appear.

The "Rabbit" appeared. He was a short man with thick glasses. He stepped through the doorway and quickly scanned the area. Having performed this ritual every year, he had become a legend in the process, and the magnitude of the moment still awed even him. Somewhere along the way, he'd been nicknamed the "Rabbit," transforming him into a mythical persona. He walked briskly and purposefully, as the small clusters of onlookers began to advance towards him, coalescing into a larger and larger crowd.

He went to the notice board and unlocked the glass doors; then he deftly stapled the four pages he'd been tightly clutching next to each other on the corkboard, closed the glass doors and turned the lock. He then disappeared into the nervous crowd that had amassed around him, having successfully completed his annual mission.

The first screams of joy heightened the anxiety of those in the back, who in turn surged forward to see if they'd encountered similar good fortune. More and more cries of elation ensued as people got to the notice board and saw their names on the list, after an initial frantic search where they seemed to find only names not their own.

In all the nervous excitement, it took Ray a few moments to find his, initially skipping down the alphabetically ordered list from Frederick Mungai to Susan Mwaniki, and feeling his body go numb before reviewing it again and seeing Raymond Kĩng'ori Mwangi, proudly occupying its place between the others. "Yes!" he exclaimed, pumping his fist, "I made it!"

"Congratulations, Kĩng'ori!" shouted Joshua Odongo, who

was also ecstatic. "Let me be the first one to call you Dr. Kĩng'ori!"

"And likewise, Dr. Odongo, congratulations!"

The rest of the evening was filled with hoarse shouts, handshakes and congratulatory high fives. And for once, first names were set aside as familiar friends referred to each other by the newly acquired titles that would define their identity for the rest of their lives.

〰
〰

After the euphoric days that followed the release of the final year results, the process of drawing lots helped determine who would be posted to the government hospitals that received interns every year. Some would train in private hospitals, while others were chosen for the handful of missionary hospitals scattered around the country. For the majority, a stint of at least a year in a government hospital was mandatory. Most of them were located in the rural and provincial towns outside Nairobi, although there were a few spots available in and around the capital. The positions around Nairobi were generally more desirable—garnering more competition—so it was unwise to count on the possibility of an internship there.

The process was simple. All the would-be interns would meet in a conference room. The self-appointed master of ceremonies from among them would call out the names of the different locations and by a show of hands people would indicate their preferences. If there weren't enough openings, all the interested parties would write their names on pieces of paper placed inside a tissue box, which were then pulled out at random until all the available slots were filled. If someone's luck failed them, and there was someone willing to swap places or relinquish the desired spot, they could make a mutually agreeable individual arrangement instead.

Some places rarely had bidders. The remote desert towns of northern Kenya seldom generated interest. Most people were from the southern half of the country and had never been up north, nor had they any desire to visit or settle there. And while the system generally worked as the basis for who was posted to which hospital, the final decision always came from the bureaucrats at the Ministry of Health, also known as Afya House.

Ray had put in his request for an assignment at the hospital in Nyeri, and he was one of the eight who made it through the balloting process. A few days later, after the selections had been made, the interns awaiting their postings converged on the ministry offices to receive the final verdict, as well as to sign their employment documents. As they sat in the conference room, waiting for the ministry official, Ray chatted with Jake Muchiri and his close friend Joshua Odongo.

"So, Jake, where are you hoping to go?" Joshua said.

Jake smiled dreamily. "Mombasa—I've always wanted to go to there, but the opportunity never presented itself. Here's my chance, and I'm taking full advantage of it."

"That sounds like a fun destination, but I hope you realize we're not going to have much of a life outside work," Joshua pointed out.

"Speak for yourself. I'm going to have the time of my life! No way I will spend a year in Mombasa, and not have a good time," insisted Jake.

"Just make sure you focus on the free things," Joshua added, with a grin, "because sixteen thousand shillings a month is all the government will pay you, and that might not even cover lunch for the three of us at one of those fancy beach hotels when we come to visit."

"Is th-th-that all they pay?" asked Ray, somewhat surprised.

The other two laughed.

"*Kwani*[26], what were you expecting? The government, in its wisdom, believes it is doing you a big favor by giving you a job and allowing you to perform uncontrolled scientific experiments on its citizens; the least they expect from you is gratitude," Jake said with more than a hint of sarcasm.

"And don't expect your salary to come in the first month or two. Sometimes it takes up to six months for your name to show up on their payrolls, then they'll pay you a lump sum and tax it at a

---

[26] Usually used at the beginning of a sentence, indicating that what follows is a question (Swahili)

higher bracket . . ."

"S-so h-how are you expected to s-survive until you get your paycheck?"

"The better question to ask is how you are expected to survive after your paycheck," Joshua countered grimly.

"We have to continue being nice to our parents and older siblings for a bit longer . . ." Jake began, his voice trailing off as the official from the ministry came through the door and a hush fell over the room.

His name was Mr. Mwathe. He was a tall, dark man in an ill-fitting suit, with a sardonic smile permanently engraved on his face. "Are you ready to go out and start working?" he said drily without looking up, as he shuffled through a sheaf of papers in his possession. There were a few affirmative answers—most people said nothing.

"I have about a hundred names on this list, which I am going to read through. These are your *final* postings—please note the use of the word "final." I am aware that you had submitted a list of where you wish to go, and for some of you that may correspond to the center that is listed on this sheet. If it is not, however, then you will make the best of what we give you. Is that understood?"

There was silence.

"Aketch?" Mr. Mwathe began, looking up. "You have been

posted to Nakuru. Amolo . . . Thika, Amunga . . . Machakos, Awiti . . ." He continued down the list in alphabetical order. When he called out Ray's name, he looked up, and his gaze met Ray's. There was a brief pause. "Mandera."

"What?" Ray blurted involuntarily, his eyes widening in disbelief.

There were a few audible snickers, but most people shook their heads in pity. As Mr. Mwathe continued reading through the list, there were a few other surprised reactions, but Ray wasn't paying attention. His mind was racing. He needed to talk to Mr. Mwathe urgently.

When the session ended, he rushed to the front of the room and caught up with Mr. Mwathe, who seemed to have been hoping for a quick getaway.

"Exc-cuse me, Mr. Mwathe, I understand what you s-said about p-p-postings being final, b-but . . ."

"Postings are final!" interrupted Mr. Mwathe waving his arm. "You go where you are posted."

"Excuse me, sir," said a voice behind Ray, addressing Mr. Mwathe. "Is it possible for me to change with Dr. Kĩng'ori. I'm from Mandera and I had applied to go there, but was posted to Nairobi. Can Dr. Kĩngori and I exchange places?" Abdi asked.

Ray felt a wave of relief starting to wash over him, but it was swiftly cut short.

"Postings are final," Mr. Mwathe repeated, shaking his head, "just like I said before! No exchanges." And with that, he turned around and headed quickly down the hallway, turning into one of the offices.

Ray and Abdi looked at each other incredulously, shaking their heads.

"I think he's angling for a bribe . . ." Abdi began to say.

But Ray was not listening. His head was spinning as he walked in the direction of the stairwell, looking for the quickest way out of the building. He felt as if the ground had suddenly given way beneath him, and the jubilation of the past five days had come to an abrupt end. Now he faced a mountain of a problem and there was no easy solution. He was sure of one thing, though—he had no intention of going to Mandera.

〜〜

After going through the final clearance process with the university, Ray returned home to Karatina with the unsolved problem of his internship posting still looming large. His parents, particularly his mother, were devastated. No one tried to persuade him to go to Mandera. It was a hot, dusty desert town at the northeastern tip of Kenya, right on the border with Somalia. It was about a thousand kilometers by road from Nairobi, and part of the drive was through hostile, barren territory where ruthless bandits armed with AK-47 machine guns sometimes lurked. Buses going there usually had to have a police escort, but it was not unheard of for the police to find themselves seriously outgunned and outnumbered by the marauders.

New doctors were usually required to report to their duty station within a month of receiving their notice. If they didn't, they faced disciplinary action from the ministry, which for a medical intern meant they were unlikely to be reassigned to a different station, in which case they wouldn't be able to complete their internship and be formally licensed as a doctor. Further, even if they somehow managed miraculously to obtain another internship and subsequent licensing, they would be ineligible for future government funding for higher level specialty training.

Ray spent most of his time at home in the aftermath of the disastrous posting, only venturing out to a tiny run-down cybercafé in downtown Karatina that offered dial-up internet services at a rate of a hundred shillings for each half-hour. Tracking down Mina Qureishi's phone number through a series of colleagues, he called her and asked her to check on whether there were any positions open at the private hospital she was assigned to. As far as she was aware, all the positions had been filled, but she agreed to ask the physician in charge and get back to him. He telephoned all the mission hospitals and spoke with their medical superintendents—who were nice and polite—but they had nothing available; they promised to keep him in mind if something came up.

He knew that the clock was ticking, and once the thirty days elapsed and it became apparent that he hadn't reported to his duty station, the threatening letters from the ministry would come. Once that process began, it would be too late. The more he thought about it, the more depressed he became. He wondered about Abdi's comment regarding the bribe. Had that been the issue? It was hard to tell with those government functionaries. Sometimes they chose to frustrate people for the pure joy of it. Rather than allow them to make a straightforward exchange that was mutually beneficial, Mr. Mwathe may have simply opted for the double pleasure of inflicting misery upon two people.

Even for those who didn't get exactly what they'd hoped for, the alternative had seemed close enough. But most people got exactly what they'd requested. Jake, for example, was probably packing his bags and hoping to head out early to Mombasa, with visions of kicking off his shoes and heading immediately for the ocean, making the most of his free time before life started to get busy.

"Why me?" Ray couldn't help but ask himself over and over. After all those years of struggling through medical school, his career as a doctor was going off the rails even before it had officially begun.

Chapter Twenty

JOEL MWANGI WAS a soft-spoken individual, the type of person someone might not remember after meeting him at a social gathering. His wife, Wambũi, was the extrovert of the two, which suited him just fine. He was a civil servant who'd been employed in the Ministry of Works for almost forty years, having started off as an accountant and rising up through the ranks to become the head of the Water and Sewerage Department.

He was a modest man and seemed content with his humble but reliable government salary. In general, these salaries hadn't risen over the years and had been vastly outpaced by inflation—so that what might have been comfortable in 1963 was far from adequate in 1999. Most employees responded to this discrepancy either by leaving government service or finding another means of generating income outside of their routine responsibilities.

For some, this meant using their official position to extort money from hapless citizens for even minor services. A water bill that was supposed to be one or two thousand shillings might be inflated by a morally derelict water-meter reader to a hundred and forty thousand shillings. And when the distraught customer went to the water department assuming this was a mistake easily remedied, they'd be informed that the records were accurate and they needed to pay up to avoid having their water turned off immediately, with a surcharge for reconnection. Taking advantage of their distress, they would next be approached by another employee, usually in cahoots with the first, who would offer to rectify the complicated situation for a small sum of four or five thousand shillings. At the end of the day, the spoils of their malfeasance would be divided among the crooked officials.

Over the years, Mr. Mwangi had observed the ethical gangrene spread through the department, but had remained untainted by it. Consequently, he found himself the recipient of an ever-increasing stream of referrals from friends and friends-of-friends, people who believed he could resolve their problems without paying a bribe. The need to devote so much time to undoing the work of his venal colleagues irked him, but it also heightened his commitment to his job. In fact, it was probably the very reason he'd remained in it so long. Whenever he considered leaving, he always asked himself what would happen to all those people who relied on his intervention.

When he married Wambũi, he was pleased deep down that she enjoyed working at the hardware store because he did not. It had always been his father's dream that Kĩng'ori and Sons would grow from strength to strength with both Mwangi and his brother Mũchoki working there, and that they would eventually take over the reins of the business when he was too old to handle it. But Mũchoki, the younger son, made it abundantly clear he had no such plans for his own life. After completing high school, he went on to Makerere to study engineering, and thereafter took a teaching position at the

University of Nairobi where he continued to thrive in his academic career. This left Mwangi in a difficult situation, as he felt under pressure not to abandon his father.

The store didn't really make much money initially, and he found himself secretly injecting funds every month into the business to keep his father's dream alive. Since he did the accounting, Mwangi made sure his father remained oblivious to the consistently negative balance on the monthly spreadsheet. That changed after Wambũi started spending more and more time in the store. Plus, his new wife connected with his father from the first time they'd met—and her obvious enthusiasm for the business was more than the two brothers could ever have mustered. Mwangi's mother had initially resented his new bride as an interloper, and regarded the warm relationship between her husband and her daughter-in-law as entirely inappropriate, well outside the bounds of custom. But over time she relented, and was completely won over when Wambũi's first baby arrived, who, being a girl, was named Mũthoni after her.

〜〜〜

One day, Mr. Mwangi's secretary, Sarah, entered his office at about four thirty in the afternoon. "Sir, there's a gentleman here to see you—Mr. Kariũki—who says he was sent by Mr. Wanyoike. He says it's a personal matter."

Mwangi nodded. He vaguely remembered a Mr. Wanyoike, who'd come to him for the kind of help he was used to rendering. When a smartly dressed, overweight man in his fifties walked in,

182

Mwangi stood up and shook his hand, showing him to a seat.

"How may I help you today, Mr. Kariũki?" he asked.

His visitor was eager to explain the problem, a slight variation on one of the usual storylines, only the sums of money at play were eye-popping. He owned a restaurant and had received a whopping water bill of five hundred thousand shillings, along with a notice that not only was he on the hook for this astronomical sum, but he was also under investigation for diversion of water from the main supply by way of an illegal connection. None of this was true, but somebody somewhere had seen a successful business that might be willing to spend a fraction of the large sum of money allegedly owed with a view to making the whole problem go away.

"I'm sorry to hear that you are in such a mess," said Mr. Mwangi. "I don't know what this world is coming to. How is Wanyoike?"

"He is doing well. He told me to say hello. He says you are the only honest person in this building, and I need an honest man to solve my problem."

Mr. Mwangi jotted down the details of Mr. Kariũki's account as they spoke. He found him an easy person to converse with and soon they were chatting like old friends. They discovered in the process that they knew a lot of the same people, many of whom they were much closer to than Mr. Wanyoike.

At some point they began to discuss their children. Kariũki

had three children, all younger than Mwangi's, with the oldest in his second year at the university and the others following behind at intervals of two years.

"Mine are all grown up now," said Mr. Mwangi with satisfaction. "My oldest is a lawyer in America. My younger one just qualified as a doctor. We're still waiting to see what will happen to him because the people in Afya House posted him to Mandera, and he has said he is not going. I don't blame him."

"Mandera? That's a tough posting. What a shame . . ." Mr. Kariuki began, and then his eyes suddenly lit up and he held up a finger as if asking Mr. Mwangi to pause for a second. He took out his cell phone and dialed a number. "Mūchiri, how are you?" he began. "I'm sitting here with a gentleman by the name of Mwangi who has a son who just qualified as a doctor, but he's having some trouble with his posting. Are you able to help?"

Mr. Kariūki listened for a couple of minutes without saying anything, after which he said, "So, he should come to Afya House tomorrow and ask for you? Okay, thanks. I'll give him your number so he can call you when he gets there . . . okay, I'll talk to you later." He hung up the phone. "That's my brother," he explained to Mwangi. "He works in Afya House—not in the same department your son has been dealing with, but he knows a lot of people there. He'd like him to go to Afya House tomorrow since he wants to help him. And don't worry, he is an honest man, just like you."

~~~
~~~

The next morning Ray boarded a *matatu* and headed for Nairobi, arriving downtown around nine in the morning; from there he hopped onto a bus that dropped him off outside Afya House. He sent a text message to Mr. Mũchiri, who texted him back, telling him to come up to his office on the fourth floor. He was a mid-level official in the ministry, and after taking down all the pertinent details regarding Ray's situation, he asked him to wait in the reception area of his office while he went down to the third floor. He returned after half an hour.

"Dr. Kĩng'ori," Mũchiri said, "the best I could do was to have you reassigned to Embu Provincial General Hospital. Is that acceptable?"

Ray was ecstatic. Embu was a reasonably big hospital, and only an hour's drive from Karatina. He thanked his benefactor profusely.

"You're very welcome, young man," Mũchiri said, before turning to his secretary. "Constance, would you mind taking this gentleman downstairs to Mrs. Ondieki's office, so that he can sign the paperwork?"

The stone-faced secretary rose to her feet. She was a slender woman, almost six-foot tall, with her shoulders hunched slightly forward. Her hair was streaked with gray. Her gaze was directed over the thin spectacles that sat on her nose, rather than through them. Ray observed she had perfect velvet-brown skin that had defied the forces of aging, and a tiny black birthmark that sat appealingly below the right corner of her mouth also caught his eye. "She must have been a head-turner in her day," he thought to himself as she stepped past him into the hallway.

"Come with me," she said.

Ray followed her downstairs, with no other words being exchanged between them, while the loud, rhythmic klop-klop-klop of her shoes echoed in the stairwell. They were stylish, medium high-heeled shoes with an audacious leopard print design. Judging from the mildly scuffed leather and the worn outer aspect of the heels, he could tell the shoes had seen better days.

"Hello, Constance!" Philip, Mrs. Ondieki's receptionist, greeted her warmly when they arrived.

"Hello," Ray's companion replied without much enthusiasm. "This young man is here for a reassignment of his duty station. I believe Mr. Mũchiri has already spoken to your boss."

"Yes, I'm aware of it," Philip said with a smile. "Welcome, young man, have a seat here while I process your paperwork."

Ray proceeded to one of the seats in the waiting area, attempting a thank you to Constance as she turned around and began walking away; but she didn't appear to have heard him.

Chapter Twenty-One

EILEEN HAD TAUGHT at Alliance Girls High School for over forty years and had witnessed the changing face of Kenya. When she arrived in 1949, it had only been in existence for about a year, trying to carve out its own separate identity from the boys' school across the valley that had already been in existence for more than twenty years. It consisted of a tiny cluster of buildings nestled in the wild thicket that was Thogoto, the settlement where the Scottish Presbyterian missionaries had built their church in 1898, and from where the mission hospital and the Alliance schools had sprung. The word "Thogoto" was the Agĩkũyũ people's rendition of the word "Scot".

Over the years the school had grown in size and become well known, taking in girls from all over the country. After Kenya achieved its independence in 1963, the staff began to transition from a predominantly British faculty to one that increasingly resembled the citizens of the exuberant, newly formed nation. When one of the early graduates from the school returned to become the first African headmistress, the seed that had been sown by the founders had finally flowered. Eileen felt an immense sense of accomplishment at having been involved in building something far bigger than herself; she finally experienced the validation that had been absent when she announced to bemused friends and family decades before that she was leaving England and moving to Africa.

As her British colleagues left one by one in the years following Kenya's independence, she didn't feel the gravitational pull from the land of her birth that they did. She waved them good-bye and wished them well as they returned home, often wondering what it would be like for them as they tried to reacquaint themselves with a place that had no doubt changed as much as they had.

Over the years, she had visited her parents, watching them slowly turn gray as they continued going through the motions of their lives. Her father, Harrold, held a steady job as a senior accountant, and her mother worked as a librarian. They were financially comfortable, but lived a life of unrelenting monotony. Eileen often wondered whether her decision to go to Africa had been subconsciously informed by a desire not to live out her life's journey in those same well-worn furrows of a predictable English middle-class existence. Most people would have considered her parents' lives desirable, even enviable, with a house that was fully paid for and an adequate pension in their sunset years—yet there was nary a hint of joy or excitement when she talked with them. It was almost as if they had made a rueful discovery, a little too late, that they had been lied to; that all the things they'd been told would bring them happiness had turned out to be nothing more than a mirage.

Harrold died in 1975, after what started as a minor irritating cough turned out on a chest X-ray to be metastatic cancer of the prostate, with a shower of innumerable white spots filling the dark spaces where his lungs occupied. Judith gave up on living a year after that. Being older and retired and having lost her only companion, she seemed to have slowly willed herself to die; and after spending twelve months wandering around in a daze, she made her quiet exit from this world.

Judith had attended the same church service every Sunday morning for decades, always occupying the same pew; so when she didn't show up one day, the vicar became concerned. The congregation was small, probably no more than thirty people, most of them over the age of sixty. After the service, he took a walk over to her house; and when he failed to get any response despite ringing the doorbell multiple times, he called the police. They found her in her bed in her nightdress, looking as if she was sleeping peacefully. What was unusual was the noticeable odor of decomposition in the air.

Although Eileen had lived for many years on a continent far away from her parents, she suddenly felt very alone after they passed on. She had never had any close cousins, aunts or uncles, and her childhood friends had moved on and changed, just like she had. But she and her parents had been close; and even though she sensed some disappointment on their part at her life choices, they still remained a close-knit family, and they had corresponded frequently over the years.

Eileen spent some time clearing out her parents' house which was now hers, then set about finding a management company that would rent it out and take care of it after she returned to Kenya. Apart from a few items of sentimental value, she had no use for most of the contents of the house; so whatever she felt was not appropriate to give to charity she discarded. Once she had accomplished everything that needed to be done, she took a taxi to Heathrow Airport and boarded a flight back to Kenya.

October is a beautiful month in Kenya wherever jacaranda trees are found, and the delicate lilac blooms festooned the driveway and parking lot at Alliance Girls, tumbling gently from the trees like purple snowflakes onto the grass and tarmac. Anyone seeing it for the first time found themselves mesmerized by the overwhelming display of color. Eileen loved it when the jacaranda trees were in bloom, and on one such day in 1989—thirteen years after her mother's death—she sauntered into the staff room after enjoying a leisurely stroll from her house. There was a folded note in her pigeonhole from Joyce Gĩchũhĩ, the headmistress, which read: "Eileen, please stop by my office whenever you have a moment. Somewhat urgent. Thanks. Joyce."

She had a warm relationship with Joyce, who had been her former student, and the two saw each other often. This made the vaguely worded note somewhat unusual. Eileen waited until the end of the day and then headed to the headmistress' office. "Hello, Joyce!" she said cheerily as she entered. "Am I in trouble?"

Joyce managed a tight smile and asked her to sit down. She opened up a folded letter and began to explain the reason for the meeting—then handed the letter over to Eileen to read for herself.

Eileen's hands trembled as she read it. Her countenance changed and she became very pale, tears started streaming down her face. "It doesn't look like there's anything we can do about it, is there?" she said, her voice shaking with emotion.

Joyce shook her head sadly. "I'm so sorry, Eileen. You know I'd do whatever was needed if it could be done."

Eileen nodded, bringing a handkerchief to her eyes to wipe away the tears.

Joyce got up from behind her desk and pulled up a chair next to Eileen, putting an arm around her shoulder. The two sat there for a long while, with only the sounds of whispering and intermittent sobbing punctuating the heavy silence.

〜〜〜

Someone had been eyeing Eileen's job. This was fairly obvious from the pressure that was coming from the headquarters of the Teachers' Service Commission. Initially, the headmistress had received a call from an individual calling himself Mr. Ngũgĩ, who stated that in the process of reviewing staff positions, he'd noticed they had a British citizen occupying a position that should have been awarded to a Kenyan. The man didn't say what was going to be done or what needed to be done, but used the word "compliance" at least fifteen times in a conversation that lasted less than five minutes. When Joyce replaced the telephone receiver, she had no idea what she was supposed to do with the information besides worry, and she made a decision to carry on as if nothing had happened.

Three weeks later, an official letter arrived in the mail that reiterated the information she'd previously received, albeit in a more threatening manner. The day after, Joyce drove to the TSC headquarters in Nairobi, not so much seeking clarification, but to find an ally who might help her sort out the situation in a manner favorable to Eileen. After being shuttled from one office to another she finally ended up in the office of a Mrs. Mbindyo, who was one of the personnel officers. She was a gray-haired, unsmiling, bespectacled woman in her late fifties who didn't speak much but seemed willing to listen.

"I am the headmistress at Alliance Girls," Joyce began, "and I'm here about one of my teachers who has been with us since the school was founded. I recently received a letter stating that because she is not a Kenyan citizen the TSC was considering replacing her. She has been an excellent teacher and actually taught me, so I was looking to see if there's any way the decision could be . . ." Joyce's voice trailed off as she noticed Mrs. Mbindyo's eyes were trained on the door, which was slightly ajar—when she immediately got up and slammed it shut.

Mrs. Mbindyo sat down and leaned across the table, beckoning Joyce to come closer. "I'm aware of the case. One of the top people in the ministry has decided that his relative will have that job, and he has people working on it to make sure that this happens.

It is very unfortunate, but I don't think you're going to be able to stop them."

"Aren't there other jobs that his relative might be interested in?" Joyce asked hopefully.

"From what I hear, his relative wants to be in Alliance Girls because it is the best school. I have no idea how qualified that person is, but that may not be the most important issue in this situation."

Joyce sat dumbfounded for a minute or two, staring at the table. "So, what happens now?"

"TSC will send your teacher a letter notifying her that her services are no longer needed; then you will get notification about the new teacher that has been assigned to your school."

"Is there any way we can fight it?"

Mrs. Mbindyo peered over her glasses, looking totally mystified. "That is not a wise approach," she said, in what was a very charitable understatement. "That is not how things work over here. If you try to stop these people, your job will go as well; and they could even make sure that the Mzungu lady leaves Kenya in a way that she is never able to return."

Knowing that was the end of the conversation, Joyce slowly rose from her seat and politely thanked Mrs. Mbindyo. As she drove back to Kikuyu, all she could think about was how she would break the news to Eileen.

∿
∿

Two days after she received the fateful news from Joyce, Eileen drove to Karatina for the weekend at Wambũi's invitation. She'd telephoned her after she left Joyce's office, and Wambũi had urged her to come visit at the earliest opportunity.

When Eileen arrived, she appeared tired and disoriented from lack of sleep. As they sat at the table for breakfast that Saturday morning, Mwangi had volunteered to work at the store that morning so the two women could catch up. Wambũi tried to make casual conversation about inconsequential goings-on around Karatina. Eileen stared glumly ahead, with no energy left over to make the polite pretense of paying attention.

"So, unless I miraculously find another job with a work permit to go with it, I'll have to return to England, which is almost as foreign a country to me as it would be to you," said Eileen.

"After all those years of service—how unfair!" Wambũi murmured softly, shaking her head.

Waithĩra, the domestic help, came into the room to see if they needed any more tea. She couldn't hear what the women were talking about, but she could tell that it wasn't good from their tone of voice and facial expressions. Eileen had visited many times before, and was usually cheerful and easy to be around. She often spent time with Waithĩra, helping her with her chores. She was able to carry on part of a conversation in Gĩkũyũ, but retreated into English when the

194

words became inadequate, a mirror-image of Waithĩra's enthusiastic segues from Gĩkũyũ into the English language.

"Have they told you when your last day is?" asked Wambũi.

"I find out this week when the letter arrives, but I imagine it will probably be a month from now, and most of that will consist of my unused leave days."

"Well, I'm here to help in any way I can; and if you'd like to stay here between the day you wind up at Alliance and the day you travel, you don't have to ask, you know that."

Eileen managed a wan smile. "I'm really going to miss this place, and I'll miss you, Wambũi."

"I'll miss you too, Eileen," Wambũi said, holding back tears.

Chapter Twenty-Two

THE AMERICAN EMBASSY looked out of place as it sat isolated on the scrubby grassland adjacent to Mombasa Road. It was heavily fortified, poised like a wary behemoth scanning its surroundings for any invisible attacker that might be lurking in the tawny vegetation. The original embassy building had been on Haile Selassie Avenue, in the midst of the hectic chaos of downtown Nairobi. On August 7th, 1998, a band of terrorists had driven an explosive-laden pickup truck into the basement garage of the building and detonated their cargo. The structure was flattened and resulted in the loss of many innocent lives, an event that scarred the happy-go-lucky East African nation that had naïvely failed to consider that not all who visited were friends; this was the land of *Hakuna Matata* (there are no troubles) after all.

The Americans, while usually more awake to the world of betrayal, scheming and international skullduggery, were also quite taken aback by this brazen and indiscriminate act of cruelty. If the first embassy building had signified an effort to engage with the local population and inhabit the same streets and endure the same traffic conditions, the new embassy symbolized a posture of aloof defensiveness, an awareness of the need to engage with the rest of the world, wherein enemies lurked among friends with no clear way to distinguish one from another.

As Ray prepared to go to the embassy to apply for a visa, he did so with a rising sense of uneasiness. He had already spent about three thousand dollars on preparation and registration for the first two USMLEs (US Medical Licensing Exams), and another twelve hundred dollars registering for the final exam that would take place in Philadelphia, which was why he needed a visa. In many developing countries, the process of obtaining a visa to travel to the United States was fraught with high drama, sudden turns and often crushing disappointment. The only certainty about it was there were no guarantees. A misunderstood statement or the misfortune of having your visa application appointment with a consular official who woke up on the wrong side of the bed, could result in a complete unraveling of your plans.

In general, it was better not to let anyone know of your plans to travel to America, so you didn't have to face myriad awkward questions when the issue came up months later when you didn't feel like talking about it. There were days in the past when prospective students would throw big going-away parties after having been accepted to universities in America, only to have those plans implode when that all-important I-20 form or visa failed to come through— often resulting in months of shame and having to hide from relentless questions about what went wrong. Over time, people had become more cautious; so that you might work in an office with someone who you'd invite to a party, and they would give a noncommittal reply and then not show up. Only later would you learn from someone else that your colleague had left the country, having kept their travel plans under wraps until they'd secured their visa, by which time they usually had just a few days to make travel arrangements and leave.

Ray's appointment was at ten am, but the general custom for all applicants was to show up before seven in the morning. Even for people who never arrived on time for work or meetings, this appointment was different. By the time Ray reached the embassy at about a quarter to seven, there was already a long line of people waiting at the security checkpoint. He got in line, clutching the packet that contained his documents. The general mood was nervous and subdued, with everyone rehearsing in their mind what they would say to the consular official when their turn came. It was a typical mild and sunny Nairobi morning, where a light jacket proved handy for the occasional chilly breeze that blew across the waiting area outside the embassy gate.

At seven o'clock, the security guards started letting people through the checkpoint, and one by one, the people ahead of Ray went past the metal detectors and out of sight. When he turned around, he saw that a long line had formed behind him, winding back towards the parking area. More people were still coming. The guards all wore an irritable scowl as part of their uniform, and they barked the same instructions at intervals whenever a new batch of applicants approached the checkpoint. It was obvious they enjoyed intimidating the crowds—especially since it was unlikely they ever received this degree of respect and attention in any other facet of their lives. Although they had no power to grant or deny anyone a visa, you wouldn't have guessed it from their arrogant demeanors.

After Ray made it through the checkpoint, he walked down a hallway until he came to a large waiting area. All the people who had disappeared ahead of him were there, seated in groups in order of their arrival and appointment times. Ray had a long way to go. Each person was called up to one of several windows to be interviewed, and those sitting in the vicinity might catch a word here or there; but it was the body language in the aftermath of the conversation that told the whole story.

Some of the unlucky ones would turn around looking stone-faced as they headed toward the exit; while others, unable to suppress their emotions, left with tears of frustration and disappointment starting to trickle down their faces—having lost all hope, they felt there was nothing to be gained in keeping up appearances. Then there were the quiet self-assured smiles of those who were pleased but not surprised with the result of their interview; some were first-timers, while others were obtaining their renewals. Even with a visa renewal there was a certain measure of unpredictability, so until it came through it could still go either way. The stakes were higher since these were people already living in the States, with financial responsibilities there, so one misstep in the process could result in complete disaster. Finally, there were those who hit the jackpot, who'd come in with low expectations and yet were granted a visa despite their lack of emotional investment. They couldn't hide their excitement, flashing huge grins and practically skipping out the door.

Ray watched the human drama from his ringside seat, knowing his turn would come. His exam was about two weeks out. He had tried to get an appointment three months ago when he scheduled the exam, but this was the earliest one available. Once the visa was a done deal, he would need to purchase an airline ticket as soon as possible. He planned on staying with his cousin, Njeri, who lived in New Jersey, traveling from there to Philadelphia for the exam.

Suddenly a swarm of armed guards appeared in the consular area and a voice came over the public-address system.

"Ladies and gentlemen, we regret to inform you that, due to security reasons, the rest of this visa interview session is canceled. You are required to exit the embassy immediately in a calm and orderly fashion. We will be contacting you with details of your new interview dates."

There were looks of confusion and panic. The people who had been standing at the counters were suddenly left staring at shuttered windows as the consular staff hastily shut down their stations and retreated into the building.

"What's going on?" an older man asked aloud to no one in particular, as people pushed back their seats, but still lingered, unsure of what to do.

"You heard the announcement!" yelled one of the guards. "Please exit the building right now!"

Ray's mind was racing as he passed through the security area alongside everyone else. There was no staff member on hand to offer information about rescheduling their appointments. He needed to get to Philadelphia in ten days' time, which didn't leave much room for maneuvering. He boarded a *matatu* on Mombasa Road and headed back into downtown Nairobi, en route to his aunt Nyokabi's house. He'd spent the night there so he could make it on time to the embassy for the early appointment. He wondered what the security situation had been about. Everything had seemed calm—no smoke, no sirens or police cars, nothing out of the ordinary—so it was impossible to guess what was going on. It was not something he'd ever heard anyone else talk about before, despite the rich body of Nairobi folklore pertaining to the embassy experience.

"*Aii*[27], they sent you away just like that!" Aunt Nyokabi said incredulously after she heard the details of Ray's morning.

He nodded. He still couldn't think straight because he was so preoccupied with figuring out what he should do next.

"Hmm, I wonder what that security situation was about," his aunt said. "Maybe there'll be something about it on the news."

They waited eagerly for the seven o'clock news, but there was no mention of any incident at the embassy. Nothing on the nine o'clock news either.

"It looks like you'll just have to call the embassy in the

---

[27] You mean to say that . . .

morning to see when they can get you in again. Is there any way for you to postpone the exam if they don't give you an appointment in time?"

"No, Aunt Nyokabi," replied Ray wearily, with a heavy sigh. "On the exam w-w-website they clearly state that the exam cannot be rescheduled and th-they do not issue refunds."

"*Haiya*! You're not serious! And how much did you say it cost to register for the exam?"

"One thousand, two hundred dollars," Ray said, shaking his head in dismay.

"*Wũi Mwathani*! (Oh, dear God!)" she exclaimed. "How much is that in Kenya shillings?"

"Ninety-six thousand," Ray said glumly.

His aunt shook her head in disbelief. "So even if your visa is delayed, they would not take that into consideration? That is ridiculous!" she declared. "Well, we're going to need to call your parents and let them know what has happened."

Aunt Nyokabi was Wambũi's younger sister, second to last in birth order. Ray's mother had helped support all her younger siblings, as well as some of the younger children in her stepmother's household. When the schools started charging fees and requiring students to purchase uniforms, the children were usually told by their parents to seek help from her. "Go and ask the teacher," they said, referring to Wambũi; "she is the one who knows about school." Implicit in this referral was the request to provide any material support necessary. Wambũi never disappointed. As the hardware store and the rental apartments grew, it became easier and easier for her to meet those obligations; and one by one these children had flown the coop and were now themselves in a position to help someone else.

Aunt Nyokabi lived alone in Racecourse, which was a large housing development to the north of Nairobi, near the Nairobi-Nyeri highway. She had a fairly comfortable three-bedroom townhouse and worked as a senior level nurse at Aga Khan Hospital. She had never married and had no children. She considered it a privilege to be able to give back to her eldest sister Wambũi by hosting Ray on this visit.

Nyokabi was very religious. Every situation had a supernatural explanation, no matter how mundane it appeared. To her mind, there was a spiritual dimension to this complicated visa situation. Before they retired for bed that night, she made a pronouncement. "Don't worry Kĩng'ori, I am prophesying over you right now, that you will not leave this house without a visa! Go to bed and don't worry about anything. Tomorrow, when you wake up and start calling the embassy, God will open a door for you."

Ray smiled politely and thanked her, wishing he could share her optimism.

The next morning after a quick breakfast, he got right on the phone. Aunt Nyokabi had already left for work. He dialed the consular number and got a busy signal. Once, twice, three times, maybe four or five—each time he dialed he got the same busy signal. He decided to take a break and turned on the TV for some distraction, meaning to try again in an hour; but he couldn't tear his mind away from the bizarre twist of the previous day and his current dilemma. It was already October sixteenth. Ray had nine days left to the scheduled exam date. A sense of dread and heaviness filled him. If everything had gone right the previous day, he would have had his visa by now.

He went back to the phone a couple of times and tried again—it was mostly busy. One time it rang, but it continued ringing unanswered and then he was disconnected. He looked through a telephone directory. There was only one number for the embassy; it was the same as the one on his visa application documents, the same number he'd been trying in vain. Ray called his mother that afternoon to update her on the situation. She encouraged him to continue trying, but she sounded worried. He spent the rest of the afternoon alternating between calling the embassy with no success, and staring distractedly at the TV or out the window.

Aunt Nyokabi returned at about six that evening and called out to Ray, who had retreated into his room. "So, how did things go?" she asked with an expectant look on her face.

Emerging from his room, Ray shook his head. He didn't feel like talking.

"Don't worry Kĩng'ori, you will get that visa," she said

defiantly. "I am declaring to you in faith that no weapon formed against you shall prosper! Not now, and not even in the journey ahead of you in America."

Ray was a little irritated by her quixotic declaration, but he knew she meant well. He excused himself after dinner and went to his room. He lay down on the bed and spent the next three hours staring vacantly at the ceiling, before turning out the lights and spending the rest of the night tossing and turning.

The next day he waited until Aunt Nyokabi had left the house before exiting his room for breakfast. After that, he resumed the same routine of the previous day, with the same results. Finally, he decided to call the main embassy line. There was a recorded message that described multiple options and stated that the line he'd reached was not for consular affairs, directing the caller to the other number—the one Ray had been using—for any visa-related issues. He was about to hang up after the message concluded, but instead decided to stay on the line.

He was startled when a female voice came on the line, asking him to state his business. He stammered uneasily and began to explain his case, hoping she would be courteous enough to hear him out. By the time he finished his story, his heart was pounding and his mouth was dry. There was a long pause at the other end, and for a moment he couldn't tell if she was still there.

"When were you hoping to travel?" she finally asked.

"M-m-my exam is scheduled for n-n-next Thursday."

"Okay, I want you to stay close to the phone. You can expect a call from someone in the consular section within the next half hour. Give them your name and details. Tell them you spoke to Lydia—that's my name."

Ray felt a smile coming on as he thanked her before she hung up.

The promised call came fifteen minutes later. The caller was all business and asked Ray for specific details; then he asked him to come to the embassy the next day at nine am with all his pertinent documents, and told him to ask for Mr. Jeffries.

By the time Aunt Nyokabi got home that evening, Ray had spent the afternoon in a happy reverie, anticipating that his circumstances were about to change.

"Did you get the appointment?" she asked, sounding hopeful, but equally prepared to launch into a scripture-laden volley of undeterred pronouncements.

Ray grinned from ear to ear. "Yes, Aunt Nyokabi—I got an appointment for tomorrow morning!"

"Praise the Lord!" she said, beaming. "Did I not tell you that you would not leave this house without a visa?"

He nodded and said, "You called it."

"Oh, ye of little faith," she said, shaking her head and still smiling broadly as she placed the grocery bags she was holding on the kitchen counter.

Chapter Twenty-Three

"LADIES AND GENTLEMEN, we have started our descent into Philadelphia International Airport. The 'Fasten Your Seatbelt' sign has been turned on. Please return to your seats in preparation for landing . . ." It was the pilot's voice over the public-address system.

Ray craned his neck and peered out the window as the plane descended beneath the clouds. He saw tiny rows of houses and streets, with numerous lines of cars moving along the roadways like zigzagging columns of ants. His whole body was tingling with excitement. After the plane landed and he disembarked, he made his way through immigration and customs. As he headed toward the exit, dragging his suitcase behind him, he found himself in the Arrivals terminal and scanned the sea of faces awaiting friends and family. He started to shiver as a sharp blast of cold air hit him as he stepped out of the sliding doors.

"Kĩng'ori!" a voice called out from his left.

Ray's cousin Njeri had come out to meet him. She lived in New Jersey, about half an hour away. Mũthoni, his sister, had stayed with her for a while when she came to the States years before. Njeri was barely recognizable in her hat and bulky winter coat. She was carrying another coat on her arm, which she handed to him after giving him a hug.

"Put this on! It's not yet November but it's freezing already. That flimsy thing you have on is not going to keep you warm here!" she said.

They walked towards the parking lot, catching up. He remembered Njeri from when they were kids. She was one of the older cousins he'd interacted with—at least to the extent that a five-year-old interacts with a sullen fifteen-year-old at the urging of parents during a family visit. She had moved to the United States immediately after high school to attend university, and had not visited Kenya since. Nonetheless, the family had gotten updates about her from her parents; and she'd had been very gracious to Mũthoni during her visit, which had resulted in a rekindling of their relationship. They'd kept in touch even after Mũthoni moved to Seattle, after her initial sojourn on the East Coast.

As they drove on the interstate towards his cousin's home, Ray surveyed the landscape. Late fall is not a particularly picturesque time once the wind has plucked the leaves from the trees, leaving gnarly, crooked branches poking out into the drab grayness like witches' fingers. Add to that seventeen hours of flight time with minimal sleep and a disorienting seven-hour time difference, Ray could be excused for finding the overall visual impression rather underwhelming. That said, he was still pretty ebullient as he reflected on how all the pieces had fallen into place at just the right time.

༈

Since Ray had arrived on a Sunday, on the following day Njeri left the house early for work—so he was left on his own the whole day.

"Kĩng'ori, time is the one thing I don't really have much of. That's just how it is in America. The fridge is full, feel free to help yourself to anything in it, and you can use the internet, TV and telephone as much as you like. I usually get home around six in the evening," she'd explained unapologetically when she was about to leave.

He understood. Prior to his leaving Kenya, Mũthoni had telephoned and prepped him for his stay. "Kĩng'ori," he remembered her saying, "Njeri is a very nice person, but please do not go to her house and sit around with your legs crossed on the coffee table waiting for her to serve you tea and *mandazi*[28]. Everybody is very busy there, and the sooner you start to make yourself useful and less of a burden, the better it will be for you—you understand?" And, of course, he did.

Njeri lived in the suburbs, so there was really nowhere to go besides a short walk in the neighborhood, which Ray did attempt briefly. But he retreated immediately after experiencing the chilly thirty-five-degree temperature that felt significantly colder from the brisk wind that whipped back and forth around him. So he spent most of his time mentally preparing for his exam on Thursday, as well as mapping out a plan as to how he would get there and back.

He'd already sent out applications to numerous residency

---

[28] Popular Kenyan snack made of fried dough, similar to a plain beignet

programs and had heard back from a few that were mostly rejections; but there was one program in Albany, New York that had offered him an interview. He was hoping for a few more so he could attend several during the six weeks he would be there. Unfortunately, part of that time included the holiday season, when not as much business was being conducted. He sent out emails to some of the programs he'd already applied to, and even made some phone calls, letting the appropriate people know he was in the country and available for an interview.

Ray found Njeri's fridge to be quite an adventure. It was packed to capacity, but most of the things inside were unfamiliar, and the variety was overwhelming. There were five different cartons of milk—soy, almond, skim, two percent and goat milk. During his orientation she had pointed out to him that the two percent milk was for him; she reckoned it was the closest thing to what he was used to, although she encouraged him to try anything else that caught his fancy. Everything was labeled "Organic," a term that was unfamiliar to him.

His eyes fell on a loaf of black rye bread, and he picked it up and studied it curiously. Ray had never seen black bread before, and he decided he would try some. He couldn't find anything that resembled butter or margarine, so he cut a small slice and took a bite, making up his mind shortly afterwards that his life up to now had been fine without it and would continue as before. From the previous night's dinner, there was a delightful chicken stew and he helped himself to it, along with something called quinoa he'd tasted for the first time the night before. The quinoa tasted different, but it was tolerable, and he'd made sure to let Njeri know that he thought it was really good. It had been a lot harder to fake affection for the Brussels sprouts and the tofu, and he had crossed them off his list for future reference after the previous night's dinner.

When he tried to make himself a cup of tea, he found himself once again beleaguered by myriad options—black tea, green tea, white tea, Earl Grey, cardamom, ginger and a host of others. When he found a box of Kenyan tea in the pantry, he settled for the familiar choice.

Njeri called around midday just to see how he was doing, and he reassured her that he hadn't yet burned the house down. She expected to be home around six thirty and planned to drive him to the mall, and also to show him the station where he would catch his train to Philadelphia early on Thursday morning for his exam.

Njeri's neighborhood was very quiet. He looked out the window multiple times, and apart from observing an occasional car coming or going, he didn't see a single human being outside. At about three, Ray reclined on the sofa and picked up the remote control, flipping aimlessly from one channel to another on the TV. . . He was suddenly awakened by the sound of Njeri coming into the house. The remote control had fallen onto the carpet. It was about a quarter past six.

"Someone's jetlagged!" Njeri chuckled. "We need to get you out of the house so you can adjust more quickly to the time difference."

She drove to the nearby mall and the two ambled aimlessly from one store to another. After getting out into the cold night, Ray was now wide awake, although much more so now than before from all the browsing. Njeri watched him looking around excitedly, especially in the electronics and clothing shops.

"So you're not tempted to buy everything in the store, let's agree that for now we'll just look around. And then we can come back tomorrow—or on another day—after you've had a chance to think about what you'd like to buy," Njeri said as they entered one of the large clothing stores.

〰〰

Everything went as planned on the day of the exam. He had no trouble getting to the exam center in time and the entire ten-hour experience was exactly as it had been described in the orientation packet.

Ray's recent followup efforts had paid off and he'd gotten responses from two other residency programs—one in Chicago, another in New Jersey. He'd already scheduled the interview in Albany, as he had received that invitation by email even before leaving Kenya. From the look of things, he would travel to Chicago from Albany. He was still trying to work out a date with the program in New Jersey. While it was closest in terms of location—about an hour from where Njeri lived—the program coordinator didn't seem

213

willing to schedule anything until after mid-January, even when he'd explained several times he'd be out of the country by then. She said she'd talk to the program director and get back to him, so he was hopeful he might do it after his interview in Chicago, since he'd be returning to Njeri's house prior to catching his flight from Philadelphia International Airport.

On the bus ride to Albany, he'd noticed what looked like white ash sprinkled on the grass, and he was churning it over in his mind when it suddenly occurred to him that it was snow. He had grown up seeing the snow on the top of Mt. Kenya, but this looked different and not immediately recognizable in this context. But by the time he got into Albany, there was more than a dusting of snow on the ground, and there was no mistaking it for what it was. He checked into the motel room provided by the program, and showed up promptly at seven thirty the next morning for his interview.

There were six other candidates waiting, all dressed in black suits or skirt suits with a white shirt or blouse and a tie where applicable—evidently the unofficial dress code for a residency interview. Ray felt painfully conspicuous in his dark blue dress shirt and tan sport coat; nowhere in the correspondence from the program had there been mention of a dress code.

"Hey, buddy, how're you doing, the name is Carlos!" said one of his fellow interviewees, taking a seat next to him and enthusiastically shaking Ray's hand. He was a confident bespectacled individual with an impeccable suit and haircut.

"I'm Ray. It's nice to meet you."

"Where are you coming from, Ray?"

"Kenya."

"Really!" exclaimed Carlos, his eyes widening. "Like, in Africa?"

Ray nodded.

"Wow, that's amazing! And here I was thinking I was a long way from home!"

In the course of their conversation, Ray discovered that Carlos was from Arizona and this was his eighteenth interview. He wanted to move to the East Coast because his girlfriend, who was also seeking a residency, wanted to live closer to her family.

"Eighteen interviews. Th-that's a l-lot of interviews!" observed Ray.

"Not any more than the average guy or gal. How about you?"

"This is my first."

A puzzled look flashed briefly across Carlos' face, but he quickly moved on. "How many more left to go?"

"One or two, maybe," Ray answered, starting to feel embarrassed.

"Well, Ray, I hope things work out for you. So, how does the process work when you're applying from outside the country?"

Ray started to explain, but was cut short when Ms. Nelson, the program coordinator, arrived to give the group directions for how the rest of the day would go. Then he met with Dr. Lewis, the program director, and one other faculty physician. There were also meetings with many of the senior residents, followed by a hospital tour. Even with nothing to compare it to, Ray was disappointed by the bored, detached manner in which Dr. Lewis conducted his interview, as well as the way the senior residents interacted with the group during the hospital tour. It appeared they didn't really care one way or another whether this group of candidates was interested in joining their program or not.

Ray felt no attraction to this place, but realized it was likely he'd have only one other interview. So he was aware that this program might be his only option—assuming they were interested in him—as there was no crystal ball to tell him how the next interview would go. But at least he learned that he needed a wardrobe adjustment for the upcoming one.

Ray decided to take the bus from Albany to Chicago when he discovered that airline tickets cost three hundred dollars, too steep a price to pay given that he had a little less than a thousand dollars in his possession. The program didn't provide any accommodations, so he'd made a reservation at a nearby hotel, which cost about a hundred and twenty dollars. He planned to take the night bus back to New Jersey after the interview so he would only have to pay for a one-night stay at the hotel. When he checked the price of suits on the internet at the public library in Albany, he'd gasped in dismay at the cost—a simple dark suit and tie would set him back at least two hundred dollars.

Chicago was a lot colder than New Jersey, and there was already three inches of snow on the ground. He had the good fortune of stumbling upon a thrift store on the way to his hotel where he found a dark suit that looked nearly new; a reasonably priced shirt and tie from a regular clothing store completed his new ensemble, which altogether came to sixty dollars.

His interview was at St. James Hospital. The next morning, he showed up there looking confident and more appropriately dressed than he'd been at the first interview. There were three other candidates waiting along with him. When he was called in to see Dr. Dean McAllister, the program director, the two connected almost immediately. He was a tan, athletic individual with unruly red hair and a mustache, and bright, expressive eyes.

"I see you're from Kenya—I've been there. I visited about twenty years ago, so I'm sure it's changed a lot since then!"

Ray smiled. "It has ch-changed. Wh-what took you there?"

Grinning, Dr. McAllister gestured at the numerous photographs on his desktop and his wall that showed him accompanied by a woman, presumably his wife—both dressed in mountain gear—standing in the snow with craggy peaks in the background.

"I've climbed a few mountains in my lifetime. I visited Kenya on the way to climb Mt. Kilimanjaro," he said, pointing at one of the pictures.

All the mountains looked the same to a casual observer, Ray thought, but he obviously attached different memories to each photo.

"I'm still hoping to climb Mt. Kenya one day," McAllister added.

"My f-f-family lives at the b-base of Mt. Kenya, s-so we can see it on a clear day from our house."

Dr. McAllister leaned forward with excitement. "Is that right! Now, tell me, I've always wondered—what does the name 'Kenya' mean, and was the country named after the mountain or the other way around?"

Ray paused to think about how to answer. "Uh . . . er . . . th-that's an interesting q-question, sir . . . the mountain was n-n-named b-before the country existed in its current f-f-form. The original name was K-kirinyaga, which I th-think means 'm-mountain of ostriches,' at l-least th-that's what my m-mother t-told me when I was little. Apparently, the B-british h-had a h-hard time p-pronouncing the original name, s-so they shortened it."

Dr. McAllister's eyes opened wide with amazement. "How incredible! Do the ostriches have a cultural significance? Are there many ostriches around the mountain?"

"N-not any m-more than in other places. What I was t-told w-was th-that the ancient p-people of my tribe had n-no concept of s-snow as it was only up in the m-mountain, and n-nobody had ever b-been up there. Th-they thought th-that the white p-patches at the t-top of the mountain were from the white p-patches on the wings of m-many m-male ostriches at the top. I d-don't know how true that story is b-but th-that's the only v-version I know."

"That's an interesting story if I ever heard one! I've certainly learned something new today," Dr. McAllister remarked, looking very pleased. "Now tell me about your medical training and what it is you're looking for in a residency program."

The interview might just as well have ended there. Dr. McAllister clearly enjoyed their meeting, which would hopefully count for something when the time came. Ray thought the tour also went well and found the residents very friendly and engaging.

As he headed back to New Jersey on the bus, Ray felt really good about his day. He would have to wait for March to find out if he was accepted, unless they contacted him before for a pre-Match arrangement—early acceptance—which he'd heard they didn't generally do.

Although Ray called them to follow up a couple more times, the residency program in New Jersey never got back to him. He didn't get any other interview offers either. So in early December, he bade Njeri farewell and boarded his flight back to Kenya, feeling faint but perceptible stirrings of hope regarding the possibility of a future trip back to the States.

Chapter Twenty-Four

AFTER RAY RETURNED from America, everything at home suddenly seemed very different. Things he'd never noticed before, or at least had never bothered him, suddenly became obvious—like the dusty roadsides with no paved sidewalk, or the total disregard for punctuality. The lack of equipment at the hospital bothered him, but not nearly as much as the placid indifference of everyone around him to the situation—patients and coworkers alike. He had suddenly become a restless misfit, no longer content with his surroundings.

"Kumagara ni kũũhĩga" is an Agĩkũyũ proverb that roughly translates to: "To travel is to become wise." Ray had stepped outside of the comfortable ignorance of his known world, and everything that was previously familiar now seemed odd and off-balance. It was impossible to settle back in as if nothing had happened, to unsee what his eyes had already seen.

The results of the October exams came out in January and he had passed. This was the final hurdle for his eligibility for a residency program. He distractedly went about his work routine at the hospital with an eye on the calendar for Match Day, when applicants were informed of where they had been accepted. It was March fifteenth, also the Ides of March, as he noted apprehensively.

About two weeks before Match Day, he received a phone call

from his mother informing him that his grandfather, Mũthee
Karanja, had died. The funeral was that weekend and he needed to
travel to Karatina. His interactions with his grandfather had been
pleasant, but mostly formal. Ray was a little ashamed that he didn't
feel more broken up at the news; his grandfather had been old, and
he'd always known that sooner or later this day would come. No one
knew exactly how old his grandfather was, but Ray knew the
members of his age group had been old enough to chew on sticks of
sugarcane—which made them at least eight years old during the great
famine— which happened around the time the Mũthũngũ arrived; he
was therefore about a hundred years old when he died.

When Ray was speaking with his mother on the phone, he
noticed her voice was shaking and he heard some sniffling, as if she
was crying. Although she was usually not an emotional person, he
knew her relationship with her father was special. She would often sit
alone with him for hours outside his hut, their conversations
sometimes erupting into laughter—he on his stool and she on a
kanga[29] spread out on the grass. He never failed to tell others of how
she'd brought him one goat after another as soon as she moved back
to Karatina and started working as a teacher; and how she'd hired a
young man called Kariĩthi to assist him with the care of his animals.
Ray knew he loved his goats. At the time of his death he had a herd
of about fifty animals he spent long hours with, following them
around as they grazed, although he was stooped over and needed a

---

[29] Multipurpose cloth used for clothing, sitting on, as a baby harness etc

cane to steady himself.

The funeral brought all the family members together, for the first time in a long while. Many of the grandchildren also attended, and Ray got a chance to see cousins, aunts and uncles he hadn't seen in years. Being Wambũi's son, everyone knew who he was; and he found himself smiling awkwardly on many occasions as he greeted unfamiliar relatives who knew his name, as well as everything about him. Most family members had received some help from his mother at one time or another and still felt indebted to her.

This included his aunt TK, the stylishly dressed architect, who arrived in her elegant purple BMW sport utility vehicle, engulfed in an aura of expensive designer perfume. She was Wambũi's youngest sister. Her original names were Truphena Nyairero—she had been named after one of Mũthee Karanja's sisters who had since passed on. She hated the sound of both names, which occasionally elicited half-suppressed snickers within her hearing. At some point while still in high school, she began calling herself Terry, and it wasn't long after that everyone began calling her "TK" for Terry Karanja. She changed her name officially at the earliest opportunity, which was as soon as she turned eighteen. TK performed very well in her high school final exam, and she went on to be the first female student accepted into the university's school of architecture. Wambũi had been instrumental in convincing her not to be daunted by the challenge of breaking new ground.

During a crisis in her first year of college, TK turned to

Wambũi for help. She'd become pregnant and appeared at their house tearful, desperate and full of shame, with nowhere else to turn. Wambũi shouldered the responsibility of breaking the news to the rest of the family, which the distressed nineteen-year-old didn't have the wherewithal to do. After the initial shock, a number of family members shunned her for a while, but Wambũi stood by her side— firm and defiant—and one by one the detractors were silenced. All this time, the worthless dandy who had sired the baby was nowhere to be seen. The baby boy—Ken, or KK—spent his early years at Mwangi's home, and Ray had many fond memories of the fun and interesting times he'd had with his "cousin-brother" during their childhood. Ken was now a lawyer in London, having completed law school in the United Kingdom.

After Wambũi helped her successfully navigate this crisis, TK had returned to college and completed the rest of her training, throwing herself wholeheartedly into every project that came her way. She had the rare ability to think abstractly in three dimensions, moving rooms and structures around in her mind without needing to put them down on paper. After she graduated from college, she worked for a large architectural firm for a few years before deciding to strike out on her own. Karanja and Associates was now a well-known firm doing important projects in Nairobi. She had five architects working with her, but there were still people who came in every now and then wanting to speak to "Mr. Karanja himself," to which she gave a firm, pleasant and well-rehearsed reply that there was only one Karanja in the group and she was it.

"Your mother is a very special person," TK often told Ray. "If it wasn't for her, I wouldn't be where I am now!"

There were a number of local dignitaries who attended the funeral, including the provincial commissioner and the mayor of Karatina. Both spoke briefly at the event, stating their connection with the family as being by way of their friendship with Wambũi, or Mama Mũthoni, as many people now called her.

One of Wambũi's step-siblings, Kĩarie, was a Presbyterian minister. So there was a large turnout from among the local clergy and elders as well, this despite the fact that Mũthee Karanja had never darkened the door of any church building.

An interesting conversation took place among the aunts and uncles that evening after the funeral, when most of the guests who were not family members had left. The group was sitting in a large circle in the grass sipping hot tea as people prepared to make the journey back home. Kĩarie, the minister, was the one who started it.

"Maitũ," he began, addressing his mother, Wambũi's stepmother, "what exactly happened on that night the Mũthũngũ policeman and his home guards came to our house, during the Emergency?"

Once he spoke, the other conversations suddenly died down, and all eyes turned to Nyina wa Kariũki.

"Which night?" she asked, with a puzzled look on her wrinkled face.

"The night they came shouting and threatening, and the Mũthũngũ had a big dog on a leash!" said her other son Mũgo, who had been about seven when it happened.

"Oh yes, I remember that night!" exclaimed Mama Peter, who was the oldest female sibling among Nyina wa Kariũki's children, and who also bore the name Wambũi. "I remember they made us go outside the house and kneel down in the middle of the night!"

"Ah, I think I remember now," said Nyina wa Kariũki, "my memory is not as good as it used to be. That was a scary night!"

"I remember the way the dog ran barking and growling towards Baba, and then just stopped and wouldn't go back to the Mũthũngũ until Baba told it to go back . . ." continued Mũgo.

There was a buzz of conversation as the few who had observed the episode firsthand began to recount it to the curious grandchildren and younger siblings who had either not witnessed it or had been too young to know what was happening.

"Baba used to talk to animals," remarked Ray's mother. "I always thought that that's what all old men did, although he was different because animals seemed to understand exactly what he was saying to them."

"His mother once told me that when he was a child, he had a dream where he saw the Athũngũ's train, years before they arrived in Karatina," Nyina wa Kariũki recalled. "She thought he was just having the silly dreams that children sometimes have, but she remembered her shock the first time she saw the train passing through Karatina and remembered what her son had described years before."

"Nyina wa Kariūki," interjected Nyina wa Wambūi, "remember the day he woke up in the morning and told us that Kĩmathi had died? It was not until two days later that someone came from Nyeri and told us the news had been announced that day."

"Oooh, yes, Nyina wa Wambūi, I remember that. That was a very strange day. I remember we couldn't tell anyone else, so we just waited, sad and confused, until everyone else got the news. Those were very difficult times."

Ray was sitting next to his mother. "S-so, w-was he like a w-witch doctor?" he asked her in a low voice.

"No, he was not a witch doctor!" she said, shaking her head vigorously.

Nyina wa Kariūki, who was sitting close by, overheard the exchange and felt the need to reiterate what had been said.

"Your grandfather was not a witch doctor, Kĩng'ori. He was a good man."

What was supposed to have been a brief epilogue before people traveled home turned into two hours of reminiscing. Ray was fascinated; he learned things about his grandfather and his mother's childhood he had never heard before. At one point, he whispered another question to his mother.

"Ask me later," Wambũi said discreetly.

He waited until the next day, when he was alone with his mother, and asked the question again. "Mom, who is the Kariũki of the other Cũcũ (grandma)? I don't think I've ever met him."

Wambũi sighed. "Kariũki was her firstborn. One day, during the Emergency, when young people were disappearing to join the Mau Mau or were being captured by the home guards, he left the village and was not seen again. We don't talk about it as it upsets Nyina wa Kariũki, and it also used to upset your grandfather quite a bit."

"S-so, n-n-nobody knows what h-happened to him?" he asked in surprise.

"No . . . er . . . well . . ." His mother hesitated for a moment, then glanced around the room uneasily before relaxing into a smile. "I don't know why I'm telling you this, because I've never told anyone—except your father. And since he's not a talker, I'm sure he's never mentioned it to anyone. You asked me a direct question, so I cannot lie to you. I trust you enough to know you will keep this to yourself."

Ray's ears perked up as his mother recounted an unusual episode that had occurred outside the hardware store, years before. A disheveled man with an overgrown beard, brown rotting teeth and matted, filthy dreadlocks had appeared one day outside the store, and peered in through the window, motionless. Customers gave him a wide berth as they went in and out. His mother was at the counter and something made her look up and their eyes met. He had been staring directly at her. His eyes were bloodshot, and his gaze remained locked on her, forcing her to look away after a few seconds. She wasn't sure why she decided to walk towards the door, but as she got closer, she noticed the familiar scar on his forehead, above his left eyebrow.

"Kariũki?" Wambũi addressed him tentatively, as she stepped out of the store. There was no flicker of recognition or acknowledgment on his part, but she was certain it was him. She went back inside and returned with a loaf of bread. When she held it out to him, he grabbed it and ripped it apart, taking chunks of bread and stuffing them into his mouth, while crumbs fell on his shaggy beard and onto the ground. She went inside to get him a drink, and when she came back he was gone.

Wambũi got into her car and drove around the nearby streets looking for him, but her search was fruitless. In the days that followed, she drove around some more, frantically scanning the roadsides and alleys for an unkempt, dreadlocked man, but he was nowhere to be seen. As mysteriously as he had appeared, he disappeared again. After discussing the matter with her husband, they decided to keep the incident to themselves, feeling that news of his reappearance was more likely to reopen old wounds than bring comfort, particularly among the frail, elderly members of her family.

~~~

March fifteenth eventually arrived; and at eight o'clock that evening, which was noon on the East Coast of the United States, Ray was frantically trying to log onto the website that would tell him whether or not his quest had been successful. As often happens when too many people try to access the same website at the same time, it crashed. What followed was a mixture of panic and helplessness as he tried to log in again and again without success.

In a state of nervous limbo, he decided to check his email. His heart jumped when he saw a new message from the organization that managed the matching process: "Congratulations, you have been matched with the Internal Medicine Residency Program at St. James Hospital, Chicago . . ."

Chapter Twenty-Five

TEDDY CRUTCHFIELD STOOD at the Arrivals area looking for his party, holding a placard in front of his chest with a name on it. The flight had landed about forty-five minutes earlier, and the first wave of passengers had made it through customs and baggage claims, emerging from the secure area of the airport, some warmly greeted by friends or family, while others confronted a more impersonal experience on arrival, making their way to one of several modes of transportation into the city. This was Teddy's third trip of the day, but the sheer variety of passengers that materialized from behind the sliding doors never ceased to fascinate him: excited tourists, nervous immigrants, exhausted returnees, restless businesspeople.

A young couple walked past him, looking tan and wearing t-shirts, jeans and sandals that had taken something of a beating in the past several days, carrying backpacks that hinted at riveting tales of rugged landscapes recently explored. They had probably been on a flight arriving from Africa. Their attire was flagrantly disrespectful of the chilly November weather, but they were locals, returning home, not about to let the perennially ungracious weather ruin the last few hours of their tropical vacation.

There was an Indian family with three young children probably between the ages of three and nine. They had two baggage carts laden with suitcases, which the father and his eldest child were pushing, with the mother attempting to assist, while alternately holding the middle child's hand and trying to push her youngest in a stroller. They were dressed in several layers of formal attire, prepared for what was likely their first interaction with the cold weather of the northern climes they knew only by reputation. The parents wore serious expressions as they scanned the crowd, hoping to spot the familiar faces of those who were supposed to be there waiting for them. They were probably immigrants making the trip of a lifetime.

The number of passengers coming off the flight was dwindling, and now there were just a few stragglers coming through the doors. He watched a gray-haired bespectacled lady with a slight frame, probably in her sixties, struggling to get her luggage cart to go where she wanted it to go; one of its wheels was misaligned and it needed an extra bit of force to keep it moving in a straight line. She didn't seem to be in a hurry as she made her way slowly across the terminal, surveying the faces of the people in the waiting area. Her eyes fell on the placard that Teddy was holding. This was his cue.

"Good day, madam—Ms. Atwood, I presume?" he asked as he reached out to take the baggage cart from her.

Eileen saw before her a hefty, muscular man with closely cropped white hair and a pleasant open face. "Indeed, I am," she replied softly and a little breathlessly, managing a smile; "and you are?"

"Theodore Crutchfield is my name, but you can call me

Teddy. It's a pleasure to meet you! I will be your driver. I trust you had a good flight?"

"I did—and I'm pleased to meet you as well."

They proceeded to the nearby taxi stand, where Teddy had parked. He opened the rear passenger door to let her get in before loading her suitcases into the trunk. He then got into his car and started the engine.

"I have your destination listed as an address on Heathside Road in Surrey," he said, looking over his left shoulder to make eye contact with her in the rear passenger seat. "Prunella from Mr. Barnes' office was the person I spoke to."

Eileen nodded.

"So, are you visiting or returning home?" he asked, trying to make conversation as they joined the M25 motorway.

"I'm not really sure I know the answer to that question," she answered wearily. "I've been away for more than forty years, so I don't really know where my home is anymore."

"Pardon my curiosity, madam," he ventured, "but were you living in different countries all that time or were you in one place?"

"I've been living in Kenya." Her voice perked up a little just saying the name.

"Oh, Kenya—that's a beautiful country from all that I've

heard!" he said enthusiastically. "I have an uncle who visited there once and he absolutely loved it. He always spoke about going back, but things never quite worked out."

She smiled and said, "That's too bad."

"What was it you were you doing in Kenya?"

"I was a teacher," Eileen said, leaving it at that.

"I notice you used the word 'was.' Are you retired then?"

"I suppose you could say that," she replied dully.

After years of striking up conversations with his passengers, Teddy had become very adept at reading between the lines; he sensed that the circumstances of this homecoming might not have been entirely voluntary. She made no allusion to family in Surrey, and the aforementioned Mr. Barnes who had contacted the taxi company was an agent with Guildford Realty Associates, which had offices scattered all over the county.

They arrived at the address—a block of flats—and Teddy unloaded her luggage. Despite her polite protestations, he picked up all her suitcases with no apparent effort, and led the way into the building to the management office, which was on the ground floor. There they encountered a young woman in her mid-twenties sitting at a desk with a bored expression on her face, turning the pages of a glossy magazine.

"May I help you?" she asked curtly.

"I'm Eileen Atwood, and I'm here for flat number 204. You should have been contacted about me by a Mr. Joshua Barnes."

There was a faint nod of recognition at the mention of the name, and she typed in some information on her computer before retrieving a large envelope from a drawer on her left. Eileen's name was written on it in bold letters.

"The keys are in the packet, as well as the contract. Please review and sign the contract and return it to me by tomorrow. Payment has already been made through a preexisting arrangement you have with the realty company. The lift to the second floor is to your right. Let me know if I may be of further assistance—my name is Amanda." And with that, she started busying herself on her computer, though in reality she was waiting for them to leave so she could return to her magazine.

Teddy picked up the bags and carried them into the elevator. When they reached the second floor, he deposited them at the door of flat number 204.

"It seems Mr. Barnes took care of everything," Teddy said, as he prepared to leave.

Eileen started fumbling in her wallet for a five-pound note, but he held up his hand and shook his head.

"Please, no tip necessary, Ms. Atwood—the pleasure was all mine. I enjoyed our conversation very much and I hope you'll do very well settling back in."

She thanked him for his trouble and as he walked away, she reached into the envelope and pulled out the key that unlocked the door to her apartment.

≈

Surrey had changed a lot since Eileen had left, though this was hardly surprising given the amount of time she had been away. After spending some time surveying her living quarters, she decided to go to the local supermarket to stock up on groceries. There was a bus stop a short walk from the apartment complex, and the bus went directly past the supermarket, two stops away. On a nice day, if one didn't have anything to carry, it would make for a pleasant walk.

As she walked up and down the different aisles in the supermarket, she tried not to compare the prices to those in Nairobi. Still, everything seemed very expensive, so she ended up at the checkout counter with only a handful of items. She would ask around to see if there were better prices to be found elsewhere. There were only two cashiers open and she took her place behind a woman who had a full grocery cart. The other queue had three people with fewer items, so it was a toss-up as to which line would get her through faster. But it didn't matter. She wasn't in a rush to go anywhere after she was through shopping.

The woman at the register was tall and blonde with short hair, who looked to be in her early twenties. She wore a big smile and had a warm, engaging voice with a noticeable Eastern European accent. She tried to make casual conversation with the customer in front of

Eileen, but the woman only grunted in acknowledgment, her face set in a hard, unyielding stare. The cashier completed the woman's purchase and gave her a receipt, cheerily wishing her a good day, a sentiment that was neither acknowledged nor reciprocated.

Eileen stepped forward and said hello to the cashier, chatting with her as she rang up the purchases. The woman smiled as she handed over her receipt, and bade her good day as she exited the store. Once outside, Eileen almost bumped into the ill-humored customer who had been in line ahead of her. She had parked her grocery cart right outside the store and was lighting up a cigarette. Their eyes met. Her gaze was cold and unfriendly. The woman gestured conspiratorially to Eileen and she drew nearer.

"These people are everywhere!" she snarled. "They're taking over our country!"

Eileen shuddered and paused for a moment, speechless, before deciding to turn around and keep walking in the same direction as before, which was towards the bus stop. The interaction haunted her for the rest of the day. And that angry contorted face kept popping up in her mind, whispering harshly to her. In the grocery store, she'd noticed people of many different ethnicities; and she considered it an encouraging sign that her hometown had come of age and become an international destination, rather than the small rural conurbation it had been when she was a young woman.

She wondered if there had been people like that woman in Kenya, whispering angrily amongst themselves when they saw her walk by. Had they stood outside an Uchumi Supermarket, pointing at her and identifying her as a foreigner who was taking over their country? She had lived in Kenya for decades and spoke Kiswahili fluently, albeit with an incurable British accent. She wondered whether, behind the inscrutable smiles of strangers, she had been viewed as an unwelcome outsider and interloper. Having lived twice as long in Kenya as she had in England, how had it been decided that this was where she belonged?

≋

When Eileen got back to her flat, she decided to call Mr. Barnes. Her connection with him had begun after her mother died, when she'd decided to put the house she inherited up for rent. She'd gotten his name from her second cousin Matilda, who lived in London and who had needed to make similar arrangements when her own parents had passed on and she had no interest in moving away from London or selling the house. Matilda had made the trip to Surrey for Eileen's mother's funeral. The two cousins had nothing in common and weren't close, but that little piece of information had been helpful.

Mr. Barnes was a thin, bald man, whose distinctive facial features might still have been noteworthy even if his pointed nose had only been half the size. The little dark line of a mustache seemed to underscore this prominent feature in the middle of his face. He spoke slowly and was eminently logical in his thinking; he could break down the most complex idea into the simplest terms so that it was easily understood. And this ability probably explained why someone of his rather ungainly appearance and uncharismatic demeanor succeeded as well as he had. His secretary, Mrs. Prunella Noble, was more outgoing, and she spoke to all their clients as if they were old friends. Eileen had enjoyed their brief interactions when she'd previously visited their offices.

The arrangement she'd made with Barnes entailed applying part of the rental income from the house she'd inherited to cover the rent for the flat she was living in. The house was fairly large and in good condition, in a very desirable location, and it had appreciated tremendously in value since her father originally purchased it. Finding someone to rent it hadn't been difficult, and the current tenant had been willing to sign a three-year lease but was only given the option of one year, which had become customary. Eileen was certain she might have gotten a cheaper flat had she looked herself; but she was coming from outside the country, a relative stranger to the area with no friend or family to do the legwork for her, so the arrangement with the realty company had seemed the best course.

The phone rang twice before someone picked it up. "Guildford Realty Associates, office of Mr. Joshua Barnes, this is Prunella Noble, how may I help you?"

"Um . . . er . . . this is Eileen Atwood . . ." she started with a stammer.

"Ms. Atwood, welcome back! How are you? I hope you had a pleasant flight, and I hope the flat is to your satisfaction," said Prunella, sounding genuinely excited. "Mr. Crutchfield, the taxicab driver, called earlier to let us know you'd arrived safely." Prunella had a very soothing and reassuring voice.

"Yes, thank you, all went very well and I like the flat. I'd like to speak with Mr. Barnes, if he's available," Eileen said.

"I'm sorry, he's out for the day," Prunella said; "but I promise to let him know you called. He'll be in touch. Meanwhile, have a good day."

Before she hung up, Eileen asked her for the name of a nearby grocery store that had better prices than the one she'd shopped at earlier, and she scribbled down the name of the store Prunella recommended. Then she started unpacking the few groceries she'd just purchased. The fatigue of her all-night flight was starting to catch up with her and before long she would need a nap. She would try not to sleep too long since she didn't want to be up all night. The apartment was furnished, which helped a great deal. She had bought a writing pad, some envelopes and postage stamps. After she'd rested, she would write a few letters to friends in Kenya to let them know she'd arrived safely.

Chapter Twenty-Six

IT WAS THE second month of internship and the blurry transition from one day to the next sometimes led to a loss of temporal perspective, so that on occasion it was difficult to tell if the instructions given by the senior resident had been from earlier in the day or from two days ago. This generated a constant sense of apprehension regarding the possibility of a forgotten assignment or a critical lab result that had not been acted upon. Lack of sleep made each day seem to drag on endlessly, while each night of inadequate rest created a craving for more—in very much the same way that a salty drink will exacerbate the thirst of a poor soul cast adrift at sea. On one morning, Ray and his fellow intern, Jan van Heerden, stood bleary-eyed at the end of the hallway, waiting for John Taylor, their senior resident, who was winding up an animated conversation with one of the senior nurses on the unit.

"Hey guys, sorry to keep you waiting!" he announced as he approached them with long strides. "You know how it is with Melvina—everything is always slightly more complicated than it really should be. She's a great nurse, but oh so nitpicky! But if I was admitted to the hospital, I'd want her to be my nurse. Alright, so what have we got? Who wants to go first?"

"I h-have a c-c-couple of p-patients on this floor, including

241

th-these two rooms over here," Ray said, nodding his head in the direction of the rooms he was referring to.

"Okay, Ray, sounds good, go ahead . . . and oh, by the way, did you switch doctors for the two patients we discussed yesterday?"

Ray nodded.

"Sweet! That Mr. Fleming is a crotchety old dude, it's impossible to make some people happy. Okay, so what's going on with the patient in Room 221?"

"H-he's a f-fifty-year-old g-guy with a past medical history of c-c-coronary artery d-disease, diabetes, hypothyroidism . . ."

"Um . . . John . . . excuse me, I'm so sorry to interrupt, but I think we need to talk about this Fleming guy," Jan said, sounding on edge. "I'm not very happy with how that situation was resolved."

Ray and John looked at him in surprise.

"Why, what's wrong?" asked John.

"Did Monica tell you why he asked to switch doctors?"

"Er . . . I didn't get into the details, but she said he was having some sort of communication issue—or maybe it was a personality thing . . . I didn't really ask her for details, this stuff happens all the time. Why, what happened?"

"Well, the guy is a damn racist!" said Jan bluntly. "I'm just going to call it out for what it is! He made this big to-do about not understanding Ray's accent; but you've listened to both of us and we're both pretty easy to understand, I think. When I entered his room, he started going on and on about immigrants with accents, so I stopped him and told him I was an immigrant from Africa. He thought I was joking, until I asked him if he'd ever heard of a country called South Africa. I asked him which continent he thought it was on, at which point he said that I was different and he could understand me."

John's face turned scarlet with embarrassment.

"Oh man, I'm sorry," he said, turning to Ray. "I didn't realize it was about *that*. It's too bad there are still people in the world like him."

"Th-that's fine," replied Ray with a nonchalant shrug. "C-can I t-tell you about the p-patient in 221 now?"

"Er . . . sure," answered John awkwardly.

"So, what happens on the day when I'm off and Ray is covering my patients?" persisted Jan irritably. "Will he stop being a racist on that day? We should not have enabled his behavior by allowing him to switch doctors."

"I get that," John said, squirming visibly. "I should have asked more questions at the outset, but I didn't. My bad!"

"If I knew h-h-he w-was a r-racist and made the request f-for the switch, would you h-have allowed it?" Ray said unexpectedly.

"Of course, I would have!"

A long pause ensued.

"Where exactly are you going with that, Ray?" asked Jan, with a perplexed look on his face.

Ray smiled cryptically, the small gap between his upper incisors coming into view. "Nowhere, I'm j-just trying to aggravate you. My p-p-point is that he needs me more th-than I need him, so it's g-good riddance for me. I hope he would have the sense not to refuse my c-c-care if his life d-depended on it. Now, can I t-t-tell you about the patient in 221?"

"Sure, go ahead," John said, sounding relieved at the idea of changing the subject.

They resumed their rounds, trying to pick up speed after the slow start. Like an odd aftertaste, the earlier discussion was never far from anyone's mind, although they all tried to carry on as if it had been forgotten.

When Ray and Jan stopped by the residents' lounge after rounds, Jan brought it up again.

"So, Ray, tell me honestly, what do you really think about what happened with Fleming?"

"It d-doesn't b-bother me," Ray said flatly.

"Are you just saying that to shut me up or is that how you

really feel?"

"A bit of b-both," rejoined Ray with a faint grin. "The g-guy hates me and he d-doesn't know me, yet he needs me more than I n-need him. Why should I b-b-be bothered about him? I d-don't know him and I don't n-need anything from him."

"That stuff drives me up the wall. I find it infuriating!"

"We all have to p-pick our battles—and th-that battle's not mine. You c-can fight that one; I'll save my energy for when I really need t-t-to fight." Ray's pager went off. He picked up the phone and returned the call. It was John. He scribbled down the information as he received it, then hung up the phone.

"Okay, enough t-talk, I have an admission in ER. I'll c-catch up with you later."

Ray left the residents' lounge as Jan flopped into an armchair and reached for the remote, aware that his call would probably be coming soon as well.

When Ray got to the ER, he hastily logged onto the computer to obtain some information about his patient in Room 15. "T-Thomas Sarkevic, f-fifty-five years old, hypertension, hyperlipidemia, with heartburn, nausea . . ." he mumbled to himself before logging off and heading to the room with his clipboard in hand.

Mr. Sarkevic was an obese man with close-cropped graying hair. He was lying on a gurney with a queasy look on his face and a basin ready in his hand.

"Hello, M-mister S-sarkevic, I'm . . ."

"You're here to take me upstairs?" the man said in a weary voice; "that took a lot quicker than I expected."

"Er, actually I'm your d-doctor, s-so it might still be a while b-b-before they t-t-take you upstairs."

"Oh well, I suspected that was too good to be true. And your name is Dr. ——?"

"Kĩng'ori."

"Wow, that's a mouthful! I'll never be able to pronounce that. Is it okay if I call you Dr. King?"

"Um . . . er . . . only if it's ok-kay for me to c-call you Mr. Sark," Ray quipped.

Mr. Sarkevic grimaced, then conceded with a shrug. "Okay, then, Kĩng'ori it is. And by the way, my name is pronounced Sarkevi*k*, not Sarkevi*ch*—everybody makes that mistake."

"Okay, Mr. Sarkevi*k*, would you mind t-t-telling me what brought you to the ER?"

He began describing his symptoms, which started off with a lot of nausea and vomiting that morning; and even after receiving intravenous fluids and multiple medications, he was still throwing up, which was why the emergency room physician had decided to admit him to the hospital until the symptoms could be brought under control.

"So, where are you from, Dr. Kĩng'ori?"

"Kenya."

"Did you go to medical school here in the States?"

"No, I went t-t-to medical school in K-kenya."

"Really!" the man exclaimed with an astonished expression, apparently delivered from his affliction, at least temporarily. "So, they actually have medical schools in Africa? That's good to know."

"Yes s-sir, there's one in N-n-nigeria and one in K-kenya. Our s-s-school was under a b-big t-tree, and sometimes the elephants would c-c-come and d-disrupt classes b-because they wanted to rub against the tree." Ray's stammer and milquetoast demeanor conferred on him an aura of innocence that often made it difficult for someone to tell when he was being facetious or sarcastic, or both as in this instance.

"Wow! That's quite a story! I didn't realize you had to overcome such hardship to get to where you are."

"Oh, I'm s-s-sorry, I was only k-kidding. There are m-m-many medical schools in Africa, and none of them is under a t-tree, as f-far as I know."

Mr. Sarkevic seemed enthralled nonetheless. "So, what's it

like growing up in Africa?" he asked.

"Um . . . l-l-let's f-first talk about why you're here, so we can figure out what we need to do for you."

They resumed the discussion about Mr. Sarkevic's symptoms and his medical history. As the conversation continued, Ray's expression changed. Something didn't add up.

"So, t-t-tell me more about the episode yesterday where you nearly p-p-passed out."

"Oh, it was nothing. I think I was just dehydrated. You know how hot this summer has been. I bet you're probably used to this kind of heat back in Africa."

"Did you actually p-pass out or nearly pass out?"

"I was getting into my car, then I felt a bit nauseous and sweaty. I'd just had some lousy pizza, which was probably why I felt so nauseous. I felt like I was going to pass out, but I leaned against the car for a few seconds and the feeling went away. It hasn't happened again since, though."

"And t-t-tell me about the discomfort in your chest . . ."

"I don't even want to call it discomfort—it's just a weird feeling, like there's a hand pressing down lightly in the middle of my chest, preventing me from taking in a deep breath. I don't know, it's hard to describe, and it comes and goes. I don't know, I think it's just psychological—I don't think it has anything to do with why I'm feeling sick and nauseous."

Ray completed the rest of his interview. There was a thoughtful look on his face. "I'll be back in a f-f-few minutes," he told Mr. Sarkevic. As soon as he stepped out of the room, Ray approached the nurse who was in charge of the care of his patient. "Larry, c-c-can we get a stat t-t-twelve-lead in Room 15?"

"Who, the gastritis guy?" the nurse said, looking confused.

Ray nodded. "I d-d-don't think it's g-gastritis."

"Alright doc, I'm on it!"

Larry disappeared into the room and emerged a couple of minutes later with the EKG printout and handed it to Ray. "Wow, look at that, doc! Look at those tombstones! You want me to grab Dr. Phillips? We're gonna need to activate a code STEMI."

Three minutes later, there was a buzz of frenetic activity in Room 15, which culminated in a stunned, disoriented Mr. Sarkevic being wheeled rapidly down the hallway in the direction of the cardiac catheterization lab, with the on-call cardiologist trotting alongside asking him additional questions about allergies and past procedures, and breathlessly explaining why he urgently needed the procedure he was about to do.

Ray watched the procession as it disappeared down the hallway, and started heading back to the main hospital building. He was walking past Dr. Phillips, the ER physician, when he stopped him.

"Are you the intern in internal medicine?"

"Yes, sir," Ray said nervously.

"Great catch! You saved that guy's life!"

≋

Hakeem had a magnetic personality. If one polled all the repeat customers at Al's Sandwiches regarding what brought them back day after day, Hakeem's name would inevitably come up. He was about six foot three and overweight, with a shiny bald head and a well-groomed beard. His smooth baritone and brilliant wit provided an excellent substrate for pleasant conversations at the lunch counter, an experience made even more enjoyable because he seemed to know all his regular customers by their first name, as well as their favorite orders.

"Ella . . . Ella! So good to see you! Where you been at? I ain't seen you in over a week! You been outta town, or you be messin' around with them low-carb diets again? You know they ain't good for you! Now Ella, you know what the good book says—give us this day our daily bread . . . so don't be tryin' to be gettin' by without no bread, you know what I'm sayin'? How you been, though?"

"I'm doing good, Hakeem, just a lot of stuff going on, you know how it is. It's good to see you!" Ella said with evident enthusiasm.

"And it's always good to see you, Ella! What you havin' today—the Ella Special?"

"I think so."

"Alright . . . Ima put in some extra chicken and sauce, so that you be thinkin' about us when they come to you with them low-carb or no-carb diets or whatever folks gettin' tripped up on these days."

"Oh, thank you, Hakeem, that's very kind of you!" Ella was grinning from ear to ear.

"Any time, Ella, any time!"

The first time Ray ordered at Al's, the experience had been a complete nightmare. He had only been in Chicago two weeks, and the numerous choices involved in selecting each component of the sandwich had completely overwhelmed him, not to mention the fact that he could barely understand what Hakeem was saying.

"What kinda bread you want? We got white, wheat, six-grain, honey-oat, sourdough, rye, ciabatta . . ."

"Th-this one," Ray had said, pointing to the wheat bread under the glass counter.

"An' what kinda cheese? We got American, Pepper Jack, provolone, Swiss, cheddar and Havarti."

"Um . . . any."

"'S'cuse me?"

"Any."

Hakeem looked up from behind the counter and hesitated momentarily, then broke into a broad smile.

"Man, that's deep! So, now *I* be feeling the pressure to pick the right cheese for you—I like that! In all the years I been here, ain't nobody ever gave me a order like that! You must not be from around here. Where you from, bro?"

"Kenya," Ray said shyly.

"Alright man, any cheese—Ima have to think about it, that's a lot of pressure you putting me under!"

From that day on, he referred to Ray as Any-Cheese, and he became a frequent customer. The shop was about a block from his apartment and it was open until eleven at night, making it a logical stop on the way home when Ray left work late. It was usually quieter in the evenings, as the heavy foot traffic tended to dwindle after about eight. In those circumstances, Ray often found himself the recipient of Hakeem's numerous questions about the Motherland, as he called it, and sometimes customers chimed in with their questions or commentaries.

"Any-Cheese, don't be takin' this the wrong way, but anytime I see somebody from Kenya, I see them skinny little folks runnin' like the devil be chasing them, always winning gold medals. So, how come you don't look like them? Are they from a different tribe?"

Ray smiled at the notion. "N-not all K-Kenyans l-look like that, th-though most of the g-g-good runners are skinny. N-not all Kenyans are runners."

"So, if I went to the Motherland, I ain't gonna find myself surrounded by a bunch of little people pointing they fingers at me? You know what I'm saying? See, I'm a plus-size like you—I don't wanna be standing out or anything like that."

"They might f-find your accent a b-bit strange, but there will b-be people in all shapes and sizes."

Hakeem started to say something, then hesitated for a moment before he continued. "So . . . um . . . if I was in the Motherland, can they look at me and tell which area or village my ancestors were from, just by looking?"

"Probably not," Ray said.

Just then two men and a woman in their twenties walked in, engaged in a boisterous conversation accompanied by raucous laughter, their voices still as loud as they'd been out on the sidewalk. One of the men staggered a little, and his speech was slurred, indicating he'd had a little too much to drink.

As they gave their orders, Ray got up to leave, nodding to another regular—Mr. Griffin— and waving to Hakeem.

"Alright man," Hakeem called out, "that's a interesting conversation! We gonna have to continue it next time."

Chapter Twenty-Seven

MARGATE COTTAGE WAS the senior care facility that Eileen had moved to after her first year back in the United Kingdom. She had managed well enough at the flat on Heathside Road, but the boredom and loneliness started getting the better of her. One day as she was shopping at the supermarket, she picked up a brochure advertising the facility. It contained attractive glossy photos of well-groomed elderly citizens living out their golden years with every whim and fancy catered to by an adoring staff of professionals. She wasn't so gullible as to believe all the claims made in the well-designed booklet, but the fact that it offered a full range of services—from independent living to full nursing care—got her attention. Her mother's death still haunted her: all alone in her house and gone, unnoticed for days. Eileen needed to be among people.

She was very thankful to her deceased parents for the house she'd inherited from them. It had appreciated immensely in value, far more than her father, the accountant, could have imagined, so she was able to live off the rent with no financial worries whatsoever. All matters related to the house were still being handled by Guildford Realty, and Eileen felt confident that the delightful Prunella Noble and her boss Mr. Barnes continued to make the best decisions on her behalf.

When Eileen moved into Margate Cottage independent living, she was among the younger residents as she was still in her sixties. Now many years had gone by and it had indeed become home. Some of the staff had been there before she moved in, and she'd gotten to know them well, learning their children and grandchildren's names and birthdates and wedding days; some had invited her to special family occasions as well. Had she not had these relationships, she would probably have withered away and died within her first two years of living in England.

She still harbored fond memories of Kenya and remained in touch with many of her friends by mail. By now, all the staff members knew the significance of a letter from Kenya, announcing it with pomp and relish as they delivered it to her personally in the common area, which is where she preferred to spend her time, rather than holed up in her room like some of the others. There were a couple of computers with internet access in the common area, and she'd gotten into the habit of reading the Kenyan newspapers online as a way to keep her connection to the country where she still dreamed of returning. But with each passing year, it had become harder and harder to imagine how a return visit would ever materialize.

"Hello, Ms. Atwood!" Karim called out to her as he reported to work.

"Hello, Karim! How are Razia and the children?"

"They're very well, thank you."

255

Karim Ansari was one of the staff members who had worked at Margate Cottage about ten years. He was gentle and soft-spoken and got along well with everyone—that is, everyone except Donna Trimble. Eileen first met Karim as he was still reeling from a savage verbal assault from Ms. Trimble.

"Hey, terrorist!" the vile woman had called out to Karim on his second day at work.

He pretended not to hear her, but she was undeterred.

"Did they send you here to blow this place up?" Ms. Trimble persisted.

When he tried to approach her merely to calm her down, she forbade him to come any closer, spewing threats and invectives, as her voice grew louder and louder. "Stop this man, he's a terrorist—he wants to kill me!" she had screamed hideously, attracting the attention of everyone in the immediate vicinity.

Karim felt helpless and mortified, and just stood there with no idea of what to do, when Rastaman—his coworker—showed up. He walked up to Ms. Trimble and put a finger to his lips, indicating to her that she needed to settle down.

"Jeremy, save me from this terrorist!" she said to him.

He merely looked at her sternly and put his index finger over his lips again. "Me no Jeremy, me Rastaman. An' you no talk now!"

Ms. Trimble let out an irritable sigh and fell into a sullen silence.

Rastaman turned around and looked in Karim's direction, signaling by a quick jerk of his head that he should follow him into the staff room, which was at the far end of the common area.

Jeremy was from Trinidad. When he first started working at Margate Cottage, he was a polite, obsequious fellow with close-cropped hair, newly arrived in the country and eager to make a good impression with everyone. After a few interactions with Ms. Trimble—she insisted on calling him Rastaman and doing a poor imitation of his Caribbean accent—something changed in him. One day he decided he would grow dreadlocks, which initially elicited surprise and fascination, with everyone convinced it was a passing fancy. But the defiant locks of hair grew on, initially standing upright; then, as a result of increasing length, hanging down the side of his head like fierce Medusa heads. Jeremy had a perfect face for dreadlocks—a long coffee-colored oval with small symmetrical twinkling eyes and perfect shiny white teeth.

Ms. Trimble might have been expected to be pleased to see him adopt her persona for him, but the reality was just the opposite. She started calling him Jeremy and begged him to cut off his locks, but he refused to answer to the name—much to her chagrin. When she complained about his hair to the management, the issue was dismissed outright. He had the right to do whatever he pleased with his hair as long as it was decent and presentable, which it was deemed to be.

Rastaman, being a keen observer, had noticed that nobody ever came to visit Ms. Trimble, even though her family promptly dealt with any of the financial matters related to her stay. Whenever she got a little out of hand, all he had to do was ask her when her family would be visiting next, and that usually set her right.

Her medical records revealed that she suffered from an atypical case of frontotemporal dementia, and anytime she said something inappropriate or disrespectful, it was attributed to her tendency to exhibit symptoms of social disinhibition as a result of her disease. But those who lived with her had strong suspicions that while she very well may have been correctly diagnosed, her boorish behavior was unlikely to be entirely the result of a medical condition.

Karim and his wife had moved to England from Pakistan the year before, and they were desperately trying to fit in. But unfortunately, most of the time that young people of the same or similar ethnicity were shown on TV, it was in connection with terrorism. When the petite lady with graying hair and glasses seated at the far end of the common area signaled to him after his interaction with Ms. Trimble, and subsequent pow-wow with Rastaman, he was unsure of her intentions; but since he didn't have the option of ignoring her, he approached. She signaled for him to come even closer, which he did.

"This is your country too. Don't listen to that witch!" Eileen whispered loudly.

Karim smiled uneasily.

"What's your name, son?"

"Karim Ansari."

"Where are you from?"

"Pakistan."

"Well, it's very nice to meet you Karim," she said, stretching out her hand. "I'm Eileen. I know what it feels like to be a foreigner—I feel like that every day!"

After that exchange, the two became friends. Over time, Karim would learn about her life in Kenya and all the people who wrote her letters, as well as of her yearning to go back to the land she considered home.

Chapter Twenty-Eight

RAY'S INTERNSHIP YEAR had progressed at a steady, hectic pace and it was already April, with the early days of spring politely inserting themselves between the sullen, fading days of winter. The remnants of dirty gray snow from prior months still sat stubbornly on the edges of the tarmac and on the empty strips adjacent to the sidewalks, where green blades of grass would soon be poking out of the ground, followed by brilliant yellow buttercups and dandelions. Every now and then the temperatures would drop, and the weather forecasters would work themselves into a frenzy, boldly proclaiming that the last big snowfall of the season was nigh, but it never came to pass.

At this point in the year, the interns were fairly comfortable and efficient doing their presentations on rounds, and had sufficiently consolidated their knowledge so the senior resident and attending physician could stand back and listen without having to make frequent interjections. For this presentation, Ray met up with Arti Patel, his co-intern for the month, as well as Gina, their senior resident, and their medical student, Matt. Dr. Lee was their attending physician for the month. When Dr. Lee arrived, the group went together to the first room, where Arti began to present her patient.

"This is a forty-eight-year-old male with a past history of

gunshot wound to the neck with resultant quadriplegia with a chronic indwelling Foley. He was transferred up from the ICU yesterday after he was admitted there two days ago with fever of 102 degrees and hypotension with a positive UA. He received IV fluids and was on IV norepinephrine for about ten hours. They started him on vancomycin and piperacillin-tazobactam which was then narrowed down to ceftriaxone yesterday when the cultures came back positive for E. coli. He lives at home with his mother and is wheelchair-dependent . . ."

Arti confidently discussed her plan, and after her concise summary, the group went into the room where Mr. Jenkins, the man in question, was watching television, with his mother nearby, nodding off in a recliner. Dr. Lee engaged the patient in conversation and he reported feeling back to normal, with his only concern being when he would be able to go home.

"We're going to look at everything and make sure there are no loose ends," replied Dr. Lee reassuringly; "and if everything looks good, we may be able to send you home this afternoon. How does that sound?"

Mr. Jenkins smiled from ear to ear to indicate his approval. His mother, who'd been awakened by the group, was a little more hesitant.

"Only if you think he's ready to come home, Doctor. We don't want to go home and have to come right back."

Dr. Lee reassured her that her son would only be discharged if all his medical issues had been satisfactorily resolved after their review.

The next patient, a couple of doors down, was also Arti's.

"This is Mrs. Summers, a sixty-eight-year-old female with Alzheimer's dementia who was admitted three days ago with a temperature of 101 degrees and a change in mental status from her baseline. Her husband is her primary caregiver, and he said she was very somnolent and difficult to arouse. She has not been started on new medications recently. Urinalysis showed moderate leukocyte esterase, and there was a questionable right lower lobe infiltrate on her chest X-ray. No history of aspiration or choking or coughing with foods, and there are no recent hospitalizations . . ."

The group entered the room. Mrs. Summers was seated in a chair, preparing to have breakfast. Her husband was seated in a chair close enough to assist her if she needed help. She smiled blankly and shook Dr. Lee's hand, and proceeded to uncover the contents of her breakfast tray as Dr. Lee started to converse with Mr. Summers, the rest of the group listening in.

"How does she look to you now compared to when she came in?"

"She looks great, doc; she is much more with it than the day we came in!"

"I'm glad to hear that," Dr. Lee said nodding. "How long has she had dementia?"

"It's been about five years. Initially it started with little things, like forgetting where she had put her keys and walking out of the grocery store without her groceries after she had paid for them—you know, the normal stuff we all do every now and then. I started to get concerned when a couple of times she got lost on her way home, even though she worked only about two miles from our house and had driven the same route for ten years. At first, no one took me seriously, not even her primary care doctor. One day I got a call from the cops after she pulled into someone else's driveway and was trying to get into their house, but the door wouldn't open with her key. The owner, who was watching from inside the house, called the cops to come over, and they were able to identify her and where she lived. I wasn't home when they brought her, but she gave them my number. After that she had to stop working—obviously."

"What's a normal day like for her?"

"She gets up and sits around all day. Eats when she's hungry and watches TV. She can watch the same show over and over—each time is like the first time."

Mrs. Summers had started on her oatmeal, looking up intermittently and smiling sweetly at the strangers in her room.

"Does she know who you are?" asked Dr. Lee.

Mr. Summers inhaled deeply then let out a big sigh. He started to talk, but his voice trailed off and his eyes filled with tears.

He quickly wiped them away and looked down, pausing to regain his composure.

"I'm sorry, doc, it gets to me sometimes. She doesn't know who I am. That's the hardest part!"

A brief awkward silence ensued until Dr. Lee extended his hand to Mr. Summers for a firm handshake, then they all exited the room. There was nothing more to be said in a situation like this one, and Dr. Lee recognized that. When they were outside in the hall, about to continue their discussions, Gina stepped away momentarily and dabbed her eyes with a tissue, taking deep breaths before she returned. Her eyes were red.

"So, how much have we been able to do for that man?" asked Dr. Lee.

"Not much," replied Arti. "We treated her UTI, but we can't do anything to give him his wife back."

"How does that make you feel?" Dr. Lee asked, looking in Ray's direction.

"Helpless."

"As physicians, this is not a place we like to be," Dr. Lee continued. "We sometimes delude ourselves into thinking we have the answers to all our patients' problems, but situations like this one remind us that being a physician is not only about fixing problems, it's also about being there for your patient even when you can't fix their problem. Speaking of which, who is our patient in there?"

Gina smiled. "Actually, there are two patients in there, and his problem is bigger than hers. She's as happy as a clam, doesn't know what is going on. He is grieving the loss of a loved one even as that same person is right in front of him, otherwise looking healthy."

"That's very perceptive of you, Gina. There is more than one patient in the room. When you walk into a room, do not assume the person in the bed is the only patient, or the sickest patient in the room, for that matter. What we saw was a woman with a urinary tract infection that has resolved with antibiotics, as well as a man with serious and ongoing emotional wounds from a complicated situation for which we have no solution. As the physician and the third person in the room, you might also become the third patient as you process your bystander grief and try to make sense of a seemingly senseless situation."

Dr. Lee's ability to inject philosophical insights into situations such as these had earned him the nickname "Confucius." The moniker, while paying just tribute to his state of mind, glossed over the fact that he was of Korean and not Chinese descent. Indeed, he was a second-generation American, born and raised in Sacramento, but still subjected periodically to annoying inquiries about where he was from.

"So, who has a better life, the quadriplegic man who is fully functional from the neck up with perfect awareness but no motor function from the neck down, or the lady with dementia who is fully functional from the neck down, but with complete loss of meaningful awareness as we understand it?" Dr. Lee asked Matt, the medical student.

Matt had a bewildered look on his face. "Um . . . I guess . . ."

"We don't know the answer to that," Dr. Lee stopped him, "so it would be unwise to speculate about situations that none of us have experienced. Both patients seem happy, and you do have an opportunity to add to Mr. Jenkins' joy by discharging him today. If you follow him in clinic, you might also have a chance to get to know him and sneak in a question or two about how he views life and what he finds valuable and enjoyable. In both those situations there is a significant caregiver burden, and helping to harness the resources to assist them would be energy well spent. The purpose of my question was to highlight the fact that we sometimes assume as healthcare providers that we know what a life worth living looks like, based on our presuppositions."

Gina glanced surreptitiously at her watch. They were falling behind time-wise. There were ten more patients to go.

"Okay, the timekeeper groweth restless! Where next?" said Dr. Lee, catching the movement of her wrist from the corner of his eye.

Matt had the next presentation.

"This is a twenty-five-year-old black male who presented to the hospital with a one-week onset of cough, sputum production and shortness of breath," he began.

"Can I stop you right there for a moment?" Dr. Lee said gently.

Gina and the two interns exchanged quick glances. This was Ray's patient—he had forgotten to tell Matt about one of Dr. Lee's signature pet peeves.

"You mentioned the patient's race. Does it have any bearing on the diagnosis?"

Matt looked puzzled.

"Let me explain," Dr. Lee continued. "When you present a patient, you are trying to build a story for me, and every piece of information matters. If you tell me you have two patients, one fifteen and the other forty-five and they come into the ER with chest pain, which one of them is more likely to have a heart attack?"

"The forty-five-year old."

"Great! If I told you I had a patient in the ER with a broken toe, would you ask me about a family history of broken toes?"

"No."

"What if I told you his father had also had a broken toe?"

Matt was not following the line of reasoning, so Ray jumped in. "I'd want t-t-to know how it happened in both the patient and his father, because for a m-m-mechanical injury, it is still more likely to have been a coincidence or an environmental issue such as a doorframe that needs to be fixed."

"Precisely—the family history is likely irrelevant in that situation. In your presentation, the mention of ethnicity presumes that you are making a case for a condition that may be unevenly distributed among races or ethnicities. If this is not the case, then you may be introducing a piece of information that is irrelevant at best, and at worst, prejudicial, given the imperfect nature of our society."

"I'm not sure I understand," said Matt.

Gina's eyes widened, knowing the discussion was going to slow down the pace of their rounds significantly.

"A relevant mention of ethnicity would be, for example, if you told me you had a black patient with choice A, sickle cell anemia, and choice B, cystic fibrosis. In the first case, this would reinforce the argument for the clinical presentation I am making as this condition is prevalent in individuals of African descent. In the second case, I would be telling my listener of a surprising clinical presentation because cystic fibrosis is typically not found in individuals of African descent unless there was DNA from someone of European ancestry higher up in the patient's family tree."

Matt's eyes lit up and he nodded as a light bulb went on in his mind.

"Kĩng'ori, you are from East Africa, right?"

Ray nodded.

"Is sickle cell disease equally distributed among all the ethnic groups in your country?"

"No. In s-some communities it is only seen if there has b-been intermarriage with someone from one of the t-tribes where it is prevalent."

"So, even among people of a similar ethnic heritage there may be significant variations in which ailments afflict some communities, and not others, in pretty much the same way Europeans of Mediterranean descent may experience illnesses that would not be found in Scandinavians. In such instances, merely saying the person is of European or African descent is, in my humble opinion, worthless," Dr. Lee summed up.

Gina cleared her throat as a signal to get the rounds going again.

But Dr. Lee added one more thing. "Alright Matt, my point to you is that you must ask yourself why you bring up each and every piece of information in your clinical history."

And with that, they finally resumed rounds, still managing to conclude before Noon Conference, much to Gina's delight. As they walked downstairs in the direction of the conference room, she asked Dr. Lee about the rumors.

"What rumors?" he asked, feigning ignorance.

Everyone had heard the rumor that the residency program might be closing down since the hospital was undergoing financial difficulties. The rumor was not new, but this time around it seemed to be picking up in intensity. One of Ray's fellow interns, Prasad, had been talking about it since the day he arrived, being known to say things like, "I hear the hospital is in trouble and may end up closing." Initially, his statements generated anxious conversation among his fellow interns, but after a while people got tired of hearing about it. The second- and third-year residents had told them dismissively they had heard similar things from the time they were interns, and the residents before them had told them of the same.

But Prasad had become so concerned about the hospital's financial condition that he'd started interviewing for a second-year residency position at other hospitals. Now as the drumbeat of rumors slowly began to crescendo, his opinion was sought after, even by second-year residents. Those in their third year were unconcerned, since they were almost done with their training. With two months left to go, even if they had to transfer, they would only need two months of elective rotations, most having completed their mandatory rotations early in the year.

It was Thursday evening when an email was sent out to all residents about a meeting at seven am the next morning with Dr. McAllister. The agenda for the meeting was not disclosed. The significance of it was highlighted by the fact that the program coordinator paged every single resident to make sure they had read the email.

Everybody showed up. Besides Dr. McAllister, all the other core faculty physicians were also present. All indicators at this point were that there was something serious afoot.

"I have asked you all here because there has been a major development that has made it necessary for us to close our residency program," Dr. McAllister said tersely.

There were gasps of shock and looks of total surprise. Even Prasad looked surprised.

"I recognize this will have a huge impact on all of you, but we have made arrangements to ensure that all of you will complete your training. You will be able to finish this training year here, through June thirtieth, so the third-year residents are unaffected. For the rest, you will be transferring into one of two larger programs in the area that have graciously undertaken to assimilate you into their ranks. You will be notified regarding which program you have been assigned to. Before I open the floor to questions, many of which I may not have ready answers to, I'd like to say that it has been a privilege working with all of you and getting to know you; and I am certain you will all succeed in your endeavors despite this."

There was a flurry of questions, many of which fell into the "why" category, which McAllister flat out could not or would not answer. Like most of his colleagues, Ray was stunned. But they were also relieved at being offered a viable way out of the situation. Without being enrolled in a residency program, most of the doctors who were there on visas would have to leave the country immediately. Dr. McAllister hadn't mentioned which programs they would be moving to, but it wasn't too difficult to guess.

One was probably County Hospital, and the other was likely University Hospital, where residents attended some of their elective rotations. County Hospital was a busy place, and it was entirely possible that working there as a second-year resident would mean working harder than they had as an intern, which wasn't the way it was supposed to be. University Hospital, while promising a more predictable workload, had some issues of its own—specifically one issue. All the non-native residents who had completed their rotations there complained they were looked down upon because they were foreign graduates; their knowledge and abilities were questioned once they opened their mouth and the faint trace of an accent was detected. So how a huge influx of them would be greeted wasn't hard to imagine; and the reassurances and protestations to the contrary of Dr. McAllister and other faculty did little to ease their minds. Residents like Gina had done their rotations there; and being American in appearance and phonation, had an excellent experience. Some of the other residents told a darker story.

They would find out the following Monday where they would be going on the first of July. Prasad had already signed a contract with a program in St. Louis and would be transferring there for his second year, hopefully for better prospects; although he had already started to express concerns about the financial health of the institution there, as well as whether the program was equipped to qualify him for fellowship training at the completion of his residency.

That weekend was a particularly difficult one, waiting in limbo for one version or another of the end of the world. Ray was not working, which in a way made it more difficult, as time seemed to drag on. He talked for a long time with his sister Mũthoni about it, but he opted not to call his parents since he didn't want to alarm them—and asked her not to tell them either. Jan, his fellow intern from South Africa, usually ran long distances to help cope with stress. He ran a total of about thirty miles that weekend.

Monday came, and after Noon Conference the residents converged on the residency office to learn of their assignments. Everyone received an envelope with a letter of acceptance from their future residency program. It was like a lottery of sorts, as they discovered whether they would face the gladiators or the marauding lions. Ray ripped open his envelope and quickly scanned the text. He was going to University Hospital. He looked around him. Arti was shaking her head, with tears welling up in her eyes. She was going to County Hospital. Jan was going to University Hospital. One by one the lottery of misery separated the group; and as they came to terms with their new assignments, they began to disperse from the residency office, many of them realizing that this would probably be the last time they would all be together as a group.

Chapter Twenty-Nine

TRANSITIONING INTO UNIVERSITY Hospital was as difficult as Ray and his colleagues anticipated it would be. Nobody there seemed particularly happy to have the new arrivals in their midst, whether it was the sulky, condescending residents or the aloof attending physicians. Everyone seemed offended by these newcomers whom they regarded as refugees, and as such would invariably taint the cachet of their beloved program.

"They're treating us like ghetto people!" mumbled Jan to Ray at their first Noon Conference. "I hate this place!"

They were distributed among the residents of the program, which only heightened the sense of isolation. Had they been at St. James, they would have been supervising an intern by the first month of their second year. But here, and this was understandable, they were initially assigned to work under a third-year resident, alongside their two interns, so they would learn the hospital system before functioning in a supervisory capacity. Unfortunately, the interns, as brand new as they were, caught the contagious toxic attitude towards the new second-year residents, considering themselves at the same level or even better. During rounds, when Ray or one of his former St. James residents answered a question or presented a patient, every piece of information was challenged and regarded with skepticism.

"Are we really sure this patient has a COPD exacerbation—or is something else going on?" a senior resident might ask.

Normally this would be a valid question, a call to others to step back and reexamine potentially premature conclusions that led them to latch onto the wrong diagnosis. And under normal circumstances "we" meant the whole team. Now, it was said to cast aspersions on the new doctor's diagnostic skills and judgment. And the "we" was really "you," which was exceedingly offensive, because it was almost as if you did not exist—as if the group was evaluating a presentation that had been deposited in their presence by a ghost; and they now had to sort through for themselves what the departed phantom had failed to do to their satisfaction.

It was going to be a long two years. Unfortunately, trying to switch programs was overwhelmingly complicated, and much more so if one was in the country on a visa; so the best Ray and his colleagues could do was buckle down and tell themselves that each passing day was bringing them one day closer to the end. All the processes were different, including the electronic medical records system, and endeavoring to master the nonmedical aspects was an investment that paid swift dividends in terms of improving efficiency and quality of life.

For the first two months of the transition—July and August—Ray spent most of his time either at the hospital or fast asleep recharging for the next day. Besides an essential trip to the grocery store or a fast food restaurant, he had neither the time nor the energy to go out to a park or movie theater. He still lived in the same apartment he was in before; the transition to University Hospital had only added about seven minutes to his commute.

He passed by St. James every day; from the outside everything looked normal, although he'd heard that everything had shut down in the early weeks of July. The story was all over the newspapers and television, and there was all manner of speculation about what would happen next to the building, the patients and the community. Ray found it worked better for him to completely tune it out, and being busy with the transition made this possible with minimal effort.

In early August, the former St. James residents were summoned to a meeting by Dr. Holzinger, the program chairman. He was a tall bearded man in his early sixties who wore bifocals, and was conspicuous for wearing bowties and suspenders. Modest and soft-spoken though he was, a cursory search of the medical literature yielded several pages of his published research. And it's possible that all those years expended on solving complex biological questions had deprived him of the ability to smile, because smile he did not.

"I trust you are all adjusting well to the program," he began, "and I do know that you have had a number of meetings with Dr. Kapoor, the program director. Do any of you have any questions regarding processes and expectations based on the four or five weeks that have elapsed so far?"

There was silence.

"We pride ourselves on graduating top-of-the-line physicians in internal medicine, and you should consider yourselves fortunate you ended up in this program, your manner of entry notwithstanding. This is an opportunity that could open up many future career possibilities. But by the same token, I would like to make it very clear that while we did make a commitment to take you in, we are not under any obligation to keep you on if you do not meet our standards. Are we on the same page?"

The terse warning was delivered in the same soft monotone that he'd started with, so if his listeners hadn't been paying close attention, they might have missed it all together. He glanced around the group to make sure they'd understood, and the half nods and disconcerted looks told him he had successfully gotten his message across.

"Well, then, if there are no questions, it's time to wish you all well. Your chief resident, Dr. Wood, whom you should all have met by now, is available to answer any questions your fellow residents cannot answer; and you may also take up any concerns with Dr. Kapoor. I'll release you now so you can get back to your work."

Nobody spoke as they filtered out of the room. That afternoon, Ray developed a splitting headache. The situation was clear now. While they were officially part of the program, they were still considered undesirable appendages at risk of summary excision if no redeeming qualities were apparent.

The first casualty came in September. Yevgeniy, whom everyone referred to as Eugene—with his permission—was a stocky, third-year resident, who could sometimes come across as overly blunt when making a point. He was from Kyrgyzstan, in the former Soviet Union, and was a highly intelligent individual. Unfortunately, he found it difficult to see the merit in anyone else's ideas if they were at odds with his own, which often made him seem argumentative. He also spoke with a strong accent, which didn't particularly enhance his communication skills.

Ray learned of what had happened to Eugene from one of his fellow residents, who'd heard it in turn from someone else. Apparently, he'd gotten into a heated discussion with a patient's family member about one issue or another, and the family member became incensed and reported it to the patient care advocate, who passed it up the chain until it ended up on Dr. Holzinger's desk. There was no one willing to vouch for Eugene from among the University Hospital residents and faculty who had worked with him in the prior three months. It was never known definitively whether his defiance and argumentative demeanor during the final meeting with Kapoor and Holzinger had any bearing on the final outcome— which most considered predetermined—but they certainly provided the doctors with a much-needed vindication.

Eugene was stunned when they gave him the news. Until that point, he had never imagined there was even a remote possibility he would be kicked out of the program. He thought the discussion was no more than a forum for the purpose of allowing him to air his side of the story, and he had been sure his case was on solid ground. Now, suddenly, he was faced with the likely prospect of having to pack up his bags and return to Kyrgyzstan with nothing to show for his two-and-a-half years in America. Without a residency program, he didn't have a valid visa to remain in the country. All he could do was check around and see if there was another program anywhere that might take him at short notice, usually one of the sweatshops willing to take on any warm body to add to their ranks of overworked, demoralized residents who had nowhere else to go. He left the hospital after first clearing his status with a clerk in the security office. Eugene, a stout muscular man, was reduced to a puddle of tears as he wondered how he would break the news to his wife and their five-year-old son.

This chilling episode rippled through the ranks of the ex-St. James residents. For the third-year residents, any hope they might skate through by dint of the fact they were in the final year of their studies quickly evaporated. Among the second-year residents, the several remaining months seemed like an eternity.

〜〜〜

Ray's first month in the Intensive Care Unit at University Hospital was a welcome break. It was much busier than on the regular wards, but somehow it seemed less stressful. Maybe it had something to do with Dr. Mordecai Goldstein, the ICU director and educator extraordinaire. He was a small man in his mid-sixties with a shock of white hair and a face that wore a permanent perplexed expression.

279

When he spoke, he usually started off in a soft monotone; but as he expounded on a topic, he began to talk faster and louder and his hands began to move excitedly. The people around him found themselves spellbound by his enthusiasm and eager to get aboard whatever intellectual voyage he embarked on. Year after year, he was voted Teacher of the Year, an accolade he considered somewhat superfluous but which he nonetheless graciously accepted.

Normally the attending physicians rounded in the ICU for one week at a time, and Dr. Goldstein came on during Ray's second week. It was a Tuesday morning, and the residents were busying themselves for rounds, which normally started at eight, when there was a minor commotion in Room 225. A number of monitor alarms went off at the same time, and the resident and intern in charge of the patient walked hastily in the direction of his room when the nurses summoned them. As they hustled inside, Dr. Goldstein appeared at the entrance of the ICU, heading towards the nurses' station, where the majority of residents had congregated.

"Good morning, everyone, shall we begin?"

Someone mentioned there was an evolving situation in Room 225.

"Oh, is that so? Well then, we'd better go there and see if they need our help," Dr. Goldstein said.

As they approached the room, Callahan and D'Souza, the resident and intern, had just stepped outside.

"Is everything okay in there?" Dr. Goldstein asked them.

"It is now, I think," said Dr. Callahan with a sigh, his eyes bloodshot and his hair in disarray. The pair had been on call the previous night and had gotten a total of about three hours of sleep between them.

"Alright, so let's talk about your patients so we can release you early to go home and get some rest."

Annie D'Souza, the intern, began her presentation. The patient was a twenty-eight-year-old man with a history of asthma, who'd come to the emergency room the night before with fevers and aches during the prior five days. He'd started coughing two days before and was complaining of sharp pains in the right side of his chest; he'd also started coughing up phlegm mixed with noticeable amounts of blood. When he got to the ER, he was restless and struggling to breathe, and the doctors there noted his blood pressure was starting to drop. He tested positive for influenza, and his chest X-ray showed areas where the lung tissue had been destroyed, resulting in multiple small cavities each about the size of a quarter. As his condition deteriorated in the ER, they decided to intubate him and put him on a life support machine; they also started him on antibiotics, as well as a medication to normalize his blood pressure. So far so good.

"Since he came up here, he's been having these episodes where he bears down and becomes dyssynchronous with the vent," Annie continued, "and he seems agitated. We're sedating him with fentanyl and midazolam, but he intermittently breaks through that and a couple of times we were unable to ventilate him, so we had to paralyze him."

"Hmm, that's interesting," Dr. Goldstein remarked thoughtfully.

Annie resumed. "He's been having high fevers, up to 103 degrees, and his hemodynamics are all over the place. He'll go from needing pressors to being hypertensive in a span of minutes."

"So, what do you think is going on, Dr. D'Souza?" queried Dr. Goldstein.

"I think he has influenza complicated by a staph pneumonia with sepsis."

"And how would you explain the hemodynamic lability?"

"I think maybe his sedation is not adequate."

Turning his attention to the resident, Dr. Goldstein asked, "Any thoughts, Dr. Callahan?"

Dr. Callahan shook his head. "I'm not sure I know what's going on, Dr. Goldstein. He did the same thing just now and was already on three hundred micrograms of fentanyl and five milligrams of midazolam per hour; that should make him pretty well sedated. He's not a drug user so far as we can tell, and he's not been on any long-term medications."

"D-d-id he have c-clonus before you paralyzed him?" Ray asked Annie.

Dr. Goldstein turned to him, his eyes widening. "Please ask that again so everyone can hear," the doctor said, moving closer to Ray and squinting to read his badge. "And say your name once so I don't have to butcher it."

"Kĩng'ori."

"Dr. Kĩng'ori wants to know if there was clonus. Why is he asking about clonus?"

His question was met with blank stares.

Dr. Goldstein looked in Ray's direction. "Go ahead and tell them."

"The patient was s-s-started on linezolid empirically for MRSA pneumonia, and subsequently on fentanyl. The h-h-hemodynamic lability and apparent agitation may be signs of s-serotonin syndrome."

"That is very likely what is going on! I'm willing to bet on it! If he were not under the influence of neuromuscular blockade it would be helpful to look for clonus. Regardless of whether or not you are able to elicit this sign, let us replace the fentanyl with an alternate sedative, and look in his medication list to make sure he's not on anything else—such as an SSRI—that could cause this syndrome. Dr. D'Souza, sometime this evening after you've had some rest, read up on serotonin syndrome and prepare to tell us about it tomorrow."

Annie nodded vigorously.

"Excellent!" exclaimed Dr. Goldstein, rubbing his hands together, "let's move on. Dr. Kĩng'ori, you're in your second year, but I don't remember seeing you last year in this ICU."

"I t-transferred in from another program," said Ray.

"Well then, it's very nice to meet you and welcome aboard. We're glad to have you!"

Ray beamed on the inside. The rest of the week went well, and he found himself paying extra attention to each of his patients so he could continue living up to Dr. Goldstein's expectations. Even after he went off service and Dr. Myers came on, the streak of good fortune continued; and that first month in the ICU seemed to be a turning point with regard to how he felt he was doing in the new program.

A new month came, and the residents switched to new assignments and the cycle continued. He was much more comfortable with the system at University Hospital now, and most of the residents now seemed to lack the energy or motivation to maintain the state of perpetual hostility towards the newcomers; so the day-to-day interactions were becoming more congenial.

One day Ray got a call from Molly, Dr. Holzinger's secretary, asking him to attend a meeting. She didn't elaborate, except to say he needed to come right away. He excused himself from rounds and went over to the administrative offices, where Molly ushered him in. Dr. Holzinger was seated at his desk with nothing in front of him; it was clear he was waiting for Ray. He told him to take a seat.

"Dr. Kĩng'ori, how's everything coming along with your training?"

"I . . . er, I th-think it's ok-kay," answered Ray, puzzled about being called in so suddenly and starting to feel a rising sense of disquiet.

"Do you remember a patient by the name of Wilbur Tomkins? You took care of him on the general medicine floor, a few weeks ago."

Ray's mind raced; he could feel his heart pounding and he was filled with foreboding. He tried to put a face to the name, but no images or memories flashed into his consciousness.

"Let me jog your memory. This is a gentleman with chronic pancreatitis who had come in with abdominal pain, which he has had multiple times. CT scan and biochemical testing was negative . . ."

"Oh, yes, I remember him!" said Ray nodding.

"Well, he lodged a complaint against you to the hospital, saying you were disrespectful and unprofessional in your handling of his case. Do you recall your interaction with him?"

Ray's head was spinning. His thoughts flashed back to Eugene being ushered out of this same building. But Mr. Tomkins? Really?

He cleared his throat and spoke. "M-mister T-t-tomkins has a history of narcotic abuse and drug-seeking behavior. He d-did n-not have any objective findings to support his complaints of abdominal pain, and specifically requested t-t-two milligrams of hydromorphone every four hours that I refused to prescribe. He was v-v-very upset at this and threatened to t-t-take action, stating that I was inattentive to his needs. I did not feel it was m-medically appropriate to issue that prescription and I still feel the same way about it now."

There was a long tense silence.

"Alright, thank you for your response. We are reviewing the case and will let you know if there is any further action to be taken."

Ray left the office angry and dumbfounded. The interaction with Mr. Tomkins had left a bad taste in his mouth, but he'd been pretty certain he did the right thing. Still, the conversation with Dr. Holzinger left him unsure of which side he was on, and what would happen next. In the days that followed, he found himself coming to work each day wondering if it would be his last, but nothing else happened. Still, he worried there might be more to come.

Unbeknownst to Ray, there had been angry words and dire threats exchanged on his behalf, and the strange encounter with Dr. Holzinger was the end result of a decision that had been wrenched out of the program chairman's hands. When Dr. Holzinger initially received the complaint, he reviewed it; and while in his heart of hearts he didn't believe it merited any consideration, he was still intent on his pernicious crusade against the intruders from St. James. Any situation that provided ammunition was fair game, and he considered at the very least issuing Ray a letter of reprimand. Unlike Eugene, whose verdict had already been decided when he met with Dr. Holzinger, he'd decided that if there was any outburst from Ray during their meeting, it could result in an escalation in the course of action—and expulsion from the program was one of the options he was considering.

Prior to the meeting, Holzinger had sent an email to the other faculty members, asking them for their input on Ray. He secretly hoped they would either be too busy to respond, or not have much in the way of positive things to say in Ray's defense. He certainly hadn't bargained on Mordecai Goldstein bursting into his office in a near-psychotic rage, demanding an explanation.

"Hold on a second, Hermann," he interrupted as Dr. Holzinger tried to explain, "a drug-seeker makes a complaint against one of our residents because he did the right thing by refusing to prescribe him the medication. And now you want to take action against that doctor who did the right thing? Am I missing something here?"

"Well, I see the issue here is how he communicated with the patient and left him feeling disrespected and abandoned . . ."

"Whoa! Time out, Hermann! Here's the real problem," Dr. Goldstein broke in angrily. "Ever since the St. James residents joined us, you've been obsessed with finding an opportunity to confirm their inferiority to the cherished graduates you selected. And being unable to come up with anything concrete, you are now clutching at straws. I have worked with that young man and I think he is an excellent physician. I will not stand idly by and watch you ruin his career!"

At this point Dr. Goldstein was visibly shaking with rage, and Dr. Holzinger sat frozen at his desk, clearly intimidated.

"Hermann," Dr. Goldstein continued, pointing a trembling index finger at Dr. Holzinger, "if anything happens to this resident, there's going to be an all-out war between me and you. And I will stop at nothing—mark my words!" And on that note, Dr. Goldstein stormed out of the office.

Shortly thereafter, Dr. Holzinger called his secretary on the intercom and asked her to reschedule his two o'clock meeting and hold any incoming phone calls. He'd never seen Dr. Goldstein in such a state before. He was usually soft-spoken and self-effacing, and while very confident in his knowledge, he never exhibited a hostile or even aggressive attitude. Something else had Holzinger worried. Dr. Goldstein was on first-name terms with Harrison Whitley III, Chairman of the Hospital Board.

The two had met about ten years before under unusual circumstances that had cemented their friendship. It was at a huge banquet celebrating the seventy-fifth year of the founding of the hospital, that had been held at the exclusive Founders' Club in downtown Chicago. Goldstein had emerged from the main dining area at the beginning of the banquet, headed for the restrooms, when he heard a thump in the hallway behind him. An elegantly dressed woman in a black ball gown had slumped to the ground, and the man beside her kneeled down, trying to raise her up. There was no one else in the corridor besides Goldstein, who rushed over to the couple.

"Let me help you, sir, I am a doctor," he said, gently laying the unconscious lady on the ground and feeling for a pulse. She had none. "Quickly, sir, call 9-1-1 and then bring me the defibrillator. It's a little box hanging on the wall that looks like a first aid kit. I saw one earlier, just around this corner," he said pointing.

The man hurried off obediently as Dr. Goldstein started administering CPR. A few moments later, he returned with the defibrillator, which the doctor attached and activated, sending a jolt of electricity through the woman's body. The next minute, the EMS arrived, barreling down the hallway. They cordoned off the area to keep out curious onlookers, while Dr. Goldstein addressed them.

"I'm Dr. Goldstein, an Intensivist at the University Hospital. This lady collapsed a short while ago and was unresponsive with no pulse. Immediate bystander CPR was initiated by myself. I attached an AED on her and she was in ventricular fibrillation, so I shocked once, and she went back into sinus with a pulse, and then you showed up. That's all I know. This gentleman may know more about her medical history as they were together."

As the EMTs prepared to move her onto a gurney and attached monitors to her, Dr. Goldstein shook hands with the woman's companion, and handed him his card. "These folks will take good care of her, sir," he said reassuringly.

Within moments the EMS had mobilized and were headed to the ambulance, with her companion following along. Dr. Goldstein watched the procession leave before heading for the bathroom, his original destination.

During the dinner, there was an announcement that the chairman of the board would be unable to attend the event unexpectedly, but Dr. Goldstein didn't think too much of it. Then his pager went off. He wasn't on call but always carried it with him in case the hospital needed him. It was the Emergency Room.

"Dr. Goldstein here. I received your page," he said, calling from his cell.

The receptionist at the ER said, "Please hold, Dr. Harrington needs to speak with you."

"You do know that I am not on call?"

"Yes sir, we are aware of it, but this was important."

Dr. Harrington came on the line. "Hey, Mordecai, sorry to call you when you're not working, but this is a rather important matter. We have a fifty-two-year-old woman here in previously good health who you encountered earlier this evening when she passed out during a V-fib arrest. No previous medical history though she was on a macrolide for the past five days for acute bronchitis. She is a runner who'd done ten miles earlier today, and may not have adequately replenished her electrolytes because her potassium was 2.7 and her magnesium was 1.2 . . ."

"But Todd . . ." interrupted Dr. Goldstein.

"Oh, I'm sorry, you're wondering why we're calling you when you're not on call," Dr. Harrington said, lowering his voice. "You see, this lady is the wife of Harrison Whitley of the Whitley family— you know, the family who owns this hospital and half of Chicago," he added a bit facetiously. "The gentleman you were talking to was Mr. Whitley himself, and he was so blown away by what you did for his wife that he was hoping you'd agree to admit her to the ICU as your private patient so we can limit the number of people involved."

"Well, I guess I don't exactly have a choice in the matter, do I?" Dr. Goldstein said evenly. "Sure, that's fine with me."

"Alright then . . . she'll be listed in the electronic medical records as Ms. Pamela Wood. But her real name is Louise Whitley."

And so was the wife of the venerable Mr. Whitley admitted to the Intensive Care Unit. Yolanda, the presiding charge nurse in the ICU, unexpectedly showed up at work on her day off to personally oversee every detail of her patient's care, working in conjunction with Ollie, the night nurse in charge. Fortunately, the night was uneventful and none of the other tests administered by the cardiologist or electrophysiologist revealed any need for intervention other than correcting her electrolyte deficiencies and discontinuing her antibiotic.

Once fully recovered, Mrs. Whitley had no recollection of the event, but thanked Dr. Goldstein effusively after her husband explained how he had saved her life. While their lives didn't cross paths again, every year the Whitleys sent Dr. Goldstein a card on the anniversary of that fateful date, with the heartfelt message thanking him for being "the right person at the right place at the right time."

Dr. Holzinger was aware of their history, as were most of the attending physicians who had been around from that time. He was also aware that Dr. Goldstein in his righteous rage could choose to bring Whitley into the situation with an undesirable outcome for Holzinger. Eventually, he settled on a simple, albeit somewhat intimidating conversation with the resident in question, fully aware it was as far as he could go without inviting further wrath from his colleague.

≈

In the few weeks that followed his meeting with Dr. Holzinger, Ray continued to wait uneasily for a follow-up call. As one week led to another it seemed less likely it was coming, so he finally stopped waiting for the other shoe to drop. There was so much else to preoccupy him with his hectic daily schedule, and he was now at the point where he would need to start applying for a fellowship program. Typically, after three years of residency training in internal medicine, his next step would entail additional training in a subspecialty such as cardiology, nephrology, critical care, etc.

Based on his experience so far, Ray had begun to gravitate towards critical care—he enjoyed working in the Intensive Care Unit, and his interactions with Dr. Goldstein and the other ICU physicians had been very fruitful in fostering this affinity. Not everyone was as fortunate as Ray; some of his colleagues were met by a distinct lack of enthusiasm from the authority figures in their chosen field, who actively discouraged them and redirected them elsewhere. Ray didn't receive any such feedback. In fact, when with some hesitation he asked Dr. Goldstein if he'd be willing to write a letter of recommendation in support of his application, his mentor broke out into a rare smile.

"Absolutely—I'd be honored to write you a letter of recommendation! I think you would do really well in this field," he said.

Ray's heart soared.

"Kĩng'ori, do you know what a 'jobby' is?"

Ray responded to the question with only a puzzled look.

"It's the Goldstein term for when you get paid to do something that you would otherwise consider doing as a hobby. That's what you should always aspire to. I found mine in Critical Care."

The first thought that came into his mind was his mother and her affinity for the hardware store; that seemed to fit the term nicely. "Thank you, Dr. Goldstein."

As they headed off in different directions, Ray heard Dr. Goldstein's voice behind him, calling him back.

"By the way, Ray, what programs are you looking at?"

Ray listed the ones he was considering: a few in Chicago, including the program he was in, as well as a number of others scattered over different states.

"Have you considered the Mayo Clinic?" Goldstein asked.

Ray shook his head.

"Make sure you look into Mayo. I trained there, and I think you would thrive there."

Ray was surprised to hear this suggestion because he knew it was a very competitive program, and he doubted his application would stand a chance against the multitude of top-tier applicants. Nonetheless, he decided to do it because Dr. Goldstein had said that he should. Before they parted, Ray thanked him for his advice.

He managed in the days that followed to obtain favorable replies from some of the other ICU physicians when he asked them for letters of recommendation. In addition, he would need a letter either from the program director or the program chairman. Normally the program chairman would have been the natural person to approach since they were higher up in rank; but in this case that individual was Dr. Holzinger. Even putting aside their unpleasant encounter, Ray had learned from the ex-St. James third-year residents that Holzinger reputedly wrote a very tepid form letter emphasizing that the applicant hadn't been part of the first batch of carefully chosen residents, but they'd managed to keep up with the rigorous expectations of the excellent training program at University Hospital. The letter was known to be glaringly devoid of approbation, written merely because he was compelled to say something positive about that individual.

Molly, his secretary, had noticed this, as she usually typed out his letters for him. The residents whose recommendations were involved hadn't expressed a wish to see the letters before they were dispatched, but Molly felt duty bound to do something. So she called them when Holzinger was out of the office, and asked them to stop by to review them before she put them in the mail. "I just wanted to make sure you were okay with my sending that letter, because if you're not, you could ask Dr. Kapoor to write you one. Most programs are fine with either the program director or the chairman."

After reviewing Holzinger's missives, every single applicant thanked her and instructed her to shred them; and that valuable piece of information was immediately circulated throughout the St. James network so that no further requests of that nature went to Dr. Holzinger. Molly, in turn, became a folk hero among the group; and over the holidays that year, her desk was covered with an array of colorful gift bags bestowed on her by the grateful residents. Indeed, when Dr. Holzinger spotted them he had assumed they were meant for him, and he approached her desk rubbing his hands with excitement.

"Are these for me?" he asked excitedly.

"Umm . . . actually Dr. Holzinger, these are for me," she replied, her eyes twinkling with mischief.

He was confused for a moment, but quickly regained his composure. "Wow, sure looks like a lot of people were thinking about you this holiday season."

"Yes sir," she echoed, smiling broadly, "it sure does look like it!"

Chapter Thirty

RAY LIVED IN a pretty safe neighborhood in Chicago, and had never had any qualms about walking home at eleven at night as there were still numerous bars, restaurants and movie theaters open at that time. It was probably why, on this particular night, he paid no attention to the voice calling out from behind him as he turned onto the quiet street that led to his apartment complex.

"Hey, I'm talking to you!" When he heard the voice a second time, he turned around to see a uniformed police officer walking towards him. "I'm Officer Flanagan, Chicago PD, and sir, it is generally not a good idea to walk away when a policeman is trying to get your attention."

"I was n-not walking away from you, and I d-d-did not know you were talking to me," Ray said, beginning to feel apprehensive.

The cop pressed on. "Could I see some ID? I'm investigating an incident that was reported in this area a short while ago, and the suspect matches your description."

Ray's heart was pounding as he fumbled for his wallet and struggled to fish out his driver's license from between a stack of other cards. He handed it to the policeman.

As the officer shone a flashlight on the card, Ray quickly

glanced around. There was no one else in the street, after a man who'd turned onto it spotted them, and immediately headed back to the main thoroughfare.

"So, what are you doing out here at this time of night, Mr. King-ury—am I pronouncing that right?"

"I . . . er . . . I live d-d-down the road," Ray said, pointing to his building.

"You sound awfully nervous for someone who just happens to be walking around in their own neighborhood," the officer said with a noticeably hard edge to his voice.

"Is there s-s-something wrong? Have I d-done something wrong?"

"Besides jaywalking and failing to heed a police officer, no," the cop said sarcastically.

"P-p-please, m-may I have my driver's license back?"

"I'll give it to you when I'm ready. Now, sit down here on the pavement with your hands where I can see them, and don't move until I tell you to!" His tone had suddenly become more aggressive, and Ray did as he asked.

Officer Flanagan pressed on his walkie-talkie and mumbled something to someone. Ray overheard the word "suspect" and felt his body go numb with terror. It seemed like only seconds later that a police car with flashing blue lights turned into the street, moving noiselessly with its siren off. It came to a stop about twenty yards away from where Ray sat, and an officer emerged from the vehicle. He was a large man, and he walked with a lumbering gait. He approached Flanagan.

"Hey, Flanagan, what's going on here?"

The cop recounted his version of events in a hushed monotone, all the while keeping a close eye on Ray, his right hand never straying too far from the pistol in its holster. He handed over Ray's driver's license to the second officer who scrutinized it carefully under his flashlight.

"Good grief, Flanagan!" he exploded. "What on earth do you think you're doing?"

Officer Flanagan was as startled and confused as Ray was.

"Hey Doc, is that you?" continued the second officer, as he approached Ray, who was still sitting on the pavement.

Ray didn't recognize the voice.

"Doc, hey, it's me, Mr. Sarkevic with a 'k.' Remember me? You saved my life about a year ago. I never got a chance to thank you! And by the way, you can get up off the street now," he said, offering an outstretched hand for support.

As soon as Ray heard the name, the memory of their encounter came flooding back to him. He felt an odd mixture of relief and disbelief as he got to his feet.

"Flanagan, we're gonna have to talk about this! What do you think you're doing picking on my doctor? Six months on the street and you're already getting yourself into trouble! Are you serious? This is the guy that saved my life when I had my heart attack! Remember how I was telling you I had a bypass last year. Well, I went into the ER and nobody else, including the senior ER doc, diagnosed me with a heart attack. It wasn't until this gentleman came in and spent five minutes in the room—just five minutes—and the next minute it was like—boom!—one thing after another! I woke up two days later in intensive care after having had a triple bypass. That's your suspect? I can't wait for you to tell me how you figured him for a suspect. I just can't wait, Flanagan!"

Flanagan was silent; and even in the dark, he was glowing with the red-hot aura of embarrassment.

Turning back to Ray, Sarkevic said, "Hey doc, I never saw you again after that day in the ER, even though I asked a couple of nurses about you when I woke up. But they didn't seem to know what I was talking about. They probably thought I was hallucinating from all the dope they were giving me. So, you live around here? Tell you what, hop in my car and we'll drive you home. Oh, and here's your driver's license back before I lose it."

"Actually, I'm only about f-f-five minutes from my apartment, so I c-can walk there—I'll be fine."

"Please sir, I insist. It would be an honor. Besides, I don't want anyone else bothering you on your way home."

"Alright," Ray acquiesced, the shadow of a smile faintly visible on his face.

Ray got into the car with Officer Sarkevic and his now sullen companion for the short ride home. The old lady who lived on the first floor looked at him quizzically as she watched him exit a police vehicle and enter the building; but he simply smiled and nodded as he walked past her and pushed the elevator button.

$$\text{\~\~}$$

"Let me give you twelve cents, so you can give me back five dollars," Ray's mother said to the cashier, beginning to fumble in her coin purse.

The young woman at the cash register looked bewildered. "Er . . . ma'am, your change is four eighty-eight."

Ray's mother stopped what she was doing and looked up. "Yes, that is why . . ." she began.

"Mom," Ray interjected with some embarrassment before turning and nodding to the cashier who was holding out the correct amount of change towards his mother. "Thank you!" he said. There were about five other people waiting behind them in line.

His mother took the four dollars and eighty-eight cents, but she wasn't done. "Okay, in this hand I have the four eighty-eight that you have just given me. I am going to add twelve cents to it. Four eighty-eight plus twelve cents is five dollars. I'm going to give this all back to you so you can give me a five dollar note instead, so I don't have to carry around all these coins. Is that alright?"

Ray squirmed uncomfortably as the cashier hesitated for a moment before slowly nodding in comprehension and pulling out a five-dollar bill from the cash register in exchange for the bills and coins that his mother handed back to her.

As they sat with their drinks, Ray's mother shook her head in bemusement. "How is it possible to have a cashier who can't count money? I know a lot of things are different in America, but cashiers who can't count money—how is that possible?"

"Well, Mom, most p-people pay by c-credit card, and even when they p-p-ay cash they just take the change the way it's g-given to them."

"So that it can sit in a big jar like the one I saw at your place?" his mother asked incredulously. "And then what do you do with that? Do you ever take that big jar and go shopping with it?"

Ray looked slightly annoyed and shook his head no.

"So, if I paid four dollars for an item that costs three dollars and fifteen cents, and put eight-five cents in a jar, I'll end up paying about twenty-seven percent more for the item since I will never use the balance."

Ray shrugged. He knew better than to tangle with his mother on the issue.

"Life is certainly more expensive in America if you pay cash, particularly if you throw away the change."

His mother was visiting him for the week, after spending about three weeks in Seattle at his sister Mũthoni's place. Ray's apartment was too small for two, so his sister had booked their mother into a hotel close to where Ray lived.

Wambũi was surprisingly independent for someone who had never been to the city before, and she seemed to have developed an unusual fetish for riding the subway—which Ray found somewhat amusing. He found it interesting how she determined her destination by glancing at the map at the start of the trip and counting down the number of stops left to go. While she was accurately able to identify her destination this way, she didn't seem to register the name of the station.

"Our station is next," she would say to Ray, "but what's the name again?"

"Er . . . La Salle," Ray would reply after checking the map for confirmation. It was an odd way to navigate the subway system, he thought, but it seemed to be working out well for her.

"So, Mom, how would you f-f-find your way if you had to d-drive or walk on the streets rather than use the subway?" he asked.

"I'd just count the streets between where I am and where I need to go. Isn't that what others do?"

"Yes, b-but not like you. How about if you were in Nairobi where the streets are not always in any particular order?"

"I couldn't get lost in Nairobi, but even if I ended up in an unfamiliar part of town, I'd just work backwards to see how many traffic lights I passed from where I started."

"What if there were no traffic signs at all?"

"I'd count trees or buildings," Wambũi said evenly. "I usually count these things without even thinking about it."

"What if there were no t-t-trees or buildings?"

"Then I wouldn't get lost because I'd be able to see across town. Without trees or buildings, though, there wouldn't really be much of a town, would there?"

〰

On her way back to Kenya from Chicago, Wambũi stopped over in England to visit her old friend Eileen. She had planned to take the train ride from Heathrow to Surrey, but Eileen wouldn't hear of it. A friend of hers had driven in from Surrey and would be looking out for her in the Arrivals terminal. He would be wearing a red golf shirt and a light blue cap; he already knew what she looked like from the photos Eileen had shown him.

As Wambũi emerged through the doors from Arrivals, a stocky bearded man in his thirties, wearing clothing that fit Eileen's description, was smiling broadly at her. He was holding a small placard with the name WAMBŨI on it. They exchanged greetings, he took her suitcase and they walked to the parking lot.

"Ms. Atwood never stops talking about you and your family," Karim said jovially. "I'm glad to finally meet you."

He was very polite and personable, and Wambũi took an immediate liking to him. Eileen had mentioned Karim and some of the other members of the staff at Margate Cottage in her letters, but he obviously knew a lot more about her than she did of him.

"Ms. Atwood talks all the time about going back to visit Kenya one day. She has told us a lot about your children in America—she carries their pictures everywhere!"

Wambũi smiled. "How about you?" she asked him. "Do you have any children?"

"I have a daughter aged sixteen and two sons aged ten and six," replied Karim. "When I first came to this country my two sons hadn't been born yet. That's about as long as I have known Ms. Atwood. She was very nice to me and gave me a lot of encouragement when my wife and I were still struggling to settle in."

It was a warm sunny day in July as they drove to Surrey, and Wambũi let her gaze roam over the undulating green landscape patterned with hedgerows and dotted with farmhouses, with cows and sheep grazing lazily in the pastures. After a forty-minute drive, they arrived at her hotel, which was about half a kilometer from Margate Cottage. Karim made sure she was checked in properly, then

told her he would return in a couple of hours to take her to see
Eileen after she'd had a chance to freshen up.

"Are you sure you don't need to be somewhere else?" she
asked him, "because I can find my way there. It's just down the road,
from what I saw when I reviewed the map with my son."

"No, Mrs. Wambũi," Karim countered emphatically; "today is
my day off and I would be delighted to show you around. Besides, it
might be a little too hot to be walking outside in the sun."

The hotel was a small comfortable place with a friendly staff;
and a shower and change of clothing brought her the rejuvenation
she needed after the seven-hour overnight transatlantic flight. When
Karim returned, he found Wambũi in the lobby engaged in a lively
conversation with the concierge.

"Looks like you've made a new friend already, Mrs.
Wambũi," Karim observed, grinning from ear to ear.

"I have indeed," replied Wambũi, bidding the smiling
concierge a good day and following Karim outside to where his car
was parked.

While Eileen and Wambũi had been corresponding almost
every two weeks for many years, they hadn't exchanged photos of
themselves recently. When they reunited at the lobby of Margate
Cottage, there was a short pause as each stood back and inspected
the other, as if to make sure the other person was real, before
stepping forward excitedly into a long tight embrace with loud

exclamations and tears of joy. Some of the residents who'd been sitting in the common room got up and descended on the lobby to see what the commotion was all about.

"My dearest Wambũi!" screamed Eileen. "I'm so thrilled to see you! This is one of the happiest days of my life!"

Laughter, more tears, endless questions and repeated hugging followed, as Karim stood sheepishly to the side, gratified to have played a role in bringing the two friends together. Eileen had aged quite a bit since they saw each other last—her hair was all gray and she looked small and frail, stooping forward a little. But she was still full of energy. Wambũi, in turn, had probably gained ten or twenty pounds in weight, and her braided hair was visibly gray at the roots.

Most of the residents at the facility knew Eileen as a polite lady who frequently spoke fondly of her previous life in Africa, but they had never seen this level of emotion in her before. Even nasty Donna Trimble was fascinated with the whole affair, and seemed baffled, if not speechless.

Seven days go by fast when one is with a beloved friend, and the days that followed were a flurry of activity, with the two sticking together from morning to evening. It was a short walk from the hotel to the elder care facility, and Wambũi enjoyed the easy stroll back and forth.

One morning, as she entered the building, she almost bumped into a man who was hastily walking out to his car. "Oops, excuse me!" she exclaimed.

"Beg your pardon!" mumbled the man politely, before proceeding towards a black Maserati that was parked a short distance from the entrance to the building.

Wambũi turned to catch a glimpse of the man as he walked away, then her brow furrowed in concentration. He was familiar to her somehow, but she couldn't figure out why.

As she sat with Eileen that morning, his face flashed into her mind again. "I saw a man this morning who looked very familiar to me, but I'm not sure where I've seen him before. He looks like he could be from Kenya, but I heard him speak and he's definitely from here." As she began to describe him, Eileen smiled.

"I know who you're talking about. He comes here every day. When I first saw him, I was excited to see him because I thought he was Kenyan. But when I went over and introduced myself, he seemed neither Kenyan nor interested in making my acquaintance."

"Good morning, ladies!" announced Karim as he walked into the common area from the staff lounge.

"Hello, Karim!" Eileen greeted him. "Say, you know the smartly dressed gentleman who comes here every day and drives a black sports car? Wambũi and I were just talking about him. Who is he?"

"Oh, is somebody looking for a husband then?" Karim asked

cheekily.

"No, my dear. I'm too old and Wambũi is married—or perhaps I shouldn't speak on her behalf."

"That's George, the Maserati guy, as we staff members call him. He's an investment banker. Nice and polite, but very bourgeois in his demeanor. He comes here to see Susan Mulligan; she's that really sweet old lady in her nineties who has dementia, the one who keeps calling me Harry. George comes to see her every single day, and on Sundays he brings her roses—every Sunday, and only red roses! Even in the middle of winter he finds red roses to bring her! From what I've heard, he used to come here with her to visit her older brother who lived here for many years until his death. I wasn't around at that time, but I remember Aggie, the tall, elderly nurse from the B-wing who usually works at night, telling us that the older Mulligan adopted him as a kid when he worked as a priest somewhere in Africa. You can ask her more about it when she's here for her shift."

Wambũi had been wondering why the name Mulligan sounded so familiar until Karim mentioned the priest in Africa. Could it be the same Reverend Mulligan who had started the mission at her village? She closed her eyes briefly and remembered that day many years before, when there was a clamor in the village and all the kids were forced to stay indoors. She remembered the adults conversing in somber whispers. It was after that incident that the police started coming and breaking into their homes and dragging people off who they thought were linked to the Mau Mau. She'd heard that the reverend had adopted the late deacon's only surviving child. Of course, that had to be who that was! The deacon's image was hazy in her mind—it was from so many years ago; but she was pretty certain from even that brief description of events that he was the son of the Deacon Mũhũyũ!

The moment Wambũi made the connection she felt her whole body tingle. Eileen was saying something, but she was distracted as a million thoughts were running through her mind while she tried to piece together fragments of memories and conversations from fifty years ago.

"Looks like I'm talking to myself," she heard Eileen say.

"Oh, I'm sorry, I was just lost in thought." Wambũi almost told Eileen about her revelation, but then decided against it. She would keep it to herself. Based on Eileen's negative interaction with the man, perhaps rousing the ghosts of one unfortunate night in 1952 wouldn't be to anyone's benefit. She would let sleeping dogs lie.

The two friends did some traveling during her visit. Karim drove them into London one day, and they did a bit of walking around Buckingham Palace and Piccadilly. And there's no way that trip would've been complete without taking a ride on the Tube; Eileen was game since she'd never been on the London Underground either. Originally, Karim was the designated guide; but Wambũi's fascination with the system along with her uncanny ability to navigate it resulted in his ceding that role to her, much to her delight. On another trip, when Karim was working, his wife Razia drove them to Stonehenge. Since Eileen was almost seventy-seven, there had been some initial concern that she might find these trips physically challenging; but she surprised them all with her strength and stamina.

"Eileen, help me understand this," Wambũi asked one day with an uneasy expression on her face. "When you get old here, they just put you away into a care home where you wait to die? This is really bothering me."

"Yes, Wambũi, it's certainly very different from what you're used to in Kenya. I remember your dad would be walking around tending to his goats, hunched over his walking stick, well into his old age—right until the day he died. I suppose it's so different here at least partly because there aren't young people around all the time to take care of you at home since they're all busy working; and it's far more difficult if you have some sort of physical limitation."

"But, Eileen, *you* look strong. Why are you in this facility?"

"I moved here because the loneliness was getting to me in my flat on Heathside Road. I had no close family, and my neighbors didn't really talk to each other. After what I was accustomed to in Kenya, the isolation was very hard for me to adjust to. Margate Cottage has an independent living facility if you don't need someone to do things for you. So you can still take care of yourself, while being part of a kind of community."

"Then if you got to where you couldn't take care of yourself, you could move to the other section?" Wambũi asked.

"That's correct," Eileen said, nodding a bit somberly.

Comprehending, Wambũi slowly shook her head. "It's very different from what I know," she said. "Do you still have a passport?" Wambũi asked, suddenly sounding upbeat.

"It's probably expired," Eileen said listlessly. "I'm sure it's somewhere among my documents. Why?"

"Get it renewed then. We need to get you back home!" Wambũi said, grinning from ear to ear.

Eileen looked nonplussed.

"Why are you looking at me like that?" asked Wambũi. "We've been talking about this for fifteen years, and none of us is getting younger. All you have to do is renew your passport and ask Karim to take you to the airport; everything else will be taken care of."

Eileen looked dubiously at her friend. But she knew Wambũi wasn't known for humor or pranks.

"Listen, Eileen," Wambũi continued peremptorily, "I'm leaving tomorrow. Start working on the passport and text me or send me an email when it's done. Plan on staying for at least three months, though you are free to stay for as long as you like."

Eileen was silent for a few moments, seeming somewhat

bewildered. She brushed away a tear that had formed at the corner of her eye, then another.

"So, you'll let me know?" Wambũi added quickly, somewhat uncomfortable with the long, emotional silence.

Eileen nodded slightly, dabbing her eyes, as a faint smile formed on her lips.

Chapter Thirty-One

EILEEN'S HEART SOARED with excitement as she disembarked from the plane at Jomo Kenyatta International Airport and headed towards the immigration desk. She bade good-bye to the new friend she'd made on the plane—a young man in his twenties named George Okundi, who was studying for his master's degree in engineering at MIT and was heading home to visit his family. They'd had a pleasant conversation through most of the flight, and he'd brought her up to date on the social, economic and political transitions in Kenya that had occurred in the fifteen years since she'd been gone. Eileen had tried to keep up to date by reading the *The Daily Nation* newspaper over the internet, but it was hard to tell what those news stories really meant without the depth and context of actually being there.

"*Sawa* (Okay), Ms. Eileen," George had said to her on parting, handing her a folded piece of paper. "That's my cell phone number. If you happen to be in Nairobi and need to get around, or just want to get together for *chai*[30] and *mandazi*, give me a call. I hope you have a pleasant stay!"

"*Sawa, asante sana* (Okay, thanks a lot)!" she replied in Kiswahili.

---

[30] Tea

The line for the immigration counter for non-East African citizens was quite long, and it moved slowly. Eventually it was Eileen's turn. She was greeted by a courteous but unsmiling young man.

"Good evening, madam, how was your flight?" he asked, reaching for her passport and landing card.

"It was very pleasant, thank you."

He scrutinized the information she had written down on her landing card. "What is the purpose of your visit?"

"I've come to visit friends and family here."

"Family?" he asked, looking up at her quizzically.

"Yes," Eileen replied without hesitation.

"This contact person you have listed here by the name Wambūi Mwangi. Who is she to you?"

"*Huyo ni dada yangu, lakini tuko na mama tofauti* (That's my sister, but we have different mothers)," she replied in flawless Kiswahili, which elicited an expression of surprise and amusement.

"*Eti umesema nini* (I beg your pardon)?" he asked.

"*Huyo Wambūi ni dada yangu* (That Wambūi is my sister)," she continued with a smile, "*unajua mimi nimeishi Kenya miaka arobaini— nafikiria hiyo ni zaidi ya miaka yako; kwa hivyo hapa ni nyumbani kwangu, na wewe in kama kijana yangu* (I lived forty years in Kenya, which is

315

probably longer than you have been alive, so this is home to me, and you are like my son)."

A hint of a smile appeared on the immigration officer's face. "*Haya, mama, karibu sana nyumbani* (Alright madam, welcome home)!" he said as he stamped her passport and waved her through.

Wambũi was waiting for her at the Arrivals area. She was accompanied by her driver, a clean-shaven man in his thirties named Ndũng'ũ. He quickly took charge of Eileen's baggage cart and walked ahead of them as they proceeded to the parking lot. It was a warm sunny morning, about seventy degrees, with an occasional light puff of wind caressing one's skin.

The weather in Kenya was one of the things Eileen had missed most in her time in England. It was predictably warm and sunny most of the time, and usually not noticeably humid—at least not in the places she was familiar with. In fact, there were so many consistently pleasant days that it was not usually deemed a subject worthy of discussion. This was in stark contrast with England, where the weather was a constant topic of conversation.

Weather concerns here were generally confined to rain— when it rained, when it was supposed to rain, or when it didn't rain. During a downpour, the Nairobians' pathological fear of getting wet was legendary; and at the first few drops of any rainfall, all the roads suddenly seemed clogged with traffic as people tried to escape the city, no matter what the time of day. If, on the other hand, the rains were late in coming, the anxious hand-wringing of farmers and weathermen became the constant refrain in the national news.

As Ndũng'ũ navigated the spacious, air-conditioned Toyota Land Cruiser through the traffic on Ring Road, heading towards Thika Road, Eileen peered out the window as she conversed with Wambũi. Hawkers shuffled between cars at traffic stops, holding up their wares, and trying to make a quick sale before the lights turned green. On the dusty roadsides were small kiosks made of wood or corrugated iron sheets, their walls adorned with banners advertising "Coca Cola," "Safaricom," or some other company or product, while pedestrians and cyclists crisscrossed back and forth, with an occasional goat or chicken blending in with the bustling scene. While this might have seemed chaotic to a first-time visitor from a developed country, it was pleasingly familiar to Eileen and she greedily took it all in.

"A lot of the old girls have been calling and wanting to know when you were arriving. They're all looking forward to seeing you again," Wambũi remarked. "Old girls" was how the alumni referred to themselves.

"I'm looking forward to seeing all of them," Eileen said with undisguised enthusiasm.

As soon as Wambũi had received confirmation that Eileen would be coming, she had telephoned Joyce Gĩchũhĩ, who was still the headmistress at Alliance Girls, to let her know. Joyce was literally delirious with excitement and she immediately sent out an email to the old girls' network to notify them. The replies from around the country were nearly instantaneous, with her former students wanting to know when to come to Kikuyu to see their beloved teacher.

It was eventually decided that the school would hold a reception in Eileen's honor, the second weekend after her arrival. About half of the teachers who had been at Alliance Girls with her were still there—as well as some of the cooks and watchmen. The news of her return had created quite a buzz of excitement, which also rubbed off on the current students who had only heard of Ms. Atwood through stories passed down over the years, or from their mothers who were alumni.

Once the Land Cruiser got past Thika, the scenery became less hectic, with densely clustered buildings and swarms of automobiles, cyclists and pedestrians giving way to rolling green hillsides, farmhouses and herds of sheep and goats. The quiet hum of the car's engine and the warm sunlight filtering through the windows worked like a powerful spell, so that Eileen—who hadn't slept well the night before—nodded off. She woke up only after the car came to a complete stop and the chimes came on as Ndũng'ũ opened the door and stepped out. They had arrived.

Waithĩra, the house-help, emerged hurriedly from the house, thrilled to see Eileen after so many years. After exchanging warm greetings and affectionate hugs, she busied herself with offloading the luggage, assisting Ndũng'ũ, whose flawless driving had made the one-and-a-half-hour drive seem like five minutes.

Eileen stood next to Wambũi on the sloping front lawn,

surveying her surroundings. "It's exactly like I remember it!" she said. "Is it okay if we go around to the back before going inside the house?"

The house was built on a gentle slope, and the backyard was splendid to behold, with its spacious well-kept lawn adorned with brightly colored shrubs and flowers. On a day such as this one, an onlooker could see across to the farms on the other ridge—and out there, towering in the distance, was the majestic mountain. In the years she'd been away, Eileen had dreamed many times of standing in Wambūi's backyard or sitting on her back porch and communing with the sublime landscape—and now she was finally here. It was overwhelming.

"I'm so glad to be back!" she whispered, turning to Wambūi, as tears of joy began rolling down her face.

〰〰

The reception at Alliance Girls turned out to be a momentous occasion, and former students flocked in from all over the country. Several new buildings had sprung up since Eileen had left, so she had an interesting time trying to remember what stood in each space that was now occupied by a new building. The students still looked the same in their dark green skirts and sweaters with white blouses and socks. Former students generated excited whispers among the current ones, as many had excelled in their careers and achieved both fame and fortune, which was evident from the number of luxury vehicles in the parking lot.

"Hello, Ms. Atwood!" said one elegantly dressed woman who approached her. "I don't know if you remember me . . ."

"Let me guess," said Eileen. "Ruth Moraa, you were in Stevenson House, sometime in the late seventies or early eighties . . ."

"Wow, *Mwalimu*, you do remember!" exclaimed Ruth.

"It certainly helps that I was the housemistress of Stevenson House," Eileen said with a grin. "So what are you up to these days?"

"I'm a cardiothoracic surgeon, based in a hospital called Groote Schuur, in Cape Town, South Africa."

"That is amazing!" Eileen exclaimed, clearly impressed. "But wait, aren't you the one who fainted in biology class when you had to dissect a frog? I think it was you. I didn't teach biology but I heard all about it!"

There was an eruption of laughter from all who were within earshot of the conversation, including the butt of the joke.

"Yes, Ms. Atwood, that was me. But I overcame my fears and turned them into an opportunity."

"You absolutely did, Ruth," said Eileen, giving her a warm hug. "I'm very proud of you!"

As Eileen and Wambũi walked on, they were stopped by a woman impeccably well-dressed in a stylish red skirt suit with matching shoes, accompanied by a young muscular man with chiseled features.

"Phyllis Aketch—how are you?" Eileen preempted her greeting.

"I'm very well, *Mwalimu*, and surprised that you remember me," said Phyllis as the two embraced.

"Of course, I remember you, Phyllis, you almost led the students into a riot. Now I hear you're a judge in the High Court—that is astonishing!"

Lady Justice Aketch was one of the most brilliant and respected judges in the High Court. In her student days, she was an activist and agitator, and she'd almost been suspended for being the ringleader in a near-riot over some issue related to the food in the dining halls. She had attended the school years after Wambũi left, so the two were meeting for the first time.

"When were you at Alliance, Wambũi?" Phyllis asked.

"I joined in nineteen fifty-three."

"Wambũi was among the early students at the school," said Eileen. "There were probably between fifty and a hundred girls in the entire school back then."

"Wow, I had no idea it had started with so few students. Where are you now?"

"I'm a shopkeeper in Karatina."

"Oh, I see," said Phyllis, somewhat awkwardly, and unsure of what to say next.

So Eileen jumped in. "Wambũi was the brightest mathematics student I ever taught. It usually took her five minutes to comprehend what took everyone else a whole lesson or two. I always imagined she would go on to be an engineer or a professor of mathematics, but she completed school at a difficult time—during the Emergency. She was a math teacher for a time, but she left the profession against my advice and went into a hardware business, where she has done very well for herself. She still exploited her talent for numbers, only in a way I would not have anticipated. Actually, you might have been at Alliance at the same time as her younger sister . . . whose name I can't recall at the moment."

"Nyairero," said Wambũi.

"No, she went by a different name," replied Eileen thoughtfully as she scanned the recesses of her distant memory, "it wasn't a Gĩkũyũ name."

"Terry?" ventured Wambũi.

"You mean TK?" asked Phyllis, her eyes opening wide with incredulity. "You're TK's older sister? Weren't you head girl in your time? I remember seeing your name on the plaque listing the names of head girls through the years."

"Yes, I was. You know TK?"

"Of course, I know TK! We were best friends—and she completely idolized you! She always talked about you!" Phyllis was shaking her head in disbelief at this discovery.

"Really, I had no idea," said Wambūi with a bemused smile.

"I ran into her about three months ago at the airport. She was going to visit her son in London."

By now, Wambūi had figured out that the man at Phyllis' side was a bodyguard, noticing the pistol butt peeping out discreetly from under the flap of his jacket. Even without the gun, the presence of a stone-faced, athletic young man hovering in the vicinity of a government official and not participating in the conversation was a giveaway.

"Before I forget," said Phyllis, turning to Eileen, "my nephew says he met you on the flight into Nairobi two weeks ago."

Eileen looked puzzled.

"A tall fellow with a goatee, studying for a master's degree at MIT . . ." Phyllis elaborated.

"Oh yes! George was his name. I'm forgetting his last name, it was either Nyakundi or Okundi," Eileen said.

"Okundi. That's my nephew. His dad and my husband are brothers. He spent many school holidays at our home. He happened to drop by my house this morning, and I told him I was coming here to see one of my former teachers. He told me he'd met a Mzungu lady on the plane who had taught at Alliance for many years and was returning here to visit friends."

"Hmm, it's a small world, isn't it?" remarked Eileen.

"That's for sure. So how long are you in Kenya?"

"Three to six months maybe . . ."

"She's here for as long as Immigration will allow her," said Wambũi.

Phyllis leaned forward, beckoning both Eileen and Wambũi to come closer. "I have a lot of people who owe me favors at Immigration, so if you need help with a Residency Pass just let me know. Here's my number. I'd be honored to help in any way."

There were several other pleasant encounters that afternoon of a similar nature, with lots of smiles, hugs, laughs, surprises and fond recollections. Eileen and Wambũi were not returning to Karatina that day; they had been invited by Joyce Gĩchũhĩ to spend the night at her house, and they had gratefully accepted.

At about four thirty, all the visitors and students gathered in the assembly hall for a brief formal session in which the headmistress gave an elegant heartwarming speech about friendship and the value of investing one's life and efforts into creating a meaningful legacy, like the one embodied in the person of Eileen Atwood. Eileen blushed and smiled and basked in the emotional warmth that enveloped her in this celebration of her life.

As Joyce spoke, Eileen's thoughts flashed back to the Sunday many decades before when she heard the missionary speak at her church, and how even as a naïve young girl she had been stubbornly certain that her destiny lay in a land she had never seen. This day was the blissful validation of a decision she had made at the age of eleven, when she was even younger than all the awestruck students gathered in the assembly hall that day.

≋

Wambũi had already made plans for Eileen, anticipating that her initial euphoria would eventually wear off, which happened when they returned to Karatina, not long after the reunion at Alliance. When she'd visited her friend in Surrey, she'd been distressed to see how old people seemed to get tossed into holding pens, marginalized by society, stripped of any freedom or usefulness they'd previously possessed—waiting to die. Indeed, as soon as Wambũi returned to Kenya after her visit abroad, with a sense of urgency she sought to find something meaningful for Eileen to do.

"Standard One pupils?" Eileen said incredulously when Wambũi informed her of the arrangement.

"I think you'll do just fine," her friend told her reassuringly. "You taught high school mathematics for over forty years, so I don't think you'll have any problems teaching 'one plus one' to a class of six-year-olds. As for teaching English, I think you have the language skills to get by. Besides, if you don't do it, they won't have anyone else—the other teacher left about six weeks ago, and it may be a while before they can find a replacement."

Eileen smiled and felt a thrill of nervous excitement. "But wait, what about a work permit?"

"You don't need a work permit because you're volunteering—you're not receiving any financial compensation."

"Are you sure about this?" Eileen asked with a note of trepidation in her voice.

"I think you'll do just fine—and have a really good time as well. You already saw this past weekend how those children you taught so many years ago never forgot you—even after they succeeded in their careers. You remained a shining beacon in their lives. Now these kids need a teacher, so I took the liberty of volunteering you." Wambũi spoke matter-of-factly as she cleared the dishes off the breakfast table and carried them into the kitchen. Eileen rose to join her in the task. Waithĩra had the day off.

"Alright," said Eileen, starting to find Wambũi's enthusiasm for the idea contagious. "Gĩchagi Primary School, here I come!"

〰〰

Wambũi had arranged it so that Ndũng'ũ would drive Eileen to the school in the morning, and then pick her up at about two o'clock. It was only about half a kilometer away, and once she was settled in, Eileen could choose to walk there and back if she preferred.

On that first Monday, Wambũi accompanied her to the

school and introduced her to the headmistress, Ms. Gathomi. She, in turn, took Eileen around to present her to the other teachers and students. It was a small village school comprising three elongated buildings on concrete slabs, arranged in a U-shaped formation, made of *mabati* roofing and siding. The "windows" were square frames of wood and *mabati* that opened outward to let in the light as well as rain, noise and occasional birds. Along the central beam on the roof ran insulated electrical wire, from which dangled a solitary forty-watt light bulb at the front of each classroom. In the middle of the "U", there was a patch of grass that served as a soccer field, with rickety wooden goalposts one was well advised not to lean against. In each classroom there was a blackboard and a few small stubs of chalk for the teacher to write with. The rooms were dimly lit, so that on a dreary overcast day in July one had to squint to see all the way to the front. On most sunny days there was enough light if one left the door and the windows open, although that sometimes resulted in the curious eyes of more distractible children wandering off in pursuit of goings-on outside the classroom.

Most of the children had never seen a white person in the flesh; and initially, before they became acquainted with Eileen, they managed to suppress the questions that were burning inside them, answering only "Yes, teacher!" and "No, teacher!" in response to her queries or instructions. That didn't last long. Once they became comfortable with her, the avalanche of questions came, some strange, some hilarious and some extremely perceptive.

The Agĩkũyũ have a hard time differentiating between the

letters "r" and "l," so that a "lion's roar" sounds more like a "rion's loar." For this reason, even though she'd been introduced to them as Ms. Eileen, they all called her Ms. Irene because that was the name that most closely approximated the sound of it as they pronounced it.

"Ms. Irene, where is your home?" one student would ask, starting a dialogue that many others joined.

"I was born in England, but I have lived in Kenya for many, many years. Even before your parents were born."

"So, is your home here or in England?"

"I suppose it's both here and in England."

"But what if you can only choose one—which one would you choose?"

"I would choose here."

"Me, I would choose America! Is England in America?"

"No, it's a different country. America is far away, on the other side of the sea."

"Are there brown people in America?"

"Yes, there are."

"Brown people like me?"

"Yes, just like you!"

"And in England?"

"Even in England."

Occasionally a child would work up the courage and ask to touch her hair, and as they did so, she would watch their eyes widen in fascination.

"Your hair is like *kĩmira* for maize!" one girl said excitedly, referring to the silky strands that flow from the tip of a fresh cob of corn.

"Ms. Irene, Mama Mũthoni is your sister?" said the same boy who'd asked her where her home was. He had bright curious eyes, and Eileen had noticed that simple answers only led to more questions from him. Wambũi was the Mama Mũthoni in question.

"Yes, she is my sister."

"But how can you be sisters when she's brown and you're white?"

"We're not sisters from the same mother and father. But sometimes if you're friends with someone for a long time, you can become like sisters or brothers."

Eileen was thoroughly enjoying herself, as were the kids. After the first couple of days, she informed Ndũng'ũ that she would walk to school and back. Wambũi didn't feel comfortable having her walk alone, so she asked Waithĩra to accompany her in the morning and meet her at the school for her return trip at the end of the day.

Waithĩra relished the task.

So was everyone now settled into their routine, with Wambũi heading off to the hardware store in the morning, Mr. Mwangi to his government job, and Eileen walking over to Gĩchagi Primary accompanied by Waithĩra. Occasionally, Eileen was invited to the homes of her former students for the weekend, who made it easy for her to visit by arranging for her transportation both ways.

She had spoken to Karim a few times to let him know how she was doing, and he was pleased to hear she was having such a good time. He assured her that nothing had changed at Margate Cottage, so she was not missing anything exciting there. She'd been forced to give up her place because the management had given her the option of continuing to pay monthly as a way to secure the room, or giving it up in the hope that something would be available when she chose to return.

One week gave way to another and it was not long before Eileen realized she'd already been in Kenya for three months. Justice Aketch had made a point of calling to see if Eileen still needed help with the Residency Pass, and she took her up on the offer. So the document was rapidly making its way through the system, accompanied by a terse whispered warning as it passed from one set of hands to another that anyone who dared obstruct its progress risked facing the wrath of the venerable judge.

In September, Eileen had an unexpected treat. Lucy Kimeu née Masika—a shy, awkward wisp of a girl who she taught back in the sixties—telephoned, having obtained Wambũi's number from Joyce Gĩchũhĩ, the headmistress at Alliance. She'd been unable to make it to the reunion, but didn't want to miss the opportunity to see her beloved former teacher.

"Please ask her if she would like to come. I'd really like to see her again!" Mrs. Kimeu told Wambũi, in an almost pleading tone.

Wambũi got home that evening with a big smile on her face, eager to pass along Mrs. Kimeu's message to Eileen.

"Kiboko Lodge? Wow! I've never been to the Maasai Mara— are you pulling my leg?" Eileen asked incredulously.

"I am not. She's the general manager at Kiboko Lodge, and wants you to spend a weekend with her at the Maasai Mara."

Eileen was stunned into silence.

"I'll take that as a yes," said Wambũi, holding up her cell phone as she began dialing Mrs. Kimeu's number. "And by the way, this is around the time of the wildebeeste migration. It's usually impossible to get a hotel room during this season in Maasai Mara. Here, the phone is ringing—you talk to her and she'll give you the details."

∿

A trip to Maasai Mara is experienced by most as a life-changing event. There, the humans are bystanders, permitted to be present only on the condition that they stay out of the way of the natives the land belongs to. The place was not created by humans for animals; the animals were always there, living their lives free from homo sapien interference. On that vast plain, myriad species of majestic birds, grazing mammals and predators of all descriptions coexist in a balance according to the predetermined rules encrypted in each creature's DNA.

Hunters survive by outrunning their prey, while the prey survive by outrunning their predators for just a few moments longer than the predator is able to keep up the blistering pace; somehow the ranks of both are miraculously not depleted. Once a cheetah slows down, unable to keep up with a Thomson's gazelle, the gazelle stops and resumes grazing nonchalantly a short distance away, as if the near-death experience from seconds earlier was nothing more than a bad dream. From a distance above, eyeing both the hunters and the hunted are the vultures, endowed with the power of infinite patience, which trumps both the speed and the power of the animals down below. The vulture knows that dinner will come at the appointed time, and calm, disciplined passivity is sometimes all that is needed for survival.

Among the land animals, the power currencies are either sharp teeth and claws, or brute strength. When a lion and a Cape buffalo confront each other in a clash for survival, the outcome could go either way. Even the king of the jungle will often beat a hasty retreat after being gored or viciously kicked by an enraged buffalo, choosing to defer the imposition of his regal authority to a more suitable occasion. Then there is the African elephant, big as a wall and willing to deploy tons of crushing force in an instant; and the graceful towering giraffe, able to see trouble coming from a mile off. No wonder the savannah is such an interesting place.

In a traditional zoo, humans isolate animals in cages and walk around observing them. But here the humans are inside wheeled cages, unobtrusively navigating their way among the owners of the land. At night, they retreat to their fenced-off encampments and lodges, safely separating themselves from the creatures that are a source of both fascination and fear.

Wildebeests are unusual creatures. With a shimmering gray coat, broad chest and skinny legs, as well as a flowing beard, they would hardly be suitable contestants in any competition where poise or good looks were winning qualities. When they run, their gait seems awkward and uncoordinated. Their magic, however, is in numbers. Take one ungainly wildebeest running, with its big chest and skinny legs, and it's a sorry sight to behold. Now imagine hundreds and thousands of these animals suddenly responding to a primal signal and starting to stampede in single file; the steady rumble of endless hoofs on the hillside as the herds make their way south towards the Serengeti, jumping recklessly with suicidal abandon into the Mara River, knowing that the crocodiles will only pick off a few and let the rest through . . .

This unrehearsed instinctive choreography on such a grand scale is a wonder to behold! Back and forth, since the dawn of time, these animals have made this journey fulfilling the destiny they were born to fulfil. Their impressive display of collective will, and the subservience of the individual to the greater purpose of the group has spawned in their human counterparts a similar migration. Every year, tourists from all over the world flock to the Maasai Mara to watch the wildebeest migration, oblivious to the ironic congruence of their own migration for the purposes of observing that of another species.

Eileen was spellbound. Nothing she had ever heard about the Maasai Mara could have prepared her for the experience. From watching a trio of lionesses hunting down a zebra, to being forced to back up their car by an irate, ear-flapping elephant who suddenly stepped in their path, she spent the day in open-mouthed awe, as their driver navigated their all-wheel drive vehicle on the rough dirt road in search of interesting sights. He communicated with other guides by walkie- talkie, so when one guide saw something worth sharing, they let the others know so they could pursue it too. Although Eileen understood Swahili, the guides used code words for the different animals, so she couldn't make head or tail of what they were talking about. Mrs. Kimeu rode with her, and they chatted in between the driver's running narration that was packed with fascinating facts about the animals and their habitat.

Kiboko Lodge was an elegant establishment with a rustic design, so its architectural style blended well with the surrounding bush. But it was fully equipped with all the comforts and amenities humans were loath to do without, such as water, electricity, swimming pools, etc. Like all the other hotels in the area, it was encircled by an electrified fence to keep out the animals; human beings, even when desirous of getting as close to nature as possible, want to feel safe as well.

Throughout her stay, Eileen felt treated like royalty by the hotel staff. And during dinner on her final evening, a jubilant procession of waiters appeared, weaving a path between tables singing "Jambo Bwana," a Kenyan pop song, a special favorite among tourists. The singer at the front carried a cake adorned with candles on it, so it was presumed to be in celebration of someone's birthday.

Eileen was enthralled by the spectacle and whispered about it excitedly to Mrs. Kimeu. As the procession made its way past their table, it suddenly made a sharp turn and came back to surround it, the sound of their singing now amplified as it was coming from all directions. The bearer of the cake placed it delicately on the table in front of a bewildered Eileen, who was now keenly aware that everyone in the dining area had turned their attention to them. Many people had risen from their seats and were snapping photos of the special occasion.

When Eileen looked down, she saw an inscription in purple lettering on the icing of the cake, surrounded by a ring of candles: *Karibu Nyumbani* (Welcome Home)! Eileen's eyes began to mist over. She turned to Mrs. Kimeu who was beaming with joy.

"You've got to blow out the candles!" the cake bearer demanded.

Eileen obediently blew out the candles to the cheers of the staff and the other guests.

The rest of the evening, and on the following day, she received smiles and congratulatory greetings from total strangers, which made her feel both intensely happy and embarrassed at the same time. Before they parted, she expressed her profound gratitude to Mrs. Kimeu for giving her the gift of an unforgettable experience.

By the time Eileen returned to Karatina on the following evening, she was in a state of bliss, exuberantly narrating her adventures to the eager listeners of the Mwangi household. This despite a throbbing headache she'd had all afternoon, which didn't seem to be getting better. She excused herself from her hosts, took some Panadol and went to her room. It was Sunday evening, and Wambūi and Mwangi would also be turning in early in preparation for the new work week.

Chapter Thirty-Two

IT WAS ABOUT eight o'clock in the morning. Wambũi had gotten to the hardware store about seven, and was getting everything ready for opening time, which was usually at nine. Two of her assistants were already there, tidying up and restocking the shelves when her phone rang.

"Hello?" she said, wondering who'd be calling her at that hour. It was Waithĩra at the other end of the line, and she was sobbing and rambling incoherently. Wambũi felt her blood curdle. "Waithĩra, *kaĩ arĩ kĩĩ* (what's the matter)!" she asked impatiently.

Waithĩra was wailing disconsolately and couldn't manage to complete a sentence, which was all Wambũi needed to tell her there was something terribly wrong. She motioned to Thiong'o, one of her most dependable shop assistants whom she usually deputized when she had to be away from the shop. "I need to rush home," she told him quickly, heading towards the door. "Something's wrong. Please look after the store for me."

_____She got into her car and raced home, bursting out of her vehicle and running into the house. "Waithĩra!"

"Over here, Mama Mũthoni!"

The voice was coming from Eileen's room. Wambũi felt her

337

knees getting weak as she was overtaken by a sense of dread. When she went inside, she found Eileen lying motionless, her usually lively amber-brown eyes stared vacantly into space, the pupils dilated. Her body was cold.

"What happened!" Wambũi screamed.

Between sobs and sniffles, Waithĩra explained how she'd been worried that Eileen had overslept and wouldn't make it to the school on time. After knocking on the door and not getting a response, she'd entered the room and found the situation as they currently beheld it.

Wambũi looked around in confusion. "Call Baba Mũthoni and tell him to come quickly!" she shouted. As her eyes surveyed the room in a panicky haze, she saw an envelope sitting conspicuously on top of Eileen's Bible on her bedside table. Peering closer, she saw that it was addressed to her. She picked it up and in her anxious rush to open it, ripped the edge of the letter inside alongside the envelope. She started to read:

My dearest Wambũi,

If you are reading this letter, then I may no longer be alive. I am sorry to have left you so suddenly, but the choice was not mine to make. About seven months ago, I went in to see my doctor because I was having headaches that had started to bother me. I had several tests and was eventually found to have a brain aneurysm. I was referred to Dr. Geoffrey Miller, one of the highly respected neurosurgeons in London, who, after reviewing everything, told me that, because of the shape of the aneurysm, I was not a suitable candidate for a less invasive procedure called an embolization. Surgery was the only option, but he was very candid with me and said that, based on the location of the aneurysm, there was a very significant chance that I would die or become severely disabled as a result of the surgery. He is a very experienced surgeon and had conferred with colleagues in London as well as with Dr. Scott Yamaguchi, an American neurosurgeon at Johns Hopkins Hospital in Baltimore, who is arguably the world's top surgeon for that particular type of surgery. All the doctors were in agreement that I had at best a fifty-fifty chance of making it through the surgery and a much smaller chance of returning to normal functioning.

It appeared that I was going to have to make a decision between living and trying to stay alive, which in this case seemed to be on divergent paths; I realized that it is possible to spend all of one's time and effort in trying not to die and end up missing out on life in the process. I asked Dr. Miller, the neurosurgeon, to give me a week or two before letting him know of my final decision.

The Lord truly does work in mysterious ways! You happened to arrive in Surrey about four days after I had my meeting with Dr. Miller. Without any prompting from me, you brought up the possibility of a visit to Kenya, something that I had wanted to do for a while but that had not seemed possible. My mother spent her final days in loneliness, and her death went

unnoticed by the community of strangers among whom she lived—
her death haunts me to this day. I did not want to die a stranger in
the land of my birth, far away from all the people who meant so
much to me.

Please forgive my presumption in withholding the details
of my medical condition from you, but I did not want my trip to
Kenya to turn into a pity party, as might happen when people are
aware that someone has a terminal condition. I have experienced
unbelievable joy since I returned to Kenya, seeing old friends and
marveling at how well so many of the girls turned out. I can truly
say that I have experienced a taste of heaven! I am glad I did not
pursue the risky surgery because I would have forgone all the
wonderful things that I have experienced.

Dr. Miller had told me that one day I might experience a
severe headache before the aneurysm ruptures, and earlier today I
developed a crushing, relentless headache that seems to be getting
worse. It's about eleven o'clock now and even after the painkillers I
took two hours ago the headache seems to be getting worse—I fear
that I may be running out of time.

I hope you understand now why I had you meet the lawyer
and Mr. Barnes when you visited—certainly not the most exciting
things to do with a friend whom you haven't seen for a long time,
but very necessary. Even if I had not come to Kenya, I did not
want to die without having someone who could help handle my
affairs after my departure.

You have been more than a friend—you are my sister.
Knowing you has meant everything to me, and I pray that the Lord
will bless you until we meet again at His feet one joyous day.

Your adoring sister, Eileen

~~~

Eileen was buried on a gentle slope on Wambũi's farm that had an unobstructed view of the mountain. Wambũi knew that Eileen would have cherished that spot. It was a beautiful clear day, and the radiant sunlight reflected off the snow-capped peaks, heightening the imposing grandeur of the mountain. The funeral notice had been posted in the local newspaper and had evidently caught the attention of many Alliance alumni, for they came in droves, parking their cars up to half a kilometer away and walking the rest of the distance. Many of the former students whom Eileen had reunited with months earlier were there, as well as a busload of current students from Alliance Girls who wanted to be part of this memorable occasion in the history of their school.

The children from Gĩchagi Primary School were there too, and shortly before the casket was lowered into the grave they broke into a soulful pitch-perfect rendition of Eileen's favorite Swahili hymn that she had taught them.

Bwana u sehemu yangu (Lord you are my portion)

Rafiki yangu wewe (You are my friend)

341

Katika safari yangu (On my life's journey)

Tatembea na wewe (I will walk with you)

Pamoja na wewe (Together with you)

Pamoja na wewe (Together with you)

Katika safari yangu (On my life's journey)

Tatembea na wewe (Together with you) . . .

Every funeral comes to a juncture where grief reaches a tipping point, when the collective dam of tears suddenly breaks and they begin to flow unrestrainedly. Usually this is when the casket starts its descent into the grave, an action that lays bare the irrevocable finality of death. But on this day, it was the sound of cherubic six-year-olds singing Eileen's favorite hymn that broke the dam, and the tears were tears of joy that flowed freely. It was as if Eileen was taking this opportunity to sing her song one last time through these children before she continued on her journey.

As the shovelfuls of earth covered the casket, the minister dismissed the congregation with a blessing. The crowd started to make their way back up the slope of the *shamba*, the moist red earth sticking to their shoes.

"Look there!" one woman in the crowd exclaimed, and the people around her turned in the direction she was pointing.

Somewhere to the north a light downpour had begun, and

with it a huge iridescent rainbow had formed against the backdrop of the sunlight on the blue-and-white peaks of Mt. Kenya. The effect was stunning. The excitement over the spectacle spread through the crowd and finally reached Wambũi, who was still in the same daze she'd been in since Eileen's passing. When she looked up and saw the brilliant arc, her tears immediately started again, but this time a faint smile appeared on her lips. Eileen was finally home.

Chapter Thirty-Three

WAMBŨI HAD TO travel to Surrey to finalize Eileen's affairs. Mr. Barnes had put her house up for sale immediately after she'd contacted him with the news. Fortunately, the current housing market was good and the house was in an excellent location, so he was already reviewing a number of offers in the range of four hundred and fifty thousand pounds. He hoped to have it sold by the time she arrived.

When he learned of Eileen's death, Karim had initially been devastated; but after some reflection he admitted it had crossed his mind on more than one occasion that this might happen. She'd spoken often to him about her dream of returning to Kenya someday—so he felt it had been a perfect ending to a life well lived. Still, he felt like he had lost a parent.

"I'll never forget the way she hugged me when I took her to the airport," he mused aloud. "She wasn't the 'huggy' type, and so it took me totally by surprise. Now, looking back, maybe that was her way of saying her final good-bye."

He was completely dumbstruck when Wambũi told him that Eileen had bequeathed him a sum of fifty thousand pounds from the proceeds of the house sale.

"Are you sure?" he asked incredulously.

"Yes, I'm sure. I reviewed the will with her and her lawyer. She considered you her son."

Eileen had traveled light in life. She hadn't left anything behind when she checked out of Margate Cottage, so her only possessions were whatever remained in the room she'd occupied in Wambūi's house. She had made it a practice to donate any clothes or belongings she'd not used in the prior year, not wanting to burden anyone who was left with the responsibility of getting rid of objects that had no meaning or significance to them.

As for what to do with the remaining proceeds from the sale of the house, Eileen had left it up to Wambūi to decide. Since she didn't need the money, Wambūi had been mulling it over since the day she'd first discussed Eileen's will with her. It was during the reunion at Alliance Girls that she finally had an idea. She'd already contacted her nephew KK, the attorney in London, to help her establish the Eileen Atwood Foundation, which would provide resources to purchase twenty-five brand new computers for the computer lab at Alliance Girls, as well as an annual scholarship to be awarded to one incoming student whose family was unable to afford the fees. She would also finance the construction of a small but elegant library with stone walls and glass windows at Gīchagi Primary, equipped with twenty laptop computers and a huge collection of children's books.

After a hectic ten days in England, Wambūi managed to tie

up all the loose ends, and arranged for Karim drop her off at Heathrow. As she sat in the Departures area, she finally had a chance to exhale and reflect on the events of the past few months. When her mind started wandering again, she picked up a free copy of a newspaper and started flipping through it. Her eyes were drawn to an interesting story about a Kenyan man in his eighties who had never been to school, and who had decided to join the Standard One class at his local primary school. Accompanying the article was a photo of an elderly bearded man in a primary school uniform—including shorts—surrounded by children the age of his great-grandchildren, and maybe even great-great-grandchildren.

"Ladies and gentlemen, we will now begin boarding for Kenya Airways Flight 117 with direct service to Jomo Kenyatta International Airport . . ." began the announcement.

Wambũi folded up the newspaper and reached into her handbag to retrieve her travel documents in preparation for boarding.

Chapter Thirty-Four

RAY, JAN AND Peter sat in the lounge taking a rare breather from their unusually hectic schedule in their final few months of residency. They were reflecting on what had transpired during the fellowship application process.

Ray had received an invitation to an interview at Mayo Clinic that had gone very well. When he met with Dr. Chris Lolgorian, the renowned—and widely published—department chair, he felt he was finally in over his head. The other candidates interviewing for the same position were from storied institutions like Harvard and Johns Hopkins and he was sure he wouldn't measure up. But Dr. Lolgorian instantly put him at ease.

"So, you're the one Mordy was talking to me about," she said with a twinkle in her eye.

Ray looked confused, wondering if there had been a case of mistaken identity.

"I'm sorry, I mean Mordecai Goldstein," she clarified. "We know him as Mordy. He trained here and we've stayed in touch and collaborated over the years. Once upon a long time ago, I was his senior resident when he was an intern. Brilliant clinician, that man! We tried to recruit him to be our ICU director, and he said he would consider it only if we were willing to move our facility to Chicago, which of course is an impossibility."

By the time the interview was over, Ray felt he did have a fair chance of being accepted by the prestigious program; so he wasn't surprised when he found out on fellowship Match Day that he was indeed going to Mayo. But most of the people around him were very surprised, and some, like Dr. Holzinger, were dumbstruck.

Jan had managed to get a fellowship in nephrology in Chapel Hill, North Carolina, and was looking forward to getting away from the Chicago winters. "These wretched winters are not suitable for us Africans," he said; then turning to Ray he added, "I wish you well in Minnesota."

Peter, who was one of the original University Hospital residents, looked at Jan quizzically. "Wait a minute, aren't you Dutch?"

"My forefathers were from Holland, centuries ago—but I am from South Africa, one hundred percent African!" Jan explained, grinning broadly.

From the TV in the lounge, a story on the news suddenly caught Ray's attention. There was a riot on the South Side of Chicago following the police shooting of one of the residents. The chief of police was holding a press conference, promising an investigation, but there was loud heckling from the crowd, after which the camera shifted to an image of rowdy youths hurling rocks at riot police. Then there was a still picture on the screen and Ray's blood froze.

". . . the victim, Hakeem Andrews, was unarmed, and his family say he was not a criminal. They are demanding justice . . ."

Ray suddenly felt lightheaded and nauseous as he recognized the man in the picture. It was Hakeem from the sandwich shop!

"Hey man, are you okay?" he heard Jan say.

He nodded weakly and buried his face in his hands. His thoughts flashed to the night he'd been stopped in the street by Officer Sarkevic's partner.

The TV news shifted to the next item, in which a young, lanky politician with a distinctive baritone voice was delivering an impassioned speech to an enthralled crowd that periodically burst into wild applause.

"There's your dude," Ray could hear Peter saying in a soft voice to Jan, in deference to the abrupt change in Ray's demeanor.

"I tell you, he's going to run for president one day," Jan whispered. "Mark my words!"

"You think so? That would be a long shot," Peter said. "I mean, don't get me wrong, I have nothing against the guy. I just don't see how he could successfully navigate a presidential election. Nobody outside of Chicago knows him."

"Well, I think he's going to run one day and surprise

everyone—you just wait . . ." Ray could hear Jan saying through the fog of his disjointed thoughts.

Chapter Thirty-Five

WAMBŨI ENTERED THE administrative building at the University of Nairobi and found her way into the office of Professor Kioko, the Deputy Vice-Chancellor in charge of Academic Affairs. The half-scowling receptionist asked who she was and what the visit was about.

"My name is Wambũi, and I'm here on a personal matter," she replied.

The receptionist asked her to have a seat and said she would pass on the message. It was nine o'clock in the morning and there was no one else in the waiting area. The walls consisted of panels of highly polished wood adorned with abstract paintings. Beyond the receptionist's desk was a long hallway with soft lighting and a series of doors.

Wambũi had brought a copy of the daily newspaper with her and she read through one story after another.

At ten o'clock, she rose from her seat and approached the receptionist's desk again.

"Please be patient, madam, Professor Kioko is very busy," she said sounding somewhat irritated.

Wambũi returned to her chair and started to flip through the pages of the newspaper again but started getting restless. She glanced at her watch. It was about midnight in Seattle—Mũthoni usually slept late. She retrieved her cell phone from her handbag, typed a brief message and dispatched it to her daughter.

Moments later, a door opened at the end of the hallway, and the clacking sound of high-heeled shoes could be heard approaching. The owner of the shoes finally appeared.

"Mama Mũthoni!" she squealed with excitement and rushed towards Wambũi, enveloping her in a warm embrace.

"How are you, Njoki?" Wambũi asked.

"I am very well and delighted to see you!"

Njoki turned to the receptionist. "Doris, why did you make my mother wait so long?"

The receptionist started to stammer out an answer, her hands fidgeting, but nothing came out—she had simply chosen not to convey the information about her visitor. At that same moment, Professor Orie, the Dean of Students, emerged from outside the building.

"Professor Orie, I'd like you to meet my mother!" Njoki exclaimed.

"Your mother?" said Professor Orie, eagerly shaking Wambũi's hand. "I'm very pleased to meet you, madam."

"After my own mother died, I used to spend a lot of time at Mama Mūthoni's house, and she became like a mother to me. Her daughter Mūthoni and I became like sisters. We went to law school together, and then she relocated to America—but we still keep in touch. A few moments ago, I got a text message from her telling me that her mother was in the reception area waiting to see me."

"Wow, that's a treat! But hold on, your last name is Kioko—I thought you were from Ukambani?" the professor said, looking puzzled.

"That's my husband," she explained. "My maiden name is Mūgo."

After the introduction, Professor Kioko took Wambūi's hand and led her to her office, leaving the receptionist smarting with embarrassment from her momentous faux-pas.

"Please, have a seat, Mama Mūthoni," Njoki said, shutting the door as they entered her office.

After making pleasant small talk, Wambūi disclosed the purpose of her visit.

"You want to enroll as a student?" asked Professor Kioko, her eyes widening with surprise.

"Why not?" Wambūi said, matter-of-factly.

"But why? You have a flourishing business and a great marriage, and both your children have been very successful in their careers. I'll obviously do whatever I can to help you, but I'm just trying to understand for myself why you've decided you want to enroll in the university at your age."

"I'm doing it for a friend," replied Wambũi with a wistful smile.

PRAISE FOR THE BOOK

". . . Githaiga introduces readers to a bevy of memorable characters that are so skillfully drawn that they effortlessly leap off the page and into readers' hearts . . ."

Booklife Reviews, Editor's Pick

"A rich, absorbing story of destinies intertwined across time and space."

Kirkus Reviews (Starred Review)

Semifinalist, *BookLife Prize*

"Best Books of 2020"—*Kirkus Reviews*

ABOUT THE AUTHOR

NDIRANGU GITHAIGA was born in Kenya and immigrated to the United States. He is a practicing physician based in Virginia. Visit www.ndirangugithaiga.com to learn more.

Follow Ndirangu at:

Facebook: https://www.facebook.com/NdiranguG/
Instagram: https://www.instagram.com/ndirangu.githaiga/

Made in the USA
Las Vegas, NV
01 July 2021